BY HANNAH MICHELL

Excavations

The Defections

EXCAVATIONS

HANNAH MICHELL

EXCAVATIONS

A NOVEL

ONE WORLD
NEW YORK

Published in the United States by One World, an imprint of Random House, a division of Penguin Random House LLC, New York.

One World and colophon are registered trademarks of Penguin Random House LLC.

LIBRARY OF CONGRESS CATALOGING-IN-PUBLICATION DATA
Names: Michell, Hannah, author.
Title: Excavations : a novel / by Hannah Michell.
Description: First edition. | New York : One World, 2023.
Identifiers: LCCN 2022059415 (print) | LCCN 2022059416 (ebook) |
ISBN 9780593596050 (hardcover) | ISBN 9780593596067 (ebook)
Subjects: LCSH: Korea (South)—Fiction. | LCGFT: Detective and mystery fiction. | Novels.
Classification: LCC PS3613.I345273 E93 2023 (print) |
LCC PS3613.I345273 (ebook) | DDC 813.6—dc23/eng/20230403
LC record available at https://lccn.loc.gov/2022059415
LC ebook record available at https://lccn.loc.gov/2022059416

Printed in the United States of America on acid-free paper

oneworldlit.com

randomhousebooks.com

2 4 6 8 9 7 5 3 1

First Edition

Book design by Fritz Metsch

For A&F,
without whom this book
could not have been written

CONTENTS

Collapse, 1992	3
Six Years Earlier, 1986	16
Twenty-four Hours After the Collapse	22
Two Days After the Collapse	26
Thirty-six Hours After the Collapse	36
Three Days After the Collapse	50
Four Days After the Collapse	61
Seven Days After the Collapse	82
Eight Days After the Collapse	89
Ten Days After the Collapse	103
Eleven Days After the Collapse	107
Twelve Days After the Collapse	118
Twenty-one Days After the Collapse	130
Twenty-two Days After the Collapse	146
Twenty-three Days After the Collapse	158
Twenty-four Days After the Collapse	168
Twenty-six Days After the Collapse	179
Thirty-three Days After the Collapse	181

Thirty-six Days After the Collapse 194
Thirty-eight Days After the Collapse 207
Forty Days After the Collapse 212
Forty-two Days After the Collapse 215
Forty-five Days After the Collapse 223
Forty-six Days After the Collapse (A.M.) 232
Forty-six Days After the Collapse (P.M.) 238
Forty-seven Days After the Collapse 247
Forty-eight Days After the Collapse 253
Twenty-two Years After the Collapse, 2014 262
Twenty-four Years After the Collapse, 2016 278
Relapse, 1992 282
One Week Later, 2016 288
Three Months Later, November 27, 2016 292

Acknowledgments 301

EXCAVATIONS

COLLAPSE

1992

Jae was a man of his word, and he had promised Sae he would be home at six o'clock. Sae glanced at the green cuckoo clock in their kitchen, waiting to see the small bird pop out to announce the hour. The last half hour before he returned every evening was the hardest. It was so close to the end and yet still so much in the thick of waiting. The children were growing tired, their careless movements more and more wild in their too-small apartment.

She imagined Jae crossing the barricades, about to board the subway, moving toward them. Hours earlier, when she was reunited with her children, she had been delighted to see them. Pausing at the preschool gates, she watched them basking in the schoolyard, unaware of her watching them. Then there was the moment she loved the most—when they noticed her and let out squeals of delight before giddily jumping into her arms.

She could not get used to being called someone's mother, the way it erased her name, made her a stranger to herself. Yet in these moments of reunion when her younger son, Hoon-min, clung to her, she felt alive and powerful—a captain rescuing those from a sinking ship—a feeling that lasted only for a while before her nerves started to fray in the unspooling hours and she began eyeing the clock for their father's return.

• • •

The boys were hungry, but she wanted to wait for Jae. For weeks his work as an engineer at Aspiration Tower had been keeping him on-site at all hours. Tonight, he had promised to come home early so they could eat together, though by six-fifteen there was no sign of him. She was like an overfilled kettle, and Hoon-min's whining was the flame threatening to boil her over. Having checked that the boys had not unplugged the phone from the wall again, Sae looked at her silent pager, feeling herself begin to rattle with fury. Shouting for the boys to sit at the table, she prepared rice and seaweed, shrugging off the guilt of offering them such a paltry meal. *It's not as though we do this every day*, Jae would say. He knew exactly how to defuse her. She felt herself soften toward him, so she willed herself to stay angry.

By seven o'clock, Sae had no choice but to surrender to Jae's absence. She considered leaving him a message on his pager, but he would call soon, she thought, with an excuse about being tied up at the Tower. Taking command of the evening, she started a bath, instructing the boys to stop touching each other's penises, to stop splashing water at her or in the other's eyes. They ignored these instructions. Seung-min wanted to get out; he was too warm, he said. Hoon-min wanted to stay in. She took a deep breath, her patience flickering like a weak flame. She sat on a low pink stool with her back against the wet tiles as they splashed around. When she could no longer ignore the ache in her back, she announced that it was time to get out, only to be ignored again.

"Listen!" she hissed. "Out!"

The knife's edge in her voice froze them instantly. Obediently stepping out of the bath, they stared at her, wide-eyed. Sae turned from them, already sorry. She hated destroying their spirits, but she felt extinguished and they needed to be in bed.

"Where's Appa?"

"I don't know."

"I want Appa."

Hoon-min began wailing. Seung-min ran out, leaving a wet trail behind him as he leapt on the bedding on the floor. Dressing the boys quickly, she turned off the light, threatening to leave them to fall asleep alone if they didn't calm down. The words had the desired effect. They both fell onto the bedding as if wounded, and Sae got down to lie between them. They writhed, tossed, and fidgeted in the heat. The boys gripped her earlobes. She was their jungle gym, their plaything, their anchor. Hoon-min's hand grew heavy as he rolled over and yawned, sleepily tugging at her T-shirt. At two years old, he was still in the habit of nursing himself to sleep, but she had resolved to wean him. She held his hand and squeezed it. *No.* Seung-min's breathing changed, calmed, but his eyes remained open at some fixed point on the cracked ceiling.

Hearing a noise outside, Sae held her breath, fearing Jae had chosen this very moment to come home. All her hard work to calm them would be undone if the boys saw their father. But moments passed. There were no creeping steps, only the sounds of the whirring, aging refrigerator in the kitchen, the low white noise of distant traffic on the freeway, the boys' rhythmic breathing. They had finally stopped squirming, their long eyelashes lay still. How beautiful and miraculous they were in the darkness, with sleep between them. The first thing Jae did when he came home late was to look in on the boys, huddled together in their slumber, like a thief reassuring himself of the safety of stolen jewels. She loved that he never took them for granted, that he did not share in her ambivalence spending hours loving them and longing to be apart from them, to be distant and present at once. She wanted them to grow up, she wanted them to stay small. Jae's devotion was a source of wholesomeness in their relationship, but in his treasuring of them she also saw a specter of a childhood spent wanting—for him family was an elusive thing—a fish slipping out of his grasp.

Stillness did not suit the boys. Sae felt an anxious tangle in her stomach. A premonition, perhaps. She left the room to resist the impulse to wake them. As she lit a green coil to ward off mosquitos, the anger she had felt slid into worry. It was eight-thirty. She paged Jae. It wasn't like him not to call. All day the air had held in its fist the threat of an unforgiving summer. Soon the monsoon season would arrive, bringing with it the unwelcome lodger, a humid creature who would come to live in their books and bedding, clothes, and cushions. There was glory in the stickiness; the way it invited them to peel off their layers, soaking in the humid evening heat, unable to sleep, suddenly open to each other. He had never been a man of many words, but for months Jae had seemed preoccupied and distant, troubled by his project at Aspiration Tower, and was even quieter than usual. Then recently, a series of power cuts had seized the city and in the evenings, when there was no light to work, they had taken to sitting on the balcony, passing a can of cold beer between them, and she had felt him return to her.

Sae stepped out onto the balcony, looking at Jae's empty seat. The countless windows of the apartments in the block facing hers appeared to her as a stack of miniature screens projecting similar lives. These glimpses were the closest thing she had to the interviews that she had conducted for work—when she'd gathered tumultuous accounts of life under dictatorship. She missed the pace of working at the newspaper, feeling the pulse and beat of breaking stories, but there was a reassuring comfort, too, in the ordinariness of her days at home with the boys.

She was pulled from these thoughts by the ring of the phone, and she picked up immediately, afraid the sound would wake the boys.

But it wasn't Jae. It was Bo-ra—who lived in the apartment two floors above her.

"Just checking in, making sure Jae got home all right. You said he was coming home early," she said. Sae could hear that she had food in her mouth and frowned, struck by the formality of a phone call.

"What do you mean?"

She heard the twist of the phone cord. Bo-ra's voice was suddenly a little louder in her ear. "He has come home, hasn't he?"

"No, he's late, actually . . ."

There was a pause. Bo-ra's voice had a strange quality to it when she spoke again. "Turn on the TV," she said and then, quietly, "It's all over the news."

The TV flickered to show the image of a car turned upside down on a street that was littered with debris. Uniformed workers were stepping over glass, their hands over their mouths. The camera panned out to display rising plumes of dust and smoke.

A bespeckled interviewer held his mic to a man who wore a suit covered in dust.

There was a loud boom, and the middle of the building just came down. I've never seen anything like it. I knew I had to get out when I first heard the noises. It was like some strange groaning animal. But there are others, he stammered, wiping the sweat from his face with his hand. There are still people trapped there.

The room began to sway, and she gripped the side of the TV stand with both hands. The phone receiver slipped onto her shoulder and she had the sensation of shifting pressure in her ears, distorting all sound. Bo-ra's voice sounded distant.

"Have you heard from him?"

Sae jerked her head to her shoulder to stop the phone from falling and pressed it against her ear.

"That's not . . . it's not . . ." Sae could not quite bring herself to say it out loud. Aspiration Tower. "When did this happen?"

"Two hours ago. What is it?"

"It's just . . . I haven't heard from Jae," Sae said.

There was a pause.

"I'm sure he's . . ." Bo-ra began.

Sae tried to say something, but a strange sound escaped her mouth.

"I'll be right down," Bo-ra said.

Sae sat with a dull ringing in her head, the receiver still in her hand. Then, calmly, she dialed his office number. There was no answer. She left another message for him on his pager and turned her attention back to the TV screen. A wailing child pointed to the ruins; people shrouded in dust limped past the camera.

Then the familiar slap-slap of Bo-ra's slippers on the outdoor stairs moments before she appeared at the door.

"He's probably on his way home," she said with a weak smile, removing her slippers before coming to sit beside Sae on the floor. Bo-ra sat formally on her knees, as though they were already at a funeral.

"There'll be a good explanation for why he hasn't called," she said. "Don't assume the worst."

But the worst had already slipped in, an uninvited guest presiding over the waiting. The news had ended, and a soap drama was unfolding without an audience.

"I have to go there," Sae said, rising to stand, feeling the blood return to her toes. She paced the room; she needed motion. Waiting without knowing, that was a thing of madness that she could not do.

"Shouldn't you wait here? He could be home at any minute."

"I heard on the news that there aren't enough relief workers," Sae said. She had the sensation of floating outside of her body, which seemed to move without instruction. "Will you stay here with the kids? I'll call you to check in every so often. Page me if you hear anything."

Bo-ra nodded, uncertainly.

At the door, she thought of the way Jae would sometimes turn on his heel before leaving the apartment to cross the room and embrace her. As though he worried she might have a change of heart before he returned. Jae. Immovable and impenetrable. Her bedrock. He would be there on-site, helping those trapped under the rubble. It was just like him to be immersed in the relief effort and forgetting to call.

Jae was a man of predictable and consistent habits, who never wavered in his path home, preferring the snaking alleyways to the crowded main roads filled with the cacophony of mopeds and the idle chatter of shopkeepers. He was a man who loved the quiet, the soft sounds of familial intimacy on residential back alleys. She could not move quickly enough, down these narrow passageways, hoping to see him as she turned each corner.

On the main road, Sae passed shopkeepers glued to the news on their TV screens, could feel the hushed rhythms of this city so used to curling into itself at the first rumblings of a crisis. At the station, she bought a subway ticket, passed through the barriers, and got on the first train to arrive, searching for Jae in the blur of faces as it pulled away.

Pressed against the other passengers, she remembered their bus rides home as students, the way they carried on their charade of being strangers after passing the checks of plainclothes officers, until he would bump up against her and she would turn her palm outward to feel his finger marking her palm. She thought of the way he had comforted the newly inducted students at the hint of violence at another protest. The way he had put his hand on the shoulder of a first year and told him, "They'll have to come through me to get to you, don't worry." The memory was soothing. She was sure she would find him with his cheek dust smeared and weary, leading someone out of the calamity.

The subway station closest to the Tower was closed, and as the carriage rolled slowly into the next station, Sae felt her heart begin to race. Several times she thought she saw him—a flash of his olive-green watch strap, the cracked black leather briefcase he refused to throw out—only to find the face of an anxious stranger blinking back at her.

At street level, a blockade had been created to allow access for emergency vehicles. Sae's heart lifted at the sight of the long line of people waiting to make a call at the phone booth. That was why, she thought, Jae had been unable to reach her. She relaxed her hands and wiped her sweaty palms against her shorts. He was probably standing in line somewhere, his impatience visible in his jaw, waiting to call her. Drawing closer to the building, she could smell wet concrete as people traipsed by her in torn and ragged clothes. The air was thick and opaque with smoke, and in her chest she felt the expansion of something oppressive and heavy.

She turned the corner and for a moment the floodlights were too bright for her eyes to take in the scene. The news report she had seen had not prepared her for it: the building standing erect in its four corners, but with its innards ripped out. For a moment she stood too stunned to move. A large broken column lay crumbled with wires sticking out like veins. Around it a wasteland of twisted steel and debris. She stepped into the dust storm, her mouth in the crook of her arm as she moved forward. The crowd was heaving forward toward the column of smoke rising at the edge of the scene, where workers were pulling objects from the rubble—concrete blocks, air-conditioning units, broken bottles of imported liquor—to attend to the voices of those trapped underground.

As she pushed past the idle spectators, looking for those clearing the rubble, it dawned on her that she had underestimated the scale of the disaster—Aspiration Tower at full height was a behemoth. The scene before her was that of a city blown apart by a bomb. It was impossible to imagine that anyone who had been in the near vicinity of the building could emerge unscathed.

A group of paramedics pushed her out of the way.

"You can't be here," one of them said as they passed her.

"I'm looking for someone," she said. The tinny quality of her voice sounded foreign to her.

A volunteer with blood-stained sleeves broke away from the group and tipped his head in the direction of the subway station. "There's a holding area for families in the gymnasium. You can wait there."

She started to protest and say that he was out among the rescue crew, but before she could finish speaking a man wearing a bright reflective vest came to report that there was a shortage of stretchers. She circled the perimeter, stepping over large blocks of concrete, shards of glass, aware of a muted siren somewhere, indistinct urgent voices, cars honking from a road nearby.

Over the din, she heard someone call her name. Turning, she saw a familiar face. She had never been so happy to see Tae-kyu. Her former colleague at *The Seoul Daily* before she had quit her job some months before, Tae-kyu was the closest thing she had to a father. In her preoccupation with finding Jae, she had not considered that he would be there.

"It takes a national crisis to see you," he said, shouting over the sound of the machinery, stepping over a pair of glasses with twisted frames. As he drew closer, she saw that his hairline was slick with sweat, and a film of ash clung to his forehead. He looked over his shoulder and gestured to the debris.

"Ever wondered what sixty-five floors looks like in powdered form?" he said.

She could not bring herself to smile, to return to their rhythm of humor as they reported on other disasters. He had reminded her of the height of the Tower and she could hardly bring herself to ask him, "But they think there are some survivors?"

"Only in the basement where there was a supermarket and maybe in the first few floors which had some luxury retail," he said. "Most of the upper floors held offices, so it will be mostly women and children down there."

When Sae said nothing to this, Tae-kyu kept talking.

"It's good to see you. I should have known you wouldn't stay at home for long. Why didn't you tell me you found another gig?"

A flattened child's shoe lay near his feet, but he did not seem to notice it. She recognized the lively expression on his face—he was his most energetic in a crisis. She didn't know how to tell him why she was there, and he seemed to misunderstand her uneasiness.

"Don't tell me you've gone to work for the *Times,*" he said, wiping the sweat from his face with the small towel around his neck.

"No, I'm not—"

"Good," he said. "You hear about the looting?" He turned to watch a team of soldiers directing a crane as it lifted a large concrete mass from the heart of the rubble. "They say there could be more than three hundred people trapped down there and all some people want to do is dig for Louis Vuitton bags. What kind of society do we live in? When looters are digging through rubble in search of designer handbags?" He glanced at her briefly. "Not that you would know. You've never owned anything designer, have you? . . . Hey, I'm kidding. Just a few months off and you've lost your sense of humor—"

He paused abruptly as he caught sight of something on the

ground. She looked down to see him looking at her feet—she was wearing only a pair of flimsy house slippers. "It's not work that's brought you here, is it?" he said, looking taken aback, putting his hand on her shoulder after a moment.

"It's Jae." She looked away. Jae had been working on the installation of a swimming pool on the top floor of the Tower. She didn't want to see Tae-kyu's face when she told him this or to see him calculating the probabilities. It was easier to stay in the realm of miracles if she didn't tell him the details. "He's working here."

This seemed to affect him visibly. Tae-kyu cleared his throat as though to say something, but silence intruded between them. Sae pushed the hair back from her forehead, unsticking her sweat-soaked T-shirt from her back.

"He's here somewhere," she said, eyeing a makeshift stretcher being loaded onto an ambulance. "I just have to find him."

Tae-kyu's momentary paralysis was unnerving; Sae had never known him to be at a loss for words. She tried to imagine what they would focus on if she was here on an assignment.

"Do they know how it happened?" she asked.

The question seemed to animate him, and he coughed before speaking. "There's some speculation that it's a gas explosion. Or maybe even a bomb."

Sae nodded. Her throat felt dry and scratchy suddenly, thinking of the Korean Air flight that had been blown up by North Korean terrorists some years before. Tae-kyu seemed to sense this was the wrong thing to say.

"I'm no expert, but the spread of the rubble doesn't seem consistent with an explosion. There would be more damage to the surrounding buildings. They say there could be a lot of survivors. It's just a question of getting them out from under all this rubble."

No sooner had Tae-kyu said this when there was a rumbling followed by shouts. There was a dulling of sound, a softening of the drills. The remaining structure seemed to be tilting sideways, the crane bending with it, the edges of the ground seeming to rise up. There was a loud crack and the remaining columns shuddered. Then all that was visible was a thick gray cloud.

SIX YEARS EARLIER

1986

Sae met Jae the year she turned nineteen, during a riot. What began as a small protest against dictator Chun Doo-hwan had spread like wildfire from one university campus to another. Helicopters had been called in at the protests at Seoul National University, and the main barricaded hall was hidden by a shroud of tear gas. Sae retreated, finding herself in an empty library. She moved past the dark bookshelves, running her fingers across dusty books, until she sensed she was not alone. Under a halo of light, a lone figure was bent over a desk. He was wearing a blue-and-white baseball shirt, his thick hair was black with wild curls cut short, rising like flames. He was statuesque in his focus, as if the protests outside were a projection of an old war film. The campus had been shut down hours before. The other protesters—her friends—had thinned into the mountains nestling the campus. The cacophony—the chants, the whistles, the drumming, the tanks—had been going on for hours. The idea that anyone could concentrate through the demonstration was astounding to her.

"We have to go," she said, shaking him lightly, seeing he had headphones on. She followed the line of his lean forearm to his shoulder, half-illuminated in the lamplight. "The police are here."

If he was startled by her presence, he did not show it and shrugged.

"I have an exam," he said.

"Can you really study through this?" she asked. The question escaped her mouth with a hiss. Students had been inducted into the movement against the government for many reasons—because of the photographs of the bodies in the unmarked graves, the possibility of arrest for possessing a book of poetry, for the torture of those who spoke out against the dictatorship. She understood those who were too afraid to participate in the movement, but his concentration felt indifferent to what was happening around them.

He flinched, hearing the accusation in her question.

"I can't fail this exam," he said.

The sound of a slamming door rang out from several levels below. Vibrations were visible in the water glass near his stack of books. She had to keep moving; she had heard the stories of what they did to the female students in the prisons. But she felt frozen, some magnetic force keeping her fixed in place.

"Don't you care about what's going on?"

"Does it matter if I care?" he said. "What will it change?"

Her face felt hot and red under her bandanna. The thundering on the stairs grew louder. She needed to go.

"I can't get involved," he said, but she thought she detected a softening of his tone.

Voices echoed at the end of the corridor. She stood frozen, unsure of which way to turn until she felt his hand on her arm pulling her toward the window.

"Over here," he said, opening a door and closing it behind her.

The janitor's closet was no larger than a bathroom cubicle. She flattened herself against the wall, disturbing some dust, which floated through a small square of light seeping in through a strip of glass in the door. Heavy footsteps were followed by muffled conversation. Slowing her breathing, she tried to quiet the rattling heart fighting inside her. Hours seemed to go by before she heard a lone pair of footsteps draw closer, then an expansion of light as the door opened.

"They've gone," he said. "Are you okay?"

The danger had passed, and with relief came an irrepressible urge to cry. Turning her face, she stared at the floor and blinked furiously until the feeling receded. When she stood up some moments later, she saw he was tall. He had the figure, she thought, of a swimmer.

"I thought you didn't want to get involved," she said, pulling her bandanna down over her chin.

"I don't have the luxury of failing this exam, okay?" he said.

Her eyes fell on his worn shoes, split like a gaping mouth at the soles. He was probably at the university on scholarship. She felt ashamed that she had misread him.

"You must resent students like us, disrupting classes," she said.

He let out a little laugh. "Why? It's so much easier to rise to the top of the class when the nation's brightest are ditching their exams to fight for their political beliefs."

She smiled a little at this. The light scent of sweat at the nape of his neck was comforting, the smell of soapy detergent a reminder of a life more ordinary. Solace had become a rarity. She was tired. Of running, of being at war with those in power. At war with her own fear.

"It's not that I'm scared," he said.

"You don't have to explain yourself to me."

"I don't know," he said. "I'm not sure how much freedom we have in poverty."

It was the kind of abhorrent sentiment that Chun and his predecessor, Park, had used to justify their ambitious economic goals, but for the first time, she could see why the dictator's vision of a wealthier country might be persuasive to a scholarship student like him. She thought of the book in her backpack—possession of it was enough to have her arrested, but she had carried it around everywhere. It was what began her search for the truth about their country. What had burdened them as students was the discovery of a system of power that held back key unsavory events in their history. They had come to the country's best institutions to further their knowledge, only to question what it meant to know at all. Part of their rebellion was a commitment to the reclamation of a more honest past.

"But how can we celebrate wealth that's been earned by slave labor? When our country's wealth has been built by silencing those who have resisted dirty corporations' sweatshops or have protested against the silencing?" She inhaled sharply and continued. "Do you really think corporations like Taehan care at all about human life?"

There was a moment of stunned silence. A helicopter was audible some distance away, and when she looked back at him, she found him searching her face, as though he were trying to decipher what she was thinking. He shifted his weight on his feet; his hands were in his pockets.

Finally, he said, "You're protesting dictatorship, aren't you? What does Taehan Group have to do with this?"

She shrugged. "I'm just using them as an example. The government and businesses are in bed together. Businesses aren't the ones who are committing murder, but they're propped up by a system that condones it."

"That's not the same as saying these companies are responsible—"

"They're complicit," she snapped, suddenly unsure of why she felt she had to persuade him there and then. There was shouting outside. The green exit sign past the row of bookshelves had begun flickering. She picked up her backpack.

"You said you don't want to get involved," she said. "I should get out of here. Thanks, for earlier."

As she moved to leave, she felt his hand on her wrist, his warm breath on her shoulder.

"Wait," he said. Outside a baritone voice was barking a message over the megaphone for students to surrender. Sae felt her face warm as he leaned toward her.

"You've got toothpaste, here," he said, reaching over. He wiped her cheek with his thumb. "Dead giveaway. The police will know you're a protester right off the bat."

"It doesn't even work," she said, with a little laugh, embarrassed. "The tear gas still burns like hell."

He continued to look at her, as if trying to piece together more information about what she was thinking.

"Listen," he said. "Maybe it's because I'm the kind of guy who needs half the class not to turn up so I can pass my exams, but I don't get it. I want to understand it better, but I don't."

She gave him a little nod and turned toward the dark stairwell. Halfway down the steps she stopped and unzipped her bag. Removing her copy of *What Is History?*, she scribbled a note for him in the margins of the title page of the second chapter, "Society and the Individual." If he was curious enough to read the book, he would find her message.

He was still standing by his desk when she returned.

"Maybe this will help," she said, handing him the book. He seemed aware that she was testing him.

Turning back to the stairwell, she could feel it burning still, the gentle touch of his thumb on her cheek.

TWENTY-FOUR HOURS AFTER THE COLLAPSE

Those awaiting news of loved ones gathered in a large school gymnasium. Thin mattresses littered the floors. Several fans had been installed; the lights were low on account of the heat. The communal microphone that announced the names of those who had been recovered had grown quiet.

"Here," Tae-kyu said, handing her a roll of gimbap. "You need to eat."

She took the gimbap from his hand but made no move to bring it to her mouth, letting the seaweed unfurl its contents onto her lap.

"You should think about getting home," he said.

Sae picked the vegetables off her shorts and calmly collected clumps of sticky rice onto her palm. "I'm not going anywhere."

"The secondary collapse has made the rescue operation more complicated. It's going to take longer to retrieve those under the rubble."

"I know that," she snapped. Tae-kyu knew better than anyone how much she hated being talked down to. He was the only one at *The Seoul Daily* who had respected her wish to be treated as an equal, to be spoken to in formal address.

"No one's going to give you a medal for sticking this out," he said, taking a sip of coffee from the paper cup in his hand. "It's been twenty-four hours. Don't you think you should be with your kids? They might start worrying that their mother has gone missing too."

"I'm going to stretch my legs and see if I hear anything," she said, her eyes sweeping the families huddled together, some rocking themselves, others weeping silently while trying to sleep. Others sat looking stonily into space. Through the open gymnasium door, Sae could see the turn in the night sky, the heat already imposing itself on the morning. An earthy, chalky smell hung heavy in the air.

Overnight a shipping container had been brought in as a makeshift office for the site. Sae approached the suited men who stood outside.

"I'm looking for someone who was working in the building," she said to a helmeted man with sparse eyebrows. "He was working for L&S Engineering?"

"You can't be here," he said. "You need to wait inside the gymnasium."

"I know that," she said, "but if there's anything you could tell me . . ." she finished, letting herself trail off. This seemed to soften him, and he wordlessly stepped into the container before returning with a clipboard moments later. He ran his finger down the list.

"What was the name of the company?" he asked, frowning.

"L&S Engineering," she said.

"I'm not seeing any L&S here." He scanned the list and flipped several more pages. "We're still a work in progress. Maybe you could check back in a few days."

Sae nodded solemnly and turned back to the gymnasium, stunned suddenly by a familiar face. It was Mrs. Bae, the wife of

Jae's business partner. Her hair was tied back, but several strands were matted to her face with sweat, her foundation melting and clustering around her pores.

"Have you heard anything?" Sae asked her. "Any news of Mr. Bae?"

Mrs. Bae shook her head, looking bewildered, her eyes darting back and forth nervously between Sae and the gymnasium door.

"He was complaining about the heat in the basement. Something about the air conditioners not working all week." Her hand trembled as she wiped at the sweat that had formed a milky mustache over her lip.

"The basement? Was Jae with him?" Sae asked. She felt a surge of relief. The secondary collapse had robbed her of hope that Jae might still be alive. His survival seemed more likely if he had been in the basement at the time of the Tower's collapse. "I thought the pool was supposed to be on the top floor. Weren't they working there?"

"Pool?" Mrs. Bae was frowning, as though she had no idea what Sae was talking about. Then a thought seemed to come, and she averted her eyes. Staring at the ground, she murmured, "Yes, the pool."

When Mrs. Bae met her eyes again briefly, Sae saw some frantic desperation in them, like a trapped bird flapping against glass. It was a look Sae had come to know well in her years of interviewing traumatized family members for the paper. Silence beholden by fear.

"I guess it means they weren't able to finish the job," Mrs. Bae whispered. "No one was supposed to know about it."

"No one was supposed to know about the pool?" Sae asked, confused.

Sae wanted to shake Mrs. Bae, to jostle some explanation out of her so that these fragments might fall together into some semblance of meaning. But it became evident that Mrs. Bae was receding into a state of shock. As though held in a trance, Mrs. Bae showed no signs of having heard her. Sae led Mrs. Bae by the elbow and helped her to sit down.

"Let me get you a glass of water," she said gently.

TWO DAYS AFTER THE COLLAPSE

Myong-hee held a cigarette in her mouth, rearranging the large lilies in the vase on the reception desk, dissatisfied with the arrangement. Song-mi, her most reliable girl, was late again for the third evening in a row. Something was brewing in her, and Myong-hee needed to know what it was. In their line of work, the absence of a girl meant something. If a girl went missing for several hours, she was usually feeling the shame slide out from between her legs, as she held on to the bed like a raft until sobriety returned. More than a day and it was likely she had decided to make a clean break from the club. Thirty-six hours, and the girl was gone for good, either lying eyes wide in a ditch or on her way there. For three nights in a row, Song-mi had arrived many hours after the club had opened, plain faced, a hesitation in her hand as she caught sight of herself in the mirror before reluctantly brushing color onto her cheeks. Unlike the other girls, she did not have a mountain of debt, but worked the rooms in the hopes that a media executive might notice her and turn her into a starlet. If the girl was losing her ambition, Myong-hee needed to know.

Myong-hee stepped back to admire her efforts. No matter how many times she removed the stems and put them in again, the flowers drooped and hung their heads, lifeless. None of her clients would notice the lilies, but the details mattered to her. The club, Myongwolgwan, was a midnight sanctuary, a place where men could relax, cut loose. Where they could say what they wanted to their superiors and be forgiven. Everything about the layout of Myongwolgwan—the antique mirror purchased from a dealer in Paris, the expensive leather sofas in the karaoke rooms, the mirrored ceilings, the velvet booths and heavy furniture—had been carefully selected to create a sense of luxury.

Each karaoke room was slightly different in size and theme to accommodate the occasion to be held within its walls. The largest one, used mostly for small teams in a department, held up to ten men and as many girls, and was painted a pale yellow. All three walls were lined with soft leather sofas where the men began their evenings with drinks before they moved to stand and dance and sing in front of the big TV screens.

Abandoning the vase, Myong-hee set about checking the rooms before the club opened for the night. Areas that moments before seemed acceptable suddenly seemed askew and off-kilter, the mirrors slanting, sudden patches of grime visible in corners she had wiped down with a rag several times before. Snapping on a pair of rubber gloves, she checked the gaps in the sofa and under the table in each room. Wiped down surfaces with bleach, enjoying the burn of it in her nostrils. She pulled out a sock with a hole in it. An empty cigarettes packet. A ripped condom. She would have to remind the girls again to insist that the men keep their trousers on until they got to the private rooms upstairs. Groping behind a cushion, she found a photograph. A woman with neat bobbed hair, a slight smile, loving almond eyes. A wife or girlfriend. One who might find lipstick stains on a collar. Who would have no choice but to accept the explanation her husband would give her. *How can I say no? Everyone else is going. This is work. Another demand of the office.* An obligation as mandatory to them all as military service. The woman in the photograph looked like Song-mi, with her porcelain skin and wide eyes. The same warmth that allowed Song-mi to turn a conversation and persuade the men to speak freely about anything.

The evening unfurled slowly, with fewer clients rolling in than usual. The collapse of the Tower two days before had affected the national mood, and men rushed home to the families they usually ignored. Myong-hee had heard the news on the radio and absorbed it, unaffected. There might have been a time when such news might have given her hope that a moment of reckoning had come for Taehan Group. But she no longer believed in karma or justice. Not when money was involved.

There was a racket at the top of the stairs and a group of men smelling of sake appeared by the lectern at the entrance of the club. Over the years she had begun to associate certain characteristics with men working in various industries. Executives conducted themselves with an air of authority, seeing the club as an extension of their offices, a relaxed space that was their earned right. Academics were the worst dressed and hid their intellectual discomfort in being patrons of room salons by being overly generous to the girls, and in effect, completely insincere. Those in service industries were kind but made demanding customers. Junior employees of any industry were the girls' preferred clients—nervous and unaccustomed to this ritual of the workplace, they were still respectful and often too drunk for sex.

A figure she recognized stepped out of the dark stairwell and into the club.

"Mr. Shim! How nice to see you," she said with her brightest smile. She had known Mr. Shim since he was a junior employee at a retail bank and kept his business as he rose through the ranks to become a senior executive of corporate loans. Hooking her arm in his, she led his group into a room.

"Who are these handsome men you've brought with you?" Myong-hee asked.

"My most important investors," Mr. Shim said. "I was bragging to them that you have the most beautiful women in all of the city."

"You told me they have the biggest breasts!" an unfamiliar man with a hooknose and liver spots on his temples quipped.

"You're too kind," Myong-hee said, smiling.

"But it looks like yours are out on a break," the man with the hooknose added with a wink.

Myong-hee covered her mouth as she laughed, her eyes falling on his gold watch and expensive-looking cuff links. This was a performance she could handle. "Well, I only work behind the desk! Someone has to organize this place! But now that I know your taste, I'll be sure to send you the kind of girls you'll like."

"I like her," he said to the men while patting Myong-hee's backside. Myong-hee helped him out of his suit jacket, noting the foreign designer label, the dry-cleaning ticket still clipped to the interior lining.

Once the men were settled, Myong-hee slipped back to the waiting room where the girls got ready, took their break, or waited to be summoned. It was a narrow space, but brightly lit, makeup littering most surfaces—including the TV that blasted the weekly music charts. Song-mi's beanbag lay crushed as she had left it in the corner. Se-ri screwed on the lid of her nail polish, and Mae closed her book and combed her hair as Myong-hee turned to her.

"The man wearing the Italian suit. He's new. Find out who he is and what he does."

After the evening's lull, it was all happening at once, with several groups arriving at the same time. Men with breath sour with soju and garlic, their suits exhaling the scent of grilled meat. Most of them were regulars. Myong-hee took care to show them that she remembered them by being attentive to the smallest of details—their favorite snacks, their whiskey preferences. She was always conscious of how much her clients wanted to spend, and was mindful not to overcharge them. There was a calculation in every gesture, designed to keep her clients coming back.

It was well past midnight as Myong-hee set about to take stock of the drinks when Mr. Li arrived. Mr. Li was a longtime Taehan Group employee, with a large square jaw and greasy hair over small friendly eyes. He stepped heavily down the stairs.

"Mr. Li," she said, her eyebrows high in surprise, the practiced look of delight. "What a coincidence! I was just thinking of you. It's quite a surprise at a time—" She stopped, realizing that it would be a mistake to call attention to the crisis at his work. "I don't know how you don't age!" she said, changing tack.

In truth, he looked haggard, worry a weighted mask against

his sagging skin, his jowls heavy and swollen, the skin of his neck like the flesh of a freshly plucked bird.

"Are you here for our company or are you expecting someone?" she asked. She had learned a long time ago that she should never assume that she knew the men's intentions for coming to her rooms.

"Is the boss here yet?" Mr. Li asked.

"No, I haven't heard from him," she replied, redirecting Mr. Li toward the most luxurious of the rooms. If Yung was coming only the best would do.

"We need a quiet place to talk," Mr. Li said, leaning into her conspiratorially. "The office is surrounded by reporters, no one can get in or out without being hounded."

"Oh?" Myong-hee asked. She was intrigued but did not ask any more. It was as she always told Song-mi—appear disinterested in work and allow the men to put their guards down. Though in truth the men were rarely worried about the women listening to their business exchanges. As they entered the room, she helped him out of his jacket and lit a cigarette for him.

"We need to figure out how to explain the Chairman's absence. I mean, think what the press will say. If they think he's taken off, what do you think is going to happen?"

This was not a rhetorical question. Mr. Li was a man who loved to be in command of information. It was likely that Taehan Group had thousands of construction projects around the world. The disappearance of the Chairman would put these contracts and future ones in jeopardy, but she feigned ignorance, to help Mr. Li feel at ease.

"Gosh, I'm not sure," Myong-hee said, a little breathlessly. "It would make the company look bad."

"We've got casualties of over one thousand dead and even more injured. No one is coming out of this with clean hands. The last thing we need is for our clients to think that we have unsafe practices. If the Chairman has gone missing at the height of the crisis, it makes us look guilty, doesn't it?"

Myong-hee nodded. The suggestion that the Chairman might finally be held accountable quickened her heart. Her cheeks felt heavy as she struggled to maintain her smile, her sight blurred slightly. She shifted uncomfortably in her seat, remembering she was mid-performance. She wanted to know more, but didn't want to seem too eager. The business of excavation was also one of timing. If Yung was in the right mood, she would be able to ask him for more details later.

"Why don't I find you some company while you wait?"

Mr. Li nodded gratefully, and as Myong-hee moved to leave, she regretted that Song-mi was not around to sit with the men when the president of Taehan Group arrived. She was someone Myong-hee could rely on who could report back on the men's conversations.

Later that evening, in a sparsely furnished room above the karaoke rooms, Myong-hee reached over Mr. Li's naked body to turn off the lamp.

"Don't," Mr. Li said. "I want to be able to see you. Have I ever told you that you remind me of someone?"

At the age of fifty, she was aware that she was still beautiful. She knew too that seduction was as much about making the other feel desired as about one's attractiveness, but still she moved her face out of the light, uncomfortable with this scrutiny. She put some oil in her palm, hoping to silence him and finish the job without him entering her, and extract whatever information she wished afterward. He reached under her bra and squeezed her breast.

"Take this thing off," he said, his voice raspy.

She did as she was told, feeling her nipples harden in the cold, but as soon as she did, he seemed to lose interest in her breasts, reaching under the tent of her skirt to put his fingers inside her. It had been a long time since she had played this role with a client. She had forgotten that half of the intimacy was in the closeness of a stranger's smell, the knowledge of someone's most recent meals in their breath. But there was also something to be gained too, a golden few minutes after he came, when he was at his most sedate, when she could ask whatever she wanted. She picked up the rhythm in her hands, encouraged by the quickening of his breath, but just when she thought he might come, he gripped her wrist.

"Not so fast. I want to finish inside you."

He raised her skirt around her waist. When she moved to lie down, he shook his head and asked her to turn over. It was both a relief and an affront that he did not want to see her face. He entered her, but his movements were half-hearted. When she turned to look at him, she could see that his face was wet, and red from straining.

"It's not working," he said.

"That happens," she said, hoping that this would not grow into an even longer evening of thwarted efforts. "You should get your wife to fix you some eel. They say it helps."

He wiped his face with his hand and gently pushed her hips away from him.

"You're under pressure," she said, sensing it would not take much for him to spill over.

He lay down heavily beside her and dug his fingertips into his eyes.

"I'm finished. We all are."

"Taehan Group has been in trouble before," she offered.

Mr. Li sat up and sighed, reaching for a drink with a trembling hand. "You don't understand, it could have been prevented. I don't know how we get out of this," he said, the remaining words seeming to congeal in his throat. "I don't want to go to prison," he said.

"Why would you go to prison?" she asked him.

"Well," he said, rolling onto his side. "Because someone has to."

He buried his head in her chest and she held him, surprised by the sudden pity she felt. She knew how the Chairman had built his empire, and how ordinary people like Mr. Li were promised more and better, only to be used and discarded. Her vision began to blur as it had earlier that evening, her body flushed, her long-buried anger stirring.

"You're trembling," Mr. Li said, suddenly tender as he stroked her face, misunderstanding. "Don't worry, I'm going to get us out of this."

Later, Myong-hee sat with her head between her legs, a cigarette in her fingers. She wanted to move but could not, hunched over, at war with an ache in her chest that threatened to expand if she allowed it. Usually she set herself in motion, to nurse herself out of it, but all the bottles had been cleared, the surfaces and leather sofas wiped down with a damp rag. There was nothing left for her but a taxi home, the lights blurring past her from karaoke rooms and love motels with hourly rates. Disposable love for disposable lives.

She lifted her head at the sound of the whining back door. Someone had come in. After a moment's hesitation, she stepped toward the back door.

"Who's there?"

A figure moved in the darkness. Myong-hee stepped back, afraid that it might be trouble. Then the rising relief at the sight of Song-mi. She had dark circles under her eyes, and even in the poor light her skin looked blotchy, her hair looked greasy and unwashed. Where was the girl with the wicked sense of humor and fighting spirit?

"Where have you been?" Myong-hee asked, though what she really wanted to ask was why she had come back, the silly girl. Why hadn't she slipped away from this life when she had the chance?

THIRTY-SIX HOURS AFTER THE COLLAPSE

The first thing Sae saw when she opened her front door was Jae's work jacket hanging over the chair by the kitchen table. She stepped into the living room, her heart in her throat. A flood of relief—he was back—it had been a bad dream. Then she heard a sigh and saw Bo-ra asleep on the sofa. Another glance revealed nothing but Jae's absence—his shoes were not set out neatly by the front door, his keys were not on the cracked china plate in the entryway. Then it came back to her—the jacket had been there for days. She had brought it out for him, insisting that it was still chilly in the mornings. He had left it at home, saying that it was sweltering where he worked.

Remembering Mrs. Bae's remark about the heat in the basement, she found herself bargaining with hope. If Jae had been working in the basement there was still a chance he was alive. Dropping her bag, she poured herself a glass of water, mulling over Mrs. Bae's uncertainty about the pool. Setting the glass down without taking a sip, she leaned over the sink. Her thoughts had taken on a looping quality, and she could no longer attempt to untangle Mrs. Bae's comments.

"When did you get back?" Bo-ra asked, her voice full of sleep.

"Just now," Sae replied, pressing her eyes with her palms. "Did the kids give you hell?"

"Hoon-min was crying for you for an hour. Seung-min fell asleep consoling him."

"I'm sorry, I should have called," she said, surveying the spread of toys in the living room—remnants of their day she had missed.

"He wouldn't let me touch him," Bo-ra said. She started to say something, seemed to change her mind, and then turned to Sae. "They kept asking for you."

"What did you tell them?" she asked, trying not to betray her alarm. She picked up the red Super Sentai figurine on the floor. Its head was missing. She looked around for it, spotting it by Jae's hanging coat.

"That Jae was tied up with work and that you had to help him," she said, massaging her right shoulder. "Have you told his family?"

"You're right," Sae said, forcing the loose head of the Power Ranger back into place, not wanting to explain to Bo-ra that Jae had no one else. "I should do that."

"Do you want me to stay?"

"No, I think I'll try to sleep."

"Do that," Bo-ra said. "I'll check on you tomorrow."

Not knowing what to do now that she was alone, Sae filled the tub and undressed. It was too hot for a bath, but she needed to shock herself out of the rotation of unanswered questions. She examined the bruises on her arms and legs. Marks she did not remember acquiring. Raising boys was intensely physical work, her body was used as a shield multiple times a day to absorb the shocks of their play. How could she do this, continue to be this for them, without Jae? There was no one else. No one to call to deliver the news. No mother who would collapse to her knees on the receiving end of the line. When Seung-min had first been born, she had pressed Jae about his family again, armed with a newfound curiosity about lineage and history. She recalled the stiffening of his shoulders, his retreat with every additional question.

She splashed her face with water and pressed her eyes shut to clear these thoughts. He would be home soon. There would be a good explanation. They would laugh about it afterward, relieved not to have lost what they now knew they had, and guilty that others had not been so lucky.

She sat in the bath, her knees like island peaks in the water. Jae had teased her about how smooth they were. *This is not the knee of a soldier of the revolution,* he said. When they had first slept together it had been in a motel with a leaking roof and flickering light from a broken traffic signal outside. Jae with his Hollywood actor jaw and cashew nut eyes when he smiled. She remembered feeling overwhelmed—the soft drip of the rain into the small stainless steel bowl, the light that kept shifting the shadows across his body, the knowledge that tomorrow would bring another protest and that they might not be so lucky to get away from the police again.

There was a sound in the corridor outside the apartment. Rising from the water, she dried herself quickly and leapt to the door. But the kitchen was as she left it—Jae's jacket still waiting for him, cradled by the chair.

The green cuckoo clock on the wall announced that it was two A.M. Almost thirty-six hours since the Tower had collapsed. Was it a mistake to have returned home instead of staying on the site, monitoring every rescue and development? Here in the apartment, she kept discovering herself suspended. She felt she was on a tightrope, unable to move forward in her waiting. She picked up the scattered toys in the living room and washed the few dishes in the sink.

Turning on the TV she found that she could not keep track of the characters or the story line. She switched it off and tipped the spines of several books before finding the book that she wanted. She traced the margin notes written in Jae's neat handwriting. For years they had left notes for each other in books that they passed between them, leaving words that felt too vulnerable to say out loud, or later, after the children were born, that there never seemed to be the right moment to say.

Once, she had picked up the novel *Immortality,* which Jae had impressed her many times that she should read and found that he had underlined the words: "In the algebra of love a child is the symbol of the magical sum of two beings." In the margins, he had written *The days feel long without you. We miss you.*

Now, she picked up the old copy of *What Is History?* and flipped through its pages, searching for the margin note she had left him.

Meet me at the clock tower at noon on Wednesday.

What Sae had not written in the margins for Jae in that copy of *What Is History?*: that she had come to university naïve, harboring the hope that her childhood friend Il-hyung might have become worldly enough to notice that her feelings for him were no longer strictly platonic. It had happened the year before he left for university—they had been lying on the pavilion by the sea in the dark when a self-consciousness had come over her. A realization that anything was possible between them—something sexual in nature, or perhaps even violent—that no one would need to know about. They had spent most of their childhood together, alone in fields or by the seaside, and it was the first time that she had wondered whether he had ever seen her as a woman, rather than as a conjoined twin. This line of thinking led her to reevaluate their friendship, and later laid the crumbs toward desire. By the time Il-hyung left for university, she was sure she was in love with him.

Sae and Il-hyung wrote to each other in the year that they were apart—he was a year older—until the letters began to peter out. At first, she thought it was because they were aware that they would spend more time together when she went to attend the same university, but when she saw him again, she sensed that he had changed. He had grown his hair long and wore wire glasses too large for his face. The first time they met on campus, where she was now a freshman, was at the corner of the university. His eyes had remained on the busy student-filled streets, on the plainclothes police officers on every block. It seemed he could look at everything but her.

He had become a student of film, and every question Sae asked him seemed to lead back to the same place.

"If you think about it, it's not just that these hostess films are cheap to make," he said. "It distracts the masses from what's going on in the country. Better to be satiated with a cheap thrill than to consider the plight of the working class, right?"

Sae nodded, though she was surprised by the turn in the conversation.

He stopped suddenly at the street corner and met her eyes directly for the first time.

"What I'm saying, Sae, is that romance is the ultimate fantasy. It's a red herring. Focusing on individual relationships is a distraction from what we can do for the community, for society as a whole."

At last Sae understood. He seemed to be trying to find a way to tell her indirectly why he had not replied to her letters. Before Sae could respond, Il-hyung pointed to a door and led her down a basement stairwell to a small underground café where a small group of students had gathered around a table.

"What do you remember being told about the Gwangju uprising three years ago?" a narrow-faced upperclassman asked them after he poured each of them a mug of hot barley tea.

Sae remembered very little. There had been a small article in the paper about a skirmish in the city. Four North Korean infiltrators had tried to incite revolution in the city.

"It was reported as a small uprising of communist sympathizers, downplayed in the papers as a small event. But there have been rumors that there was a lockdown. That thousands of ordinary civilians were killed by the military. Some were buried in mass graves outside of the city," Il-hyung said. Turning toward Sae, he said, "Doesn't it unsettle you that something like this could have happened and that we knew nothing about it?"

The upperclassman threw a book into Sae's lap. The photocopied pictures were grainy, but the violent motion was clear. The blurred baton swinging in from the edge of the photograph was a second strike. The pregnant woman was lying on the ground, her head in a halo of blood.

"This is what our fascist government is willing to do to anyone who dares to dissent."

Sae looked up at Il-hyung, sickened, unsure why he was subjecting her to this. Then she remembered the student who had confronted a professor about his lecture on the circumstances of the dictator's rise to power. "What about Gwangju?" he had asked. "Are we going to talk about what happened there?" The professor had dismissed them early, and the student had not shown up in class again. At the time she had not given it much thought—it was easier to believe that he had become disillusioned with the professor and had given up the class. Now she saw another possibility. That he had been silenced. And suddenly she did believe it—that an entire city could be held under siege while the rest of the country was deaf and blind.

"It's time to wake up and confront what has been sacrificed in the name of progress. History," Il-hyung paused, his eyes meeting Sae's, "is not as we have been told.

"They told us extremists and rebels stormed the city. They lied. They told us no civilians were killed. They lied. These were students and civilians who had gathered to call for the end of martial law. These were students our age, gunned down by paratroopers. Demonstrators and innocent bystanders were slaughtered. The families of those who were missing were too afraid to go to the authorities. How can it be that the deaths of so many can go unnoticed? Can be forgotten so easily? How can it be that we are learning about what happened from foreign newspapers?"

Two students in the group had begun weeping; others were looking at Il-hyung, studying him intently as if they were unsure whether to believe him. She was not used to this new, serious version of him. In high school, Il-hyung's tendency had been to resort to humor in moments of tension. She did not know what to make of this authoritative persona, this newfound charisma, and could only hope that the mask would come off in private. But even as she maintained her suspicion of his performance, she was deeply troubled by what had been revealed at the meeting. So when, several hours later, the upperclassmen invited them to consider becoming involved in a book group where they would study banned texts, she agreed immediately.

As she got up to leave, she felt Il-hyung's hand on her shoulder. He handed her a book wrapped in newspaper.

"You should read this."

When she tried to unwrap it to look at the cover, he stopped her.

"Wait until you get home, and don't get caught with it. We'll discuss it next week."

Back at her desk, in her dormitory, Sae switched on the light and removed the newspaper from the book jacket. *What Is History?* and the author's name, Edward Hallett Carr, were embossed in gold lettering on the hardback. She read as fast as she could, flipping through the Korean-English dictionary to look up the words she didn't know.

> When you read a work of history, always listen out for the buzzing. If you can detect none, either you are tone-deaf or your historian is a dull dog. The facts are really not at all like fish on the fishmonger's slab. They are like fish swimming about in a vast and sometimes inaccessible ocean; and what the historian catches will depend, partly on chance, but mainly on what part of the ocean he chooses to fish in and what tackle he chooses to use—these two factors being, of course, determined by the

> kind of fish he wants to catch. By and large, the historian will get the kind of facts he wants. History means interpretation.

Sae drew back in her chair. A small scrawl at the corner of the page caught her attention. *Who wrote our history textbooks?* In all their years in education, had they ever been invited to interrogate anything or anyone? History was equated to science. The facts were simply facts. Irrefutable. What had happened at Gwangju proved that what they knew of events had been distilled, facts buried. If they did not know what was happening in the country, then they had no grasp of history. If they had no grasp of history, they did not know who they were. Carefully placing the book back in its newspaper cover, she slipped out of the room and onto the roof. Her heart raced; she was terrified by all that she could not answer. Down in the garden, the day's laundry remained on the line. Farther down the mountain, the bright lights of downtown Seoul burned with industry. No doubt there were still people working throughout the night to reach the ambitious deadlines their employers had set them. Even as students they were expected to work from dawn until dusk. There was never time for rest or leisure, let alone contemplation or to challenge the way things were.

After her father's death, Sae had decided that she would do everything she could to leave Mallipo, go to Seoul National University, and then return to support her mother. She became a workhorse, mechanically memorizing what she needed to know for the exams—going straight to her desk as soon as her school hours were finished and studying late into the early hours of the morning. She did not allow herself to feel—not hunger or thirst or loneliness. She imagined university to be the antidote to their descent into poverty; she hoped it would reroute her mother's walk. Each day, her mother took the long path home from the market to avoid a confrontation with her debtors. There was a practical reality promised by a degree, but university also held the promise of a completely different experience from the days of rote learning in her high school classes—the hope of feeling inspired, witnessing an impassioned debate with a professor, freedom, the decadence of discussing a theoretical idea. University held the promise of intellect being pushed, and wonder being nurtured.

When her first professor, a small man wearing a neat knitted vest despite the late August heat, entered the classroom and began speaking in a soft, shaky voice, her hopes dissipated. They had been tricked into industrious studiousness and sold a false dream. As the sociology class unfolded, she saw that the class was an extension of those she had in high school. They were there to listen and focus on preselected texts. Any time a student raised their hand to ask a question, the instructor would shut it down. Later she would learn that the presence of state agents in the lecture halls had stifled everyone.

After that first meeting Il-hyung had invited her to, Sae soon discovered that the education that mattered was taking place underground. Her classmates studied texts they smuggled in, like Lenin's *What Is to Be Done?* They had animated discussions, drawing parallels between the industrial development described in Marx's *Capital* and what was happening in South Korea. No one had been allowed to criticize the government's ambitious economic agenda, but in these groups the seniors spoke openly and critically about how the economic development of their country was based on what was equivalent to slave labor. Sae got much more from the close readings and discussions of these texts than she got in any classroom. She was undecided about whether communism was really the best system for society but thought people should have the opportunity to decide for themselves. What really bothered her was the suppression of truth, the idea that they were inculcated into a system that hid texts and withheld key facts to present a heroic and clean version of history. She believed knowledge shouldn't be an instrument of power but something that was freely available to everyone. They were told that resistance to unjust authority was a waste of their youth and their privilege. After all, they were lucky enough to have the opportunity for an education while other college-aged workers struggled to make a living wage.

The necessity of dismantling the dictatorship was the only thing Sae was sure of; it became the most important thing to her. She stopped going to her classes. Her schoolwork seemed trivial. She and others in the student movement used every opportunity to voice their resistance and disapproval of the dictatorship. They believed it was the right use of their privilege, to not simply tend to their own interests and status but to look after others.

In her first year in the movement, there were small protests on an almost-daily basis. She was responsible only for the gathering of pebbles to throw at the armed guards during the protests. Older classmates would tell her when and where to be for the next demonstration, often a mere half hour before she was to be there. After that first summer she was introduced to more members of the underground family, senior students who had organized the protests for years. They taught her how to make Molotov cocktails, gave her more books to read, listened and engaged in meaningful debates with her. By her final year of university, she was responsible for recruiting and educating younger students. Slowly, she felt herself detach from Il-hyung. She couldn't help but notice that he often asked the female students to prepare snacks and meals while the male students pored over the texts, or suggested that they offer childcare while the male students helped farmers with their farmwork and learned about their production cycles. The other female students thought her to be arrogant because she refused to make coffee for the older senior male students during the meetings. One of the older female students told her off for causing faction within the movement with her feminist principles. Who had time for women's rights, they said, when democracy was at stake?

They had been working for a cause that should have brought them a sense of unity. Instead, she had felt alone. Part of the alienation was intentional. They were not to become too familiar with one another, so that there would be nothing to reveal in an interrogation should they get caught.

Over time Sae began to feel weary, having absorbed the anguish and resentment of the parents whose homes she cleared of evidence whenever one of her classmates was arrested. One mother had thrown a cup of water over her, blaming her for her son's involvement in the movement. For the interrogation that the whole family would endure as a result.

So when she found Jae waiting for her at the clock tower, a

week after meeting him, the first thing she had felt was shame. Had she been sincere in wishing to induct him into the movement? She had only wanted to see him again.

"You found my note," she said.

He was wearing a wrinkled plaid shirt and a pair of faded jeans. The same pair of split-soled shoes from when they had met in the library. He seemed nervous, looking over his shoulder every now and then. In the daylight his face seemed narrower, his features more delicate than she remembered.

"I wanted to see you again," he began, his eyes still roaming the crowd of students around them. "I mean . . ." he said, putting his fists into his front pockets. "I wanted to talk to you about the book. It's left me with a lot of questions."

He held in his eye a raw weariness, as if looking upon the world through a new filter or lens. It had happened to her, too. That look that questioned everything. She wanted to put him at ease. To be able to comfort him with the touch of a hand.

"Why don't we take a walk? Go somewhere a little quieter?"

He gave her the smallest of smiles and let her lead the way.

They crossed the campus, toward the forest trail. He began to talk about what he had read. How it made him question power completely differently. How he had also not considered that the history they had been taught might have convenient omissions. She liked how thoughtful he was. His words were measured, fully considered. She liked that he asked questions and engaged with her responses, instead of lecturing her, as Il-hyung liked to do.

"There's more to it, though, isn't there?" he said. "You didn't give me the book just to make a philosophical point about who authors history."

She hesitated. There was something undernourished about him. The hardest thing about knowing the truth was that there was no way to unlearn it, that nothing was ever the same again. "There's a group of us who gather every week. We read books that have been banned. Sometimes we talk about events that aren't reported on the news. About the government and what we can do to resist."

Their steps slowed. The regal blue sky was now hiding behind a blanket of clouds. Sae sat down to lean against a rock and studied him against the bamboo grove. He looked down at his shoes.

"It's a personal decision whether you want to join or learn more," she said, realizing how little he had told her about himself. "I don't know anything about you. It's going to come at the cost of your family life. I don't know anyone who has been able to save their relationship with their parents. I don't know—"

"There's nothing to save," he said hastily.

"Oh," she said, looking at the tear in the buttonhole of his shirt. She had already sensed something of this story, his loneliness in the library. "I'm sorry."

The rock Sae was sitting on was uncomfortably hard. She rose to her feet and flattened the collar of his shirt, thinking how his hand on her cheek in the library had felt like a gesture of protection. It was not until years later that she understood that she had sought in him an ally, a refuge from the alienation she felt within the movement. She was not to know, at that moment, that he was to become one of its most fervent members.

THREE DAYS AFTER THE COLLAPSE

"When is Appa coming back from his trip?" Seung-min asked. He had refused to go down to the playground while Hoon-min napped, intent on sticking himself to her thighs. He felt too warm against her bare skin, too heavy on her lap, but no suggestion would deter him or move him more than three paces from her.

"He'll be home soon, as soon as he's done with work."

Beside them Mrs. Song sat silently stripping withered strands of spring onion from the stalk. Since Sae had returned home from the site of the collapsed rubble, she had hardly been alone, with a neighbor or two always in her living room, doing some chore or other. These were neighbors that she had recently befriended, stay-at-home wives who spent their afternoons complaining about their lives—the hollowness of their marriages, their sweet turned bitter husbands. About the circularity of their days, the unending cycle of the dishes, their mother-in-law's endless nagging, the side dishes—pickled cucumbers, sesame oil–soaked spinach, pickled radishes—which took so long to make but disappeared as soon as they turned their backs. What was the point of paying attention to what they wore, or their appearance, they said, when no one saw them anymore. They had become Invisible Women. She listened to these stories with the manner of a journalist undercover, as if she were on assignment again; not quite accepting that she might now be one of them, having given up working at the paper.

During these gatherings, they eagerly waited for Sae to toss in her complaints about Jae. How could she tell them that he was not like any of their husbands? That he treated them as treasures—the family he never had as a child? If he was tired, he never complained. He could appear serious and cold to others, but in the presence of their little family, he was animated and playful.

"Will he bring back lots of presents?" Seung-min asked.

"Yes," she said, without much conviction. She wanted to peel him off her, to mute his never-ending questions. She didn't know how much longer she could contain the looming eruption, her frustration with waiting, the lack of space, the sense that she could hardly be alone with her fear.

"But how many?" he asked, climbing onto her lap again.

"Why don't you go play outside, Seung-min?" she said, untangling herself from his grasp.

He placed his finger on the edge of her nose. "Why are your eyes so red, Omma?"

"Seung-min? Will you go upstairs to my apartment and see if Soo-ah has finished her homework? If she has you can both go and get some ice cream," Mrs. Song said.

Seung-min looked to Sae before reluctantly leaving to find Mrs. Song's daughter.

As soon as he had disappeared upstairs, Mrs. Song asked her, "Still no word?"

"No," Sae said simply. Three days had passed and her calls to the hospital had been fruitless. Mrs. Song opened her mouth to say something and then seemed to reconsider before setting her attention to peeling the onion in her hand. Just then, the phone began to ring and Sae leapt to it.

"It's me," Tae-kyu said. "Have you checked the hospitals?"

"Not since last night."

"They've heard some voices underground, they've got a team removing concrete right now," Tae-kyu said. "They've got a pipe down there, got some drinking water to them."

"I'll be there as soon as I can."

"No, don't come just yet. I didn't get any names, but I think they were part of a janitorial department. But it's good news; it means there are still people alive down there."

Sae gripped the receiver a little more tightly. The hope that rose in her chest was weighed down by a growing pessimism.

"They've ruled out a bomb. They think it might be something structural. They're investigating the foundations as we speak."

Sae's thoughts returned to Mrs. Bae's remarks. If the infinity pool was being built on the sixty-fifth floor, what had Mr. Bae, and possibly Jae, been doing down in the basement? She could not remember if he had mentioned having an office in the Tower. Why would they have been working in the basement? Had they been called to check on the foundations of the Tower?

"I have to go," she said, letting the receiver slip down her cheek.

She tried to call Mrs. Bae, but the line was busy.

Mrs. Song was staring at her expectantly, waiting for news. Sae felt ungenerous, suddenly resentful of her neighbors' watchful attention, no longer sure whether they were there to help or to witness her slow unraveling.

"They think they may have found something at the site," Sae said, picking up her purse. "Will you watch the kids?"

The elevator in Mrs. Bae's apartment building was broken, and so Sae took the stairs. Glimpsing the sudden downpour through the window, she thought of those waiting to be cut out of the rubble. A survivor who had been uncovered the day before claimed to have survived on rainwater. It was coming down now in heavy sheets, and pools of water were forming on the roads. How many more lay waiting under layers of earth? Waiting for that crack of light in the darkness? The sound of another's voice?

At the top of the stairs, she had to stop, feeling winded and dizzy, and placed her head in her hands. She took several moments to catch her breath and waited for the granite corridor to come back into focus. Only a week before she had sat with Jae on the balcony in the sweltering heat, feeling the transfer of sweat from his upper lip onto hers. He kissed her, but his thoughts were elsewhere. Pressing the cold beer can in her hands to his bare chest, she made him jump as she summoned him back to her.

"Where are you? It feels like you're not here, even when you're sitting right next to me."

He looked down at the can before meeting her eyes. "I'm here."

"You've been preoccupied lately."

"It's work," he said, raising the beer to his lips. In the silence that followed, Sae had the sense that he was organizing what he could tell her and what he should leave out. Finally, he put his arm around her. "When this is all over, we should get out of the city."

She smiled. "Where would we go?"

"Jeju-do? Pusan? Anywhere, so long as we're together."

"And when would that be?"

"Every day feels like it could be the last."

"I didn't know you were so close to finishing?"

"That's not what I mean."

She frowned. "What do you mean?"

"I don't even know where to start," he said, fiddling with the top of the beer can.

"Start anywhere," she said with a smile. "I'm not looking for an award-winning speech."

"We should never have agreed to do it, all right? This whole thing about the swimming pool isn't—"

"Appa, you're home," a sleepy voice said from behind them. Seung-min stood rubbing his eyes. "Why is it so dark?"

"I'll lie with him," Jae said, rising to his feet.

She had waited for him, but he had never come back. When she had gone to check on them, she had found Jae fast asleep between the two cherubs, cocooned in their nest of wings.

After several rings of the doorbell, Sae knocked on the door only to find it falling open.

"Anyone home?"

There was no answer. The apartment was smaller than she expected and had a nostalgic, wistful touch. Of faded honeymoon hopes and neglected aspirations. Pink fabric wallpaper clung to the walls, rippled by humidity. It was only as Sae slipped off her shoes that she heard the dial tone and crossed the living room to replace the receiver back on the hook. The sink was full of dishes. Water stains had whitened patches on the floor from the kitchen to the living room.

The remaining daylight illuminated a layer of dust on the cabinets. In the bedroom the radio was still on, turned down low, and several winter coats were laid out on the bed. She pulled the mirrored closet door aside to find skeletal hangers suspended on the rail. Drawers hung open, slack-jawed and uneasy in the telling of a hurried departure.

Sae closed the closet doors and opened another, moving more quickly from one room to another. She checked the balcony, opened the closet in the hallway, scanned their second bedroom. Noted gaps in the rack by the door where only a few shoes had been selected for the journey.

She went back to the hallway closet and stood in front of it as though it were a window overlooking a scene from a great height. Sae thought of Mrs. Bae's reluctance to meet her eye, her palpable fear. The realization was like an electrical surge in her veins; Mr. Bae was alive, because his clothes were gone, too.

9 A.M., August 26, 2016
Chairman's residence, Gugi District, Seoul

If there's one thing that I had to master in order to become a successful businessman, it is how to read people. You've bought a new suit for this job, your shoes look new, but the way you sit suggests that you are ill at ease with me. I thought you were supposed to be the fearless reporter and I, the defensive subject of inquiry. You should feel comfortable asking me anything if you're going to work for me.

You may have heard things about me, so I understand that you may feel intimidated. Throughout my career I've been called all sorts of things. Tycoon. The father of the South Korean economy. A reporter at *The Korea Times* called me the commander of miracles because of what I have achieved with Taehan Group. That tickled me. It's true that whenever someone tells me that something is not possible, I get a tingling in my gut, an overwhelming whole-body itch to prove them wrong. After all, there is nothing more foolish than to suggest that something is impossible without even trying. Why make your world narrow and small by sticking only to familiar terrain? A pioneer is a person willing to throw themselves against the limits of possibility and, in doing so, widen the scope of the world.

You want to ask me where I was in the days after the Tower's collapse. So much has been made of the fact that my whereabouts were unknown for several days after the Tower fell. There were rumors that I fled the country, attempting to shirk my responsibility for what happened. It has been suggested that my absence during this time is evidence of my guilt. But I assure you that I was not in hiding.

It is no longer a great secret that at that very moment I was staring my own mortality in the eye as a young doctor showed me the damning shadow on the X-ray, revealing stage three lymphoma, which had formed a fist around my liver and heart.

At that moment, I asked myself, what did I have to regret? I was seventy-five and had built an empire of sixty businesses and services in construction, automobiles, shipbuilding, electronics, petrochemicals, oil refining, engineering services, high-rise apartment complexes, department stores, hotels, and media. I had done more than enough in my lifetime to retire.

I asked the doctor how long I had. The doctor replied, "Six months, sir," while examining my face for signs of distress. He seemed worried that I had not fully comprehended my condition. That he might be liable to a lawsuit in the future. But my silence was simply a defiance in the face of death. I had commanded the construction of the shortest possible highway between Seoul and Pusan. If I could not move mountains, I tunneled through them. I refused to be told how and when I was going to die. I called for my secretary, who was waiting outside for me in the hallway. I instructed him to ensure that no one would hear of my test results. We were days away from a deal with the city to begin a major construction project, repaving city hall and pedestrianizing it. I could not have the mayor suspecting that anything was amiss. And I couldn't have the stock market wreaking havoc with my company's share price based on false news. Because I felt, at that moment, perfectly fine. Heartburn troubled me from time to time, and I had recently found myself loosening my principles around money—allowing myself a chauffeur to drive me the three miles to my office on chilly mornings when my leg bothered me, as well as a second pair of shoes.

I'm not a superstitious man, but it did occur to me to wonder whether it was the loosening of my principles that had led to the cancer. Or perhaps such uncharacteristic impulsiveness was a symptom of the cancer. I decided this diagnosis was not a cause for concern, but merely an excuse to indulge in opening the bottle of Macallan M scotch whisky I had received from an American commander I met during the War.

I went back to the office and tended to business—calling my managers in Abu Dhabi, Tokyo, Dallas, and Detroit to get their daily reports on the construction projects underway. Then I instructed my secretary to consult three of the most prominent specialists from three different continents to examine the X-rays and for them to negotiate a cure among themselves. I told him that I was not to be disturbed under any circumstances. As confident as I was that I would beat the growths in my body, the appearance of them seemed to be a sign for me to take a moment's break to contemplate everything I want to achieve in what time I have left. I dismissed my driver and drove three hours south of Seoul, into the mountains.

I have a modest plot of land there. It is my ambition that when the remains of my family in North Korea are found, I will bury them here so that we might finally be reunited. As yet, there is only one big burial mound—my youngest son Geun-ye's grave. How lonely it looked! How tempting it was to allow myself to perish so that he would have some company. I don't know how long I stayed there, at his grave, turning over and over again the strange circumstances of his death, as I always do when confronted with his grave. I then drove to the country house nearby and read over the factory manager's notes, trying yet again to make sense of what had happened.

This house in the country is modest. A replica of the home I grew up in with my father. There is no phone there. It had been a long season of endless work, and I knew that if I was to keep up this pace and maintain a fight for my life, I needed to rest. It can't have been longer than a day when I saw my secretary's car appearing on the horizon.

He came in, sweating profusely from his oily, balding scalp. I saw that he came with bad news. Over the years, I've become all too familiar with Mr. Gong's tics. His extreme discomfort with his role at being the bearer of bad news. It begins with a neck twitch, which he tries to smooth with his right hand before shaking out his wrist as if he is throwing down a small feral animal that had been gnawing at his shoulders. He had done this when a landslide had taken the lives of some of my laborers when they were tunneling through a mountain during a highway construction project and when a construction manager had been taken hostage in the Middle East.

Mr. Gong entered the courtyard and pinched his trousers at the knee before sitting on the maple wood floors to remove his shoes. He was taking great pains not to make eye contact with me.

"What is it?" I asked, annoyed that he had disobeyed my instructions that I should not be disturbed and even more so that it could only be news of the most disastrous kind.

"Aspiration Tower has collapsed."

My first thought was on the necessity of acting quickly. All of Taehan Group's resources had to be directed to the rescue effort. In a crisis you have to be levelheaded and systematic in your approach. You have to know how to fight battles on multiple fronts. Maintain a bird's-eye view and see with clear vision how all of the pieces need to fall. But suddenly it was as if some old dog had dug up the raw bones of my grief, exposing it to the light. That personal tragedy seemed to explain how even the Tower could have fallen. Mr. Gong was looking at me, waiting for a response. I cleared my throat and tried to speak, but no sound came out. All I could think at that moment was that none of it would have happened if it weren't for Geun-ye, my youngest. It wouldn't have happened if Geun-ye were still alive.

I hope this satisfies your question. My last biographer was a fool. Perhaps you journalists are all the same. Looking for the meatiest part to carve away from bone, to reshape it, to cook it and flaunt it as evidence of something else. How you like to serve up stories that suit your interests. Such a disinterest in context. In history. Do you understand now? I was not in hiding, I was grieving. You will have seen my secretary's instructions. Remember, you're not working for the paper now. You're working for me. A ghostwriter is merely a scribe, taking down the facts. You see this home? All glass and light. I asked my architects to build it for me as a testament to my transparency. As my biographer, you have my promise. I am only telling you the truth. History as it happened.

FOUR DAYS AFTER THE COLLAPSE

"Where are we going?" Seung-min asked, tugging on Sae's hand as they rose from the subway station. The heat of the roads felt like hot breath on her skin. They cut through the covered market, and Seung-min paused as they passed the stainless steel bowls containing small live octopuses, the tank full of eels. At Sae's prompting, he skipped along, drawn to the weeping glass of the orange and pink slushy machines.

"Come on," Sae said urgently. At Jae's office, at least, she was likely to find some answers.

Hoon-min sank down and sprawled on the ground. Sae glanced at her watch. It was later than she thought. She kept losing track of time, her thoughts dissolving before they could solidify. She opened her bag and brought out the carrier, put Hoon-min on her back and wrapped him tightly, feeling the spike of heat as his warm body lay against her sweating back. Seung-min ran ahead to the open grill where skewers of chicken lay roasting in the blast of the afternoon sun.

Seung-min ran his fingers along the edges of tables, the spicy offerings of kimchi, the large bowls of greens. He was about to poke out the center of a row of gimbap when Sae snapped at him.

"Stop touching everything!"

Seung-min shrank back, held ransom by the sharp edge in her voice, and began to cry.

His tears eroded her. She bent down to cup his shoulder. "Are you hungry?"

He shook his head. "Carry me too, Omma, I don't want to walk anymore."

"Just a little bit longer," she said quietly. "We're almost there."

His cries got louder, and she pulled him firmly by the hand toward the low-rise building at the end of the market. Seung-min broke off, letting go of her hand, brightening as he recognized where they were, his figure a blurred line as he zipped through the crowded stalls.

"Appa! We're going to see Appa!" he said with delight as she caught up to him at the stairs. His excitement at the prospect of seeing his appa was so convincing that Sae allowed herself, for a moment, to believe that they might find him there, at his office.

By the time Sae caught up with him at the bottom of the stairs, she saw that he was pressing his face against the glass door, sullen.

"What is it?" Sae asked.

Seung-min did not answer. When she reached the top of the stairs, she saw that the small office space had been rearranged. In place of the four desks that had been there, there was now a tower of boxes.

They were greeted by a young woman Sae did not recognize. She was dressed formally in a short-sleeved blouse and navy skirt. As she stepped out from behind the desk, Sae noticed her white socks poking out from her slippers. The woman turned on a second fan.

"Can I help you?"

Sae shifted Hoon-min on her back, and felt the unpleasant sensation of her damp T-shirt where he had been pressed against her. "Isn't this . . . L&S engineering?"

The woman brightened, happy to know the answer.

"No. We've just moved in," she said, snapping the gum in her mouth.

Jae had never mentioned that they were moving their office. Sae closed her eyes for a moment. Was this a slip of memory? Even if they had been speaking over the children, a move seemed like something she would have remembered. An event that would have been mentioned more than once.

"Do you know when the other company moved out?"

The woman shook her head. "Maybe six months ago? I'm not sure. But I heard they went bust. Just couldn't compete with the bigger companies, I guess."

This was news to Sae. She looked around at the pile of leaflets promoting some kind of medical equipment. Two large posters with photos of a machine and X-rays hung on the walls. Sae thought of Mr. Bae's cleared-out drawers. Was it possible that Mr. Bae had asked Jae to keep the move a secret? To conceal a change in the company's circumstances? Sae had never trusted Mr. Bae, a small pig-faced man with roaming eyes, the way his eyes would drift across the room and over to women, evaluating them while mid-sentence about something else. But Mr. Bae seemed well-connected and had taken Jae on despite his record of arrest and his unfinished engineering degree, when he needed a job the most.

Sae thought back to the winter, trying to recall if Jae had mentioned that he was worried about money. It was around that time that he had signed the contract to work on Aspiration Tower. He had seemed strangely ambivalent about the project, and she wondered whether he was anxious about working for the notoriously difficult and well-established Taehan Group.

"And you are?"

"I'm the . . ." she hesitated, then decided to continue. "Wife of someone who used to work here," she said. "Do you have any details of where the last tenants might have gone? Or a phone number?"

She shook her head. "I don't know what to tell you. We just moved in. You could talk to the owner of the building. He might know something."

The woman wrote down a phone number and snapped the gum in her mouth sharply as she handed it to her.

Just as Sae turned to leave, the woman asked her to wait and handed her a box.

"There were a few things they left behind. I don't know if it's useful, but you might want them."

Seung-min looked at Sae as she took the box before following her back into the stairwell.

"Where's Appa?" he asked, this time more quietly.

"I don't know," Sae said, lingering a moment in the stairwell, momentarily blinded by the afternoon light. The weight of Hoon-min's sleeping body pressed heavily against the base of her spine. Seung-min gripped Sae's hand. The noises from the street filtered in through the door at the bottom of the stairs, the horns and alarms from the road rose sharply above the layers of other sounds.

"Omma?" Seung-min asked, tugging on her fingers.

She hung there for a moment, trying to steady herself with

her hand against the wall. Was Jae about to tell her about this—that the company was moving or that the project wasn't going as planned—when they had been interrupted by Seung-min the week before? New uncertainties flooded in as she caught sight of the cracked paint on the small window between levels, the underlay of color revealing that the interior walls had once been a lime green rather than the white they were now. She removed her hand and with it came a small film of paint. She picked at the edge of flaking paint on the wall, wondering what else would come away if she kept chipping away at it.

By the time they returned home, it was past eight-thirty. Her heart dropped at the sight of the dark living room as she swung open the front door. Every hour announced by the clock without news from Jae seemed to reverberate with ominous possibilities. It was only when Seung-min kicked a toy car across the room and thrashed around the small living room that she was moved to remember that the boys had not had any dinner. A tantrum was gathering fuel, anger circling hunger, building like a tornado. Sae would have to move quickly to snuff it out. The chicken soup on the stove had spoiled in the heat, the top layer congealing like jelly, and in her urgency she felt grateful for the neighbors who had put other soups in the fridge to reheat. The beef and radish soup would work. She set it in a pan and turned on the fire, her thoughts pulled to the office, the box that she had been given there. It was only when the soup bubbled over that she returned to her senses. Spooning rice hurriedly into bowls, she set them aside and washed up two others for the soup before calling the boys to come to the table.

"No," Seung-min said, refusing the soup in front of him.

"No?" she asked, puzzled.

"It's broken."

She noticed the chip at the edge of the bowl. Seung-min was a high-energy child, but also a picky eater. His protruding spine and sand ridge ribs had attracted many comments from the neighbors and Sae had indulged his every whim if it meant that he would eat, but now she was too tired.

"It doesn't matter, just have the soup," she said.

"No, I want a different one," he began to whine, pushing the bowl across the table. It spilled on the floor. His wails rose to a hysterical scream. All she wanted was a moment's quiet to be able to pick out a single thought from the roar in her head and follow the thread of it. The wave of frustration she had been trying to ride washed over them, and she wanted to strike something. She yanked him from his chair, feeling the stretch of the joint in his shoulder where she gripped his arm.

"We all have to deal with what we are given, whether we like it or not, do you understand?"

The fear in his eyes terrified her. She let go, watching the patch of white on his arm recover blood. All of the stories of bad mothers on the news programs, all of those brutal acts, began like this. If she had been a good mother before, it was because she had never been tested, not by anything significant. Snapping out of her anger, she stepped back, horrified by her own rage.

"I'm sorry," she said. If Jae were in the same position, he would have elaborated, explained things calmly to Seung-min. But she could not. Instead, she pulled him gently to her chest.

"I want Appa," he said.

"I know, me too."

"When is Appa coming back?"

"I don't know," she said.

Wasn't that the truth? To assume the worst was to tell a lie.

The box the secretary had given Sae contained a few items: a file from some old construction projects in rural cities, a few old handwritten invoices from contractors, and a diary from the year before. There were names and phone numbers written in the back, but there was nothing that meant anything to her. Nothing indicated that L&S Engineering was in serious financial difficulty.

As soon as the boys were asleep, Sae felt for the light in the small second bedroom they used as storage. Several of the boxes stacked under the window were hers—files that she could not bring herself to discard from the paper. There were only one or two boxes belonging to Jae that she had never bothered examining. Inside were some old books from when they were students, some poetry, and a few early photographs from when Seung-min was first born. She found a sketchpad full of architectural drawings and a detailed sketch of an old hanok home drawn with fine black lines. When she had first met Jae, he had often sketched buildings.

Looking at the detailed sketch of this hanok home, it struck her that he was able to see things as composites of very small details. She was struck by his neatness, the intention in every line. She was messy unless she was forced to tidy up. She felt her way around decisions; he reasoned through them, often postponing making important decisions because he hated to make the wrong one. If there was one source of tension in their home, it was that she was not organized like he was. She understood it was because she had grown up comfortably until her father's death, while Jae's every expenditure had involved a negotiation or sacrifice of some other resource.

As she looked through the boxes, she came across the books from their university years. A crumpled piece of paper had the poem "We Threw the Book Ten Times Over," for which the poet Yang Song-U had been sentenced to five years in prison. She had watched as he read the words with steady hands: *We threw the book ten times over / Because of the army, because of the secret police / And now, because of hunger.* Later, other equally dangerous works by Engels, Orwell, and Lawrence were passed between them. The pages were dog-eared with passages underlined in pencil. An occasional note or question in the margins.

In the beginning, she had tested him to see which provocation—the book of North Korean poetry, the critical history of America's involvement in the Korean War—would be the one to drive him away. But he always returned the books to her, the pages lined with more questions. With every book he handed back to her, he seemed less uncertain of his involvement. During the meetings where they discussed working conditions in the factories, Sae saw that expression of intense focus on his face that she had first noticed in the library.

It wasn't until some months after that first encounter in the library that he handed her a work of fiction: *The Unbearable Lightness of Being* by Milan Kundera. Before this, they had only ever exchanged nonfiction—historical or theoretical texts. A work of fiction felt like an invitation of a different kind. She returned to her dorm room and flipped through its pages, searching for his margin notes and the passages he underlined, which she had grown accustomed to, and found only one:

"You don't know how happy I am to be with you." That was the most her reserved nature allowed her to express.

For weeks afterward she had the sense that he was avoiding her, and that she had misunderstood his intention in handing her the book. The next time they found themselves alone it was a month later as they ran down a shuttered alley near the university. Over that summer, the protests against the dictatorship intensified. A student had been killed during an interrogation, his trachea crushed against the edge of a bathtub while the police held him underwater. Now it was not only students taking to the streets but taxi drivers, office workers, factory workers. The city had become used to absenting itself at the sound of the soldiers' tread. The outdoor markets—the clock stalls, the booths selling black market American candy, the pails of salt water with sea urchin and fresh octopus—were rolled away and hidden from view. But now shopkeepers abandoned their posts and took to the streets, no longer hiding away.

"It's a dead end," she said to Jae as they turned a corner. The riot police were not far behind. Just as they rounded the corner, she felt him pull her through a door. For a moment they stood in darkness, hearing only the sound of their breaths, the rapid fire of footsteps outside. Then a small window opened, and a man shone a torch in their eyes.

"Power's out," he said with a razored voice. "Rooms are three thousand won for the night. You got any money?"

Sae pulled out the $100 bill she kept in her back pocket for emergencies.

"American dollars? I don't have change for that," the innkeeper said, taking the bill anyway. He had a lean face but a swollen neck that reminded Sae of a toad. He closed the window and opened a door, pointing them in the direction of a long corridor.

"I'll give you the best room in the house," he said with a grin, clapping Jae on his shoulder. "You can take your time, stay as long as you like."

The room had frosted windows and a ceiling with brown hexagonal shapes. As soon as the innkeeper left Sae collapsed onto the floor, feeling the exhaustion of a swimmer who had been treading water for too long. Jae opened the window and surveyed the alley below them.

"We're probably safe here for now," he said. Then after a long pause, "They've arrested Jong-hwan."

"I know," she said softly. "We'll have to go and clear out his house, tell his family."

"It should have been me," he said, his breath sounding labored. "It wouldn't matter then, I mean for him and his family . . ."

"It looks like they got you, too," she said, seeing a bloodstain on his denim jacket. She pulled at it and pressed up his sleeve. "You're bleeding."

He seemed not to hear her. "I mean if it were me . . . it would be okay. It would be okay."

"Take this off," she said gently, not knowing how to calm him. He was radiating a kind of panic that she had never seen in him before. "We should try to stop the bleeding."

She helped him unbutton his shirt. The rolled-up bedding in the corner was suddenly suggestive and she tried not to think of the guests who had used these rooms before them. Opening her backpack, she found a spare T-shirt and ripped it into strips and wrapped it around his bicep, feeling the tensed muscle as she tightened the bandage.

"I read the Kundera," she said, trying to distract him. "Franz reminded me of you." She was not quite brave enough to mention the words he had underlined. "The way he was disappointed by language, how he never was able to say what he wanted to."

She could hear his panicked breath beginning to slow. He was quiet for so long she began to think that perhaps she had misread him. For days after he had given her the book he had been unable to meet her eye. Had she misinterpreted what he meant by it? It was, after all, a secondhand copy. Another reader might have underlined those words. Perhaps he hadn't been trying to tell her anything at all.

"Do you think Il-hyung feels that way?" he said after a while.

"What does he have to do with anything?" she asked, surprised by the question.

"You're a couple, aren't you?"

"No," she said. "You don't really believe that?"

"He's in love with you," he said.

She laughed at this. "No way. He doesn't believe in love. He thinks that's some bourgeois invention."

She helped him put his shirt back on. He put his hand over hers, pressing it against his chest. She could feel the fast drumming of his heart, the furnace of his skin.

"Do you think that too?" she asked quietly. "That it's an invention?"

"It doesn't matter what I think," he said. "I know what I feel. You asked me the other day what I am afraid of . . ."

"I dare you to say it," she said with a smile. "Franz."

He leaned in closer to her, hesitating for a moment before he was so close that she could feel the soft bristles of his upper lip, his warm breath on her nose. His lips felt full and warm, and she felt what she had felt once before, when she had swum too close to the edge of a waterfall, and realized she was going to fall.

"You wanted to know what caused the Tower to collapse," Taekyu said as soon as she picked up the phone. "There's going to be a statement first thing in the morning."

"Well?"

"They've ruled out explosives. It's a structural problem. I called it, didn't I? I don't have the name of the company yet, but the working theory is that there was a fundamental miscalculation of the weight on the load-bearing beams."

"Of what?"

"I didn't catch the exact details. As you can imagine, Taehan Group wants to be in control of the announcement. But it sounds like it was a retrofit that stressed the Tower."

Everything seemed to slow down and become heavy. Sae pressed her temples and closed her eyes. All the windows to the apartment were open and she could hear the sounds from the units around her, a dog whining in the heat, a cartoonish scream, faint shouts over music.

"A retrofit," she repeated.

"An addition of something, like an extra floor, or—" he said.

"A swimming pool," she said, thinking of Mr. Bae's emptied-out closets.

"Yes," he said with a note of surprise in his voice. She heard the shuffling of papers, as though he were looking for a note that might confirm this.

Sae had not told him about her exchange with Mrs. Bae.

"Wasn't Jae working for an engineering company? What did you say he was doing there?"

As soon as she put down the phone, she crossed the living room to the closet and pulled out a travel bag. She crept into the bedroom where the boys lay curled into each other and grabbed a few T-shirts and shorts from the drawers. There was only one place she could think of to go. How long did she have before the news broke that L&S Engineering was responsible for the collapse of Aspiration Tower? Once the reporters learned who was responsible, they would be like vultures, circling her apartment for any scrap of information. There would be no keeping Jae's disappearance from the boys then.

11:30 P.M., September 27, 2016
Chairman's residence, Gugi District, Seoul

You can make a writer out of a journalist, but you can't take a journalist out of the writer, it seems. Was it Ronald Reagan who said "Trust, but verify" in his negotiations with the Soviet Union? While I hope you do not see us as such adversaries, if it will help us to move forward, I am willing to revisit the facts of the collapse of Aspiration Tower.

Aspiration Tower was less than five years old, but it was due for an upgrade. Until recently the citizens of our great country had been so hardworking that the concept of leisure was something of a luxury most could not afford. But everyone needs time off now and then. My eldest son, Yung, suggested that we should build an infinity pool on the top floor of the Tower to cater to the growing class of people who would part with their money for leisure. We outsourced the project, bringing in an engineering team who specialized in remodeling. The project was going well. We had a date set for the opening at the end of the month. They filled the pool so that the employees could enjoy a dip before the official opening. That's when the cracks emerged. They call it "structural overload." The engineers had been experts in remodeling but had not calculated the weight of the water in the pool.

At Taehan Group, we have a special emphasis on being meticulous. There is no substitute for precision. When I began my first business at a cement factory, for example, it was essential that we checked blueprints to confirm the correct ratio of cement to water for the structure in question. There are contractors who will cheat or try to save money by diluting a concrete mix. But if it's one thing that every successful entrepreneur knows, it is that trust is essential in business. One can succeed by swindling a partner, but a serial liar will have a poor reputation, and reputation is everything when it comes to long-term success.

People think that I began Taehan Group to make money. They see me as a maverick who leapt at any opportunity given to him because he has nothing to lose. Nothing could be further from the truth. Anyone who thinks that it is money that drives my company is misinformed. I began Taehan Group because of my family. Every family in this country has had someone taken too early by a national catastrophe. The people of our nation have endured oppression at the hands of the Japanese, war, poverty, the division of our one nation over two generations. We all have our ways of dealing with loss. Taehan Group was mine.

These days we have all sorts of events—Christmas, Valentine's Day, White Day, birthdays, public holidays, New Year's Day, Lunar New Year—events that my consumer businesses treat as important occasions to bring out special products to sell. An event creates urgency. What is better for making a sale than urgency? That's why we put in the extra resources to mark these important days. But before you accuse me of being profit hungry, let me share a thought. It occurred to me in reflecting on my childhood that these celebrations are also landmarks in the year that give you a sense of the passing of time, like little pins on the map of memory. You see, when I was growing up, every day was the same, and my father instilled in us that we should work hard no matter what season it was. And so, though we knew what time of year it was because of the seasons, there was a timelessness about my childhood that stretched out our endless hunger.

We grew up during the Japanese occupation of Korea, in a place we now call North Korea. I can't tell you exactly when things began to change. Soon we found ourselves bickering more, the younger children were quicker to tears. When we began to quarrel, our father stopped intervening and soon began to disappear. It was almost as though he couldn't bear the noise, couldn't stand the sight of us. Our hunger made us irritable—our rice bowls became more watery with every meal, and the few vegetables we had, divided nine ways, were not enough to sustain us.

That was the beginning of my father's desertion of us. Every night, after he thought we were all asleep, he would get up, put on his thick vest, and go outside and then return before we woke at dawn. I knew he would be angry if any of us followed him out, so I resisted the urge, but I knew he was out there trying to dig up even a small scrap of crop to feed us.

The winter that Bok-nyuh, my youngest sister, began to scream and faint with fever, we were at the lowest ebb. The harvest that autumn had been spare after the monsoon had washed away all our hard work during the planting season. We had gathered little to trade.

"We need a doctor," my mother said, rocking Bok-nyuh.

"We don't have the means," my father said.

"They won't turn us away, just look at her," my mother said. "Why won't you try?"

My siblings and I exchanged startled glances, because we had never heard my mother speak to our father like this before. My mother stood up and went to the old dresser where she kept her needle and thread and removed a scrap of worn linen. She pulled out a silver hairpin and handed it to my father.

He shook his head. "If the Japanese find out that we have valuables we've been hiding from them, there's no telling what might happen."

"It's your daughter's life."

My father reluctantly took the hairpin, looking at it as though this piece of jewelry was the root cause of all our misery.

He put on his thick vest and I jumped to my feet, saying that I would go with him. It was a full day's walk to the nearest village, the terrain often rough and uneven on the mountain path. He would need help. We retrieved the wheelbarrow we had used in plentiful harvests for moving crops from the fields back to our storehouse. My mother brought out several thick blankets, and we nestled Bok-nyuh inside. Her face was burning red with fever despite the cold. We started on the long walk using the force of our weight against that heavy wheelbarrow. We hoped that Bok-nyuh would fall asleep, but she arched her back and screamed. I picked her up and put her on my back as my mother often did, and she quieted.

We had walked like this for a long time when I saw that my father's rubber shoes had split and that his socks had become wet in the snow.

"Why don't we sit for a moment?" he said, winded. There seemed to be something else that pained him.

"What is it, Father?"

"Perhaps we should stop here," he said. Thinking the pain in his feet was unbearable, I offered to go on without him. Bok-nyuh was still asleep on my back. I had not been to the village often, but I knew that we were about halfway there. I wasn't entirely sure of my direction but made my best effort to sound confident.

I expected him to say no, but instead he began to nod slowly, as if it made all the sense in the world. We had only one lamp between us, but we decided that I should take it. I left the wheelbarrow with my father and walked away from him, leaving him in the darkness.

Several times I almost turned back, finding it hard to carry the increasingly heavy weight of my sleeping sister. I knew that if I stopped, it would be too hard to start again, so I kept walking, until I caught a glimpse of the straw-thatched roofs of the village in the distance. A patch of warmth spread on my back. Bok-nyuh had urinated through her clothes. I had not brought a change of clothes for her, so I did my best to wrap her in blankets so she would not be cold.

A man with an ox and cart was approaching me on the widening dirt path.

"I need a doctor. It's my sister," I said.

The man looked at us for a moment.

"Where have you come from?"

I told him I had been walking all night and he took pity on me, offering to take us in his cart. It was only when I sat down that I realized how sore my legs and feet were. Bok-nyuh's cheeks were bright red, and she was so weak that she no longer seemed to have the energy to moan.

It turned out to be glandular fever. "She is malnourished," the doctor said, "and dehydrated." He asked me where we lived and why it had taken so long for me to seek help. My mother's silver hairpin was burning a hole in my pocket, but I didn't want to give it up. So I lied and told him that we were orphans, that we had come from the mountains. The doctor took a long look at us and told me that he would waive his fee. He fed us and told me to come back in a week; that he would find work for me.

My father had told us that we had had a poor harvest, so I thought it would be difficult to find food or that it would be very expensive, but as we left the doctor's home to return to the family, we walked through the market, surprised to see sweet potatoes, potatoes, spinach, eggplants, and dried fish. I had never seen such abundance—mats filled with dozens of rubber shoes, copper bowls, colorful linens.

A strange, unsettled feeling took hold of me. I carried Bok-nyuh on my back and sang to her to keep her spirits up, though mine were beginning to sink. It was probably then that it started. The doubt. You see, before this trip to the village, I didn't know that there were other ways of living. Poverty is a condition that takes on new meaning when you see that it is only one of many possibilities. That's when it becomes unbearable, like an itch in some unreachable corner under a shoulder blade. That journey to the market cast a light on the way we lived. I saw that faces could be rounder, that there could be lightness and laughter. Suddenly I found myself restless and eager to go back, to explore this other world. But I discarded these thoughts whenever they sprang to life. Because a son does not defy his father.

My siblings were so happy to see us as we returned. Several of them were crying to see that Bok-nyuh was alive. My mother stroked my head and squeezed my hands, too overwhelmed for words. But my father said nothing. He did not congratulate me or even seem to register that we had returned.

Suddenly everything about the house I had loved looked different. I couldn't stop picturing the doctor's house, the shine of the wooden floorboards in his hanok home, the crispness of his hanbok, so clean, so new. Until that foray into the village, I did not have anything to compare our living standards to. Now I saw that everything was either broken or had been worn down to its bare threads.

As soon as I got the chance, I went to the storeroom next to the hearth where we kept our grains and vegetables. The large earthenware pots were filled with red pepper paste and soybean paste, but I could not find more than one sackful of rice and barley to last us until the end of the winter. When I returned to the house, I saw my father sitting on the edge of the porch, looking over the frozen fields. I wanted to ask him how we were going to survive the rest of the winter but was afraid of what his answer might be. We had not yet paid the taxes we were supposed to hand over to the Japanese every month, and I was not sure what would be left for us after.

"Isn't it good news, Father, that Bok-nyuh is feeling so much better?" I asked.

My father did not look at me.

"Father?"

"Don't worry," he said. "I will look after us."

But the way he said it gave me a chill. There was a vacant look in his eyes. It occurred to me that maybe he was thinking that if the worst had happened to Bok-nyuh there would be one less mouth to feed.

That night I woke up to find my father gone from the room we all shared together. I went outside, calling for him. I tried to see the path ahead of me through the fog of my own breath. I found him in the field, digging at the frozen ground with his bare hands, frantically, his hands reddened and bleeding, but he kept at it like some ferocious animal.

"Aboji, Aboji," I said, over and over, but he did not seem to see that I was there. The faraway look in his eyes scared me. I tried to shake him out of his trancelike state, but he seemed paralyzed.

Sometimes, when you are forced to act, that movement comes from a force within you that's instinctual. I've never been a person to overthink. It's all gut and feeling. And that's when I knew, just like I've known over the years—when to gamble on a business, when to walk away from a man who could not be trusted—that I had to leave right then. I was the oldest son. I had to do something for my family. When my father came back to himself, I thought he would be proud of my actions.

I went back into the house and wrote a note for my family. With the moonlight as my only guide, I slipped past my father and out onto the mountain path. My mother's silver hairpin, still in my sock since we had come back from the village, would become the down payment for what would become Taehan Group.

Everyone loves the expansive possibilities of a rags to riches story, yet you seem unmoved. I see now that journalists and entrepreneurs are more similar than one would first think. An entrepreneur with a seedling of an idea is a restless man, unable to sleep, able to think of little else. There is something that you wrestle with; I can see that in your face. Go on, you may ask me anything. That is how we build trust. After all, there is nothing more crucial in any relationship—business or personal—than building trust, wouldn't you agree?

SEVEN DAYS AFTER THE COLLAPSE

"I thought you'd forgotten about me," Myong-hee said with a mock pout as Mr. Li entered the club.

"I've been living at the office," he said. "Maybe you don't watch the news?"

"So long as it's work that's keeping you and not some other woman," she said, playfully pinching his arm, forcing lightness. In truth, she had been avoiding the news. What use was it to watch a predictable fight, when it was always the same winner? She hooked her arm in his and led him down the corridor.

"What are we in the mood for tonight?"

"Just someplace where we can be alone," he said in a low voice. "I came in to talk to you."

"Me?" she asked, the act dropping for a moment, surprised. She smiled uncertainly at him, releasing his arm. He placed his hand on her face and she caught it, wary, unnerved. It was one thing to be looked at in these rooms, another to be seen.

"What's on your mind?" she asked, struggling to find the rhythm of her playfulness.

He stepped back, a look of minor irritation passing over his face. "Can we sit down?"

"Of course," she said, grasping his arm and leading him to the smallest, most intimate room in the club.

When she returned with a tray of drinks and snacks, she found Mr. Li pensive, sitting with a cigarette between his fingers, stroking his lip with his thumb. She filled the glass with whiskey and handed it to him.

"Has something happened?" she asked, feeling strangely protective of him. She forced a smile and put a finger between his eyebrows, teasing out the wrinkle there.

"It's not looking good," he said, raising the glass to his lips.

Myong-hee shifted her weight on the sofa, which suddenly felt too soft.

Mr. Li swiveled the ice in his glass. "There was a memo going around, an hour before the building's collapse, saying that the management should evacuate. Some of the managers said the building was making strange noises for weeks."

Myong-hee let this sink in. "You mean that some people knew the building might collapse?"

"There's going to be an investigation. If they find out that I've destroyed evidence, I'm going to be in the line of fire."

"What evidence?" she asked.

"Never mind that," he said. "That's not why I'm here."

He shifted to face her and held his drink in both hands. "I've worked for most of my life taking orders from my superiors. I don't want to go to prison for them, too. I'm leaving for Los Angeles tomorrow. I've got some money set aside. Once I'm settled there, I'll have someone sell my place here, and it should be enough to last for a while."

Myong-hee looked up at him, puzzled, unsure why he was telling her this.

Mr. Li set down his glass and rubbed his hands, as if resolving to do something. "They say the food is very good there. The weather is more temperate. The traffic's just as bad. Why don't you come with me?"

Myong-hee let out a laugh to hide her surprise. "To Los Angeles?"

"I found an old company photograph while I was clearing out my desk. That's when it came to me. Why you look so familiar."

Myong-hee bit the inside of her lip, unable to say anything.

"You used to work at Taehan Group, didn't you? What happened?"

Myong-hee forced a tight smile and gathered her hands in her lap, pressing the nail of her thumb into the edge of her index finger. What had happened to that young woman she had been at Taehan Group? Her naïvety all those years ago was humiliating. When the Chairman had invited her to dinner, she had allowed herself to believe it was because she had been noticed for her efficiency at work. She had failed to notice that women did not rise to senior positions. That was the thing about being young, she thought. One always thought that one was exceptional.

The Chairman had approached her at a lunch event held to celebrate the company's thirtieth anniversary. His eyes were warm. The fine lines around his mouth suggested he laughed easily and often.

"Myong-hee-shi?" he had said. She turned to him, surprised that he knew her name. "Perhaps you might consider having dinner with me? We could talk about your future."

The Japanese restaurant they went to had private rooms with sliding rice paper doors. He placed his hand on her waist as he gently pushed her inside. They sat on the floor with their legs in the bunker beneath the table, their toes occasionally touching.

"Tell me where you grew up," he said, pouring her drink. The Chairman was not wearing a tie, and the top button of his shirt had been unbuttoned. His relaxed attire made her less shy. He felt like an older brother, though he was old enough to be her father.

She spoke of her upbringing in the countryside. How they had moved to the city after the death of her mother.

"It must be lonely to find yourself in the big city. I know what it's like to be alone without family in a big city like this."

As he told the story of how he had come to live in Seoul, never knowing what had happened to his family, he had the look of a lost child. She wanted to hold him. Comfort him.

As they left the restaurant, the Chairman told her that he wished to see more of her.

"We countryfolk have to look after each other," he had said. He shook her hand. Held on to it a moment longer than seemed polite. She blushed and looked down at the street. The feeling had been mutual, then. The longing to protect. She felt she had found a kindred spirit in him.

She had been touched by his kindness, too naïve to know any better when she received the secretary's note that the Chairman wished to see her at the Plaza Hotel.

"Did he need me to bring something for him from the office?" she asked, puzzled.

"That won't be necessary," the secretary said, not quite looking at her.

The instructions were for her to meet him at the penthouse.

She glanced up at the height of the hotel before stepping through the gold-rimmed circular doors. Perhaps, she thought, he wished to show her the view. To tell her about the places countryfolk could reach if they worked hard.

She pressed the bell for Room 1101, the presidential suite. The Chairman opened the door, holding the phone receiver to his ear. He allowed her to pass by him, gesturing for the sofa, and then retreated into another room, the long telephone line trailing behind him like a leash. She sat obediently on the hard sofa, waiting for his return. From where she sat, all she could see were the peaks of the mountains against the shock of the bright blue sky.

When the Chairman reemerged from the other room forty minutes later, there were no apologies or explanations. He offered her a cigarette, which she declined.

"I like that you don't smoke," he said. He offered her a drink, which she gladly accepted, though she wasn't sure whether this would be approved by him. He came to sit beside her.

"It's nice for us to spend some time together alone like this," he said. "It's not often that I get the privilege of beautiful company. There's not much time for anything else in this business. Sometimes I worry that I'll just disappear."

He gave her a hurt look, and she put her hand on his face. She understood. He had sought her out as a refuge from his loneliness. He kissed her and put his hand inside her skirt. She drew back in surprise, her hand instinctively gripping his. This seemed to delight him.

"I want you to be my companion. It's a lonely business. You know better than anyone."

She nodded, confused. Obedience to authority, to elders,

was what had been drummed into her as a child. Myong-hee had never been able to say no if someone needed her help. The drink blurred the edges of the scene. She couldn't quite believe it when he carried her, sliding the door aside to reveal a large bed in the adjoining room. He did not seem to expect her to do anything. He carefully removed her clothing as though she were a gift. As he spread her blouse open, she felt her cheeks glowing against the lamplight. He removed his shirt and whipped out his belt. The darkness of his nipples surprised her. She could hear him unzipping his trousers, but she did not want to see what he was to bring out. He pushed up her skirt so that it hung about her waist and ripped her underwear. There was a long pause. Myong-hee dared not look at him in her shame. All she knew about what was to happen next was patchy and theoretical. She was ignorant of the mechanics and the physiology. Her breaths were shallow and rapid. Her stomach and breasts were cold. The roughness of his hands against her ribs, the firmness of their grip, illuminated a sudden doubt. Was he a protector, a friend? He pressed against her. When she cried out in pain, and wriggled from under him, he pinned down her wrists. Persisted with his hardness until she was broken, the hard eggshell cracked, the yolk spilling out. He was frantic in his movements, not man but bear, burrowing deeper and deeper inside her.

After he caught his breath, he said, "They say the first time is the worst. You won't hurt so much next time."

Myong-hee did not know what to say. Only then did she notice that in the bedroom there was only a narrow window the length of the room. Lying in the bed there was no view of the mountains. Only a dark navy sky.

• • •

"Come with me to America," Mr. Li said. "I've got some money. I'll be good to you."

The offer was like a warm bed for a weary body. No more late-night encounters with men, consenting to touch she didn't want. The endless worry about money, a misstep with the police that might finally put her behind bars. To take flight and set foot on the same soil as her daughter.

"I need a little time to think it over," she said.

"I'll have a ticket ready for you," he said, taking her hand. The tenderness of the gesture brought blood to her cheeks. "I'll be waiting for you at the airport tomorrow night."

EIGHT DAYS AFTER THE COLLAPSE

Sae gazed at the thin line of morning light rising over the rice paddies visible over the highway partition. The boys had been wild with excitement as they got on the bus, and it had taken her an hour to settle them. Now that they were asleep beside her, she had time to think. To turn over the possibility that the Tower had collapsed on account of a mistake made by the engineers. Sae thought of Jae's careful sketches, committed to paper in black ballpoint pen, never revising a line, never making a mistake. Jae was the type of person to check the work of others meticulously. Yet the announcement aligned with the fact of Mr. Bae's disappearance, which could only be interpreted as evidence of his guilt.

Seung-min murmured in his sleep, and Sae pulled her cardigan over his shoulders. She rested her head against the window. Mrs. Bae's comments outside the gymnasium gnawed at her. What had Mrs. Bae meant when she had said that they hadn't been able to finish the job? Was it possible that Jae had gone into hiding because he was complicit in a mistake? She wanted to believe that he would not leave her in the dark in this way—he was no coward—but he had deserted her once before.

• • •

It had happened a year after they had begun seeing each other. Sae had just scraped by and finished her degree, and she had begun working as an intern at *The Seoul Daily*, a newly formed newspaper started by dissident journalists who had been purged from the newspapers controlled by the authoritarian government. Sae had loved the promise of the paper—its commitment to holding the government accountable to the truth. She had been disappointed to find, however, that though their political values were in line, most of the senior journalists were unkind and arrogant. Tae-kyu was the only one who treated her with any respect.

Jae had taken some time off from school and found work at a cement factory in Ansan, an hour and a half from Seoul. For six months they lived for the weekends when he would take the train to see her. One afternoon she stopped by at the factory on her way back from conducting interviews in Gwangju. She had hoped that it would be a good surprise, but he seemed jittery and distant.

"You don't seem happy to see me," she said. "What is it?"

"The Chairman came by for a tour today," he said, his eyes drawn to the imposing factory gates. It was as though he feared the Chairman's return. "Everyone's been on edge."

"Let's get out of here," Sae suggested brightly. "If we leave now we can make it back to Seoul."

But when they arrived at the station, they learned they had just missed the train, and found themselves in a country inn where the innkeeper scowled at them disapprovingly when they said they needed only one room. Jae had been subdued since they had left the factory. She tried to engage him with a story about what had happened to her earlier that day when interviewing a witness about what he had seen during the uprising.

"Tae-kyu has been trying make contact for months. He was reluctant to talk to us. We assured him that it was for an archive, we all know we can't publish anything about it now. It wouldn't be safe to. Anyway, Tae-kyu wanted me to leave the room, thinking the guy would talk if they were alone. I go into the kitchen and his wife tells me everything that she saw. No one had thought to ask her!"

When Jae didn't smile, her own smile faltered.

"You've been really quiet since we left," she said. "Did something happen?"

He picked up the copper kettle in the room and poured them both a cup of warm barley tea.

"What does it mean to you?" he asked. "All this?"

She tensed, unsure of what he was referring to. In the dwindling afternoon light, Jae's reticence seemed to take on new meaning. "All this?"

He gave her a small smile. "The protests. Our work in the factories. What does it mean to you?" He took several gulps of the tea and poured himself another cup. "Would you still see me in the same way if I wasn't involved in the movement?"

It was with some relief that she understood. For weeks Jae had been planning a protest with the workers. The Chairman's visit had spooked him.

"No one has done more for the movement than you," she said.

He had helped students infiltrate the factories by forging their identity numbers. He had helped others organize after-work education programs. He had worked in the factory himself. And things had shifted for the better. After the dictator announced that direct presidential elections would be held later that year, workers were emboldened to continue pressuring for better working conditions. There was momentum in the labor movement. She didn't think there was any shame in him wanting to quit.

"You didn't answer the question."

"Jae," she said, taken aback. How could he doubt it? "You're not serious?"

"You're with me because you think I'm a certain type of person."

"What do you mean?"

"Because I'm involved in all of this. If I weren't, you'd look at me differently."

"No," she said, picking up his hand. "I wouldn't."

On their first walk after the library, he had told her that he was studying to be a structural engineer, but that he had really wanted to study architecture. In the months that followed, the movement demanded that they become workers, to make the ultimate sacrifice in their education. Many had refused, but Jae had not. Sae had marveled in the way he had walked away from his degree, as though it were nothing to him. Now she wondered if this was something that he regretted.

"You should finish your degree. Do architecture. Is that what this is about? Are you afraid that the others might think you sold out? Or gave in? What is it that you're afraid of?"

He said nothing for a while. Sae was beginning to tire of his silences.

"You don't trust me," she said.

"What are you talking about?"

"You never tell me about yourself. You won't say what you're afraid of. In fact, you never tell me anything!"

"What is it that you want me to say?"

"Things that people tell each other. About how they grew up. Stupid things they did as a kid. That kind of thing!"

Under the harsh glare of the naked lightbulb, he looked stone-faced.

"Are you asking because you care or because you want to satisfy your own curiosity?"

She felt as though he had slapped her. He had never said anything that had hurt her in this way, and she knew it only hurt because she recognized the truth in it. She trespassed others, not respectful of the places within them they dared not go themselves. But the idea that Jae might think this of her was doubly painful. "Am I a burden to you?"

"You ask so much of people. Have you ever considered what it costs them to answer?"

"Am I a burden to you? I'm not asking just anyone. I'm asking about you. I love you."

She saw him wince as if she had struck him. She had never said this to him before. When his eyes met hers they were full of tears. "Don't say that."

She tried to steady her trembling lip. "Don't you love me?"

"Have you ever considered that 'love' means something different to me, Sae?"

She tried to touch his cheek, but he flinched.

"He used to line up the boys. I was the youngest. I learned not to offend. But that didn't stop me from having to watch. Do you know what it's like? To smell the blood of another kid as they're being beaten? Is this the kind of thing you want to know?"

She wanted to ask who he was referring to but did not want to push him. She placed her palm on his shoulder. He let her touch him then.

"There's nothing you can tell me that would make me change my mind about you."

To her surprise, he began to cry, his hands over his face.

"It doesn't have to hurt," she said. "I would never hurt you. I love you."

She fell asleep in his arms, only to wake to an empty room, blue dawn light streaming in through the inn's rice paper doors. Beside her, a note: *I'm sorry. I think we should stop seeing each other.*

She ran out of the inn room with the blanket around her nakedness. The innkeeper was feeding the chickens and hardly looked at her as he spoke. "He left an hour ago. What is it? Did he forget to pay you?"

Sae shot the innkeeper a look and got dressed. She thought back over the evening before. She had driven him away with her questions. It was her fault. She had to find him. It was still early. She thought she might be able to find him at the factory. But when she spoke to his manager he said that Jae had not come in to work. She went to the train station, thinking that she might find him there, but it was empty. She spent the next day trying to find him, asking friends if they knew where he might be, but no one seemed to know.

And then, two days later, she heard the news. He had been arrested.

• • •

In the months following his arrest, Sae found herself unable to sleep. Nausea had become a constant companion. At night she lay awake, aware of every odor, filthy human smells that filtered in from the street. She felt sick with the world. The National Security Law was invoked to discipline anyone who challenged the establishment. Those who were suspected of fueling unrest were dragged out of their houses at night, blindfolded, and taken to the anti-communist bureau of the National Police. Some were tortured in hotel rooms. They were told that if they died while being tortured, they would be reported missing. Or driven to the border, forced to cross, and shot for trying to defect.

During the day she worked at the paper, while also making inquiries about where Jae might be held. She searched the prisons, scribbling messages in magazines that sympathetic guards smuggled through bars. They were sent back with scrawls from her friends on the inside. No one had seen him. She feared the worst. Imagined the coroner's reports tossed over flames. *The trachea was damaged before the drowning occurred.* His veins ruptured by the voltage. An unmarked grave.

On weekends, she returned to the factory where he worked, interviewing workers, trying to find anyone who might know something. No one seemed to know what had happened to him.

Months later, she met a former classmate she had not seen in some time. He had been arrested many years before and had aged prematurely, his hair flecked with gray, his mouth full of gaping holes. He told her of Joguksa, a temple where some students fleeing from the police had found shelter.

"You were close with Jae, weren't you?" he said. "He was there."

Her heart dropped like fruit that had begun to rot on the vine.

She went straight to Seoul station, going against the crowd at rush hour, to get on a train to a mountainside town. She walked in solitude on a steep and rocky path, guided by the sound of the bell tower at its summit, the occasional echo of a wooden fish gong.

At the temple entrance, a monk greeted her with a bamboo bowl full of water. He led her across the dirt courtyard to a smaller temple with red paint flaking off its pillars. Jae was repairing the roof. He worked bare-chested and held two black tiles in his gloved hands. She watched him, hardly able to contain herself, wanting above all else to touch him. When he noticed her, his surprise was visible. Swinging down from the roof, he landed gently on the ground. He came closer, but did not embrace her.

"How did you find me?"

He seemed to be concerned that if she had found him, others could do so, too.

"Min-young told me he saw you here."

He leaned over a water pump and rinsed himself, pressing his eyes for a long moment before allowing himself to look at her.

Later, they stood outside the bell tower at dusk. Near the temple that had presided over political power shifts for more than three hundred years, on a ground with gingko trees older than their republic.

"Why have you come here?" he said. There was an unfamiliar flatness in his voice. She was taken aback by the question.

"How can you ask me that?" she said.

The outline of the mountains glowed red against the setting sun. The juniper trees looked frozen as if permanently set by a harsh wind. Was it possible for something to be permanently changed, she wondered, by a moment's impact?

The only clues to what those months of separation had been for him were in the nervous tic of his eye, the calluses on his hands. In his leanness he appeared both taller and more frail, his shoulders hunched, like a man coming in from the cold.

"I've been looking everywhere for you."

"You shouldn't have," he said, his eyes fixed on the ground.

"I thought you were dead," she said, louder than she intended. The echo of her voice rang out in the valley, and several birds took flight. She had the urge to push him, to make him look at her. Was he so empty of feeling that he could not imagine why she was there?

"I—I almost lost my mind," she stammered. "I got you into this. How could I not look for you?"

"I don't blame you for any of it, if that's what you're worried about. There, you've cleared your conscience. You can go."

"What did they do to you?" When she reached to touch his face, he stepped out of reach.

"If you leave now, you'll still make the last train back to Seoul."

"I'm taking you with me," she said.

"I'm no good, Sae. I can't give you what you want," he said. He swallowed hard and murmured something she could not hear. When their eyes met, she saw that he was holding back tears.

Her heart lurched. It was the first sign that he still felt something.

"Did they hurt you?"

"Will you leave, please?" He reached for her elbow, as if to turn her away.

"Not without you," she said.

"Go now, before I lose my nerve. Just try to forget me."

She freed herself of his grasp and shook her head, resolute.

"I can't," she said. "I'm pregnant, Jae."

The bus driver announced that they would be making a rest stop. Seung-min kicked the empty seat in front of him, and when Sae put her hand on his leg, he looked up at her with sudden curiosity.

"Is she our real grandmother?" Seung-min asked.

"Yes," Sae said, eyeing the truck on the road beside them whose wobbly cargo looked as though it would spill over at any moment. She opened the window, though the air-conditioning was on. She needed air, something to relieve the pressure in her head.

"Why hasn't she come to see us?" Seung-min asked.

Sae noticed his scuffed shoes and dirty shorts. What would her mother think? She had always imagined that she would return home as her happiest self. To prove her mother wrong.

"She's been busy," Sae murmured.

"Is she mean and scary?" Hoon-min asked.

"Not always, no," she said.

"Can she do magic?"

"I don't think so," Sae said, as the bus pulled into a rest stop.

The boys excitedly jumped out of the bus. Seung-min bolted ahead, Hoon-min closely following behind, until his foot caught on the uneven asphalt, and he fell. Sae picked him up as he wailed and was trying to console him when she caught sight of the TV screen. There was a photograph of Mr. Bae's face on the news. The newscaster announced that there was a warrant out for his arrest.

"Omma? Why are you shaking?" Hoon-min asked.

She looked past the hungry travelers as they gathered around the food stalls, searching for a diversion. She needed to find space to think. A toy-vending machine at the other end of the concourse seemed to offer the answer. Herding the boys along, she put a few coins into the slots and removed two plastic eggs each containing a small Transformers figurine. She placed one in Seung-min's hand and the other in Hoon-min's.

"You can have these if you stop asking questions," she said.

In Mallipo, they stepped into the smell of the hot sea air and walked down the narrow strip of shops with sliding metal doors and green plastic awnings where once the villagers had hung a congratulatory banner for her and Il-hyung when she had won a scholarship to Seoul National University. Past the stretches of roadside where the day's catch of small shrimp were laid out to dry. There wasn't a part of their path, or any of the paths that broke off the road they walked on, that she didn't know like the back of her hand. In the days immediately after her scholarship was announced, villagers would yell their congratulations through the rain or cross the road to shake her hand. On the hillside pavilion she had parted with her mother as she had wept. Had waited for Il-hyung at the village shop every morning so they could walk to school. To most, her hometown was a place known best for its stretch of beach and soft sand, the romance of its melting sunsets. It was the piers that loomed largest in Sae's memory, where she had waited for her father's boat to come in every afternoon, studied his face to see whether they had a large catch. The comfort of returning to her hometown was stained with the sadness of knowing what had happened in the years after she left.

At the top of the hill, at the end of the dusty path, was the familiar cinder block wall and blue gate. She knocked and, when there was no answer, pushed it open and urged the boys forward into the courtyard. Her mother came out of the living room and stopped short when she saw them. She was wearing a light-yellow knitted cardigan despite the heat. Her hair had been freshly dyed and permed. She had been afraid that her mother would have aged beyond recognition in the time since they had seen each other, but there was still a youthfulness about her. The only hints of age were in her unevenly freckled cheeks, the slight curve of her fingertips.

"Is that you, Sae?" she said. Sae could see her mother resisting an impulse to meet them at the gate, her eyes lingering on the boys for several long moments, before taking off her slippers to step into the house.

Sae clenched her boys' hands in hers until they winced.

"What are you doing just standing there?" her mother asked. "Aren't you coming in?"

Sae had forgotten about the heat in the countryside and could feel sweat pooling along the edges of her bra straps, the hem of her shorts. As if able to read her thoughts, her mother set down an icy glass of mixed grain powder and water for them, bringing the fan from the edge of the room to cool them. The gesture felt formal, as if she were the unwelcome guest that Jae had once been. Sae remembered her mother's refusal to look at him, staring only at his cheap shoes, her shudder at the revelation that he was an orphan who had served time in prison. Sae had been ungovernable even before she met him, but her mother had blamed him for her participation in the student movement. "He'll ruin you!" she screamed. As if the warning alone would form a net strong enough to hold her, out of the riots, out of the line of fire, out of the current pulling her into his arms.

How could they begin a conversation that had been on hold for six years? Carefully, skating the surface of the past, to a time before Jae. Her mother spoke of the town, of all the people who had packed up and moved to the city, of her brothers, all the while never quite looking at her. The children played with the toys her nephews had left behind, delighted by the sudden shock of space in this countryside home.

"Grasshoppers!" Seung-min said, red-faced, as he came to them for a gulp of water.

"If you go to the edge of that gate there are frogs, too," her mother said, patting his backside. Sae found herself envious of the natural affection, unsure if her mother's love for her had eroded after so many disappointments. She was relieved, too, that whatever had happened before the children was not held against them. Her mother, who could not pass a baby on her path without indulging in its cheeks, who had always had an affinity for young children, seemed to share a secret language with them. It also explained her refusal to see them, knowing that once she saw them, she would not be able to hold herself back from them.

The boys leapt in the direction of the gate.

"They're getting big now, the toughest years are over," her

mother said, looking at her directly for the first time. "But you look like a ghoul. When's the last time you ate a proper meal?"

Sae looked down at the gap between panels on the wooden floor. "You heard about the Tower" was all she was able to say.

"It was on the news," her mother said, puzzled.

"I haven't been able to find him," she said, her voice suddenly hoarse.

A strange cry escaped her mother's mouth. The boys turned to look in their direction. At first, she thought her mother was generous to weep for the loss of a person she had been so vehemently against, until she realized as her mother grasped her hand the tears were for Sae.

Here in the safety of her childhood home that she had returned to after so many years in exile, she felt a lurch in her stomach, as if she was falling. Until that moment, she had led the charge, she was her best self in a crisis, but she now felt unable to breathe, suspended. She closed her eyes, waiting for the delayed sensation of impact, much like the way that as a student she would wake up alive with pain in her back, only registering injury after the shock had worn off, days after being struck by the baton of a state trooper.

Sae collapsed into her mother's arms, grateful she was there to catch her.

TEN DAYS AFTER THE COLLAPSE

Sae held the phone receiver to her ear, listening to the ringing while watching Hoon-min squatting behind her mother's large earthenware kimchi pot, hiding from Seung-min. The sun was setting, leaving only a pleasant and warm wind in the air. She found herself imagining telling Jae about the boys—barefoot and carefree, the day a blur of browned legs and happy shrieks. She found herself thinking that he would love it here; Jae himself had a particular talent for nurturing plants. How he would love to dirty his own hands in these fields.

She felt a lump in her throat at the thought and could not speak when Tae-kyu came on the other end of the line.

"Hello?"

"It's me," she said. "You're a hard man to pin down."

"I've been tied up," he said. His voice sounded distant, as though he was holding his face away from the phone.

"I've come to my mother's," she said. "I thought we should get out of the city for a bit."

He cleared his throat and said quietly, "It was a good call."

"Is there any more news? Why's there a warrant out for Mr. Bae's arrest? Didn't they announce that what happened was a mistake?" Sae asked, watching as Seung-min crept toward Hoon-min with a water hose in his hands.

"There's some evidence that he was using substandard materials, diluting concrete to save costs. The police want to pull him in for questioning, but they can't find him. It doesn't look good."

There was a clipped quality in the way he talked, and Sae knew him to be like this when he was holding his tongue. Hoon-min let out a shriek as Seung-min doused him with water. The wind no longer felt pleasant, carrying with it animal smells and the scent of rot. She imagined that this is what it would feel like to be hit by the hot blast of a bomb detonation in the next town over, knocking the breath out of her.

"There's something else," he said. "They've cleared more of the site and uncovered the basement parking lot."

For a moment she wasn't sure what he meant by this.

His voice was gentle after a long pause. "There are quite a few bodies that they haven't been able to identify, Sae."

She didn't know how long she stood there, numb and immobile, the boys' giggles muted, watching the sky grow heavy with darkness. She thought of Jae's unhappiness in the evenings, the Baes' bare closets, the emptied-out offices. She kept arriving at the same point: Jae was so careful. So precise in his work. And then there was Mrs. Bae's discomfort in the gymnasium. That look of confusion at the mention of the swimming pool. Her stomach tightened, curling into a fist. A feeling like lead in the gut. That there were violent things happening in the world just at the edge of her awareness. Happening silently in the next room. It was a familiar feeling that sometimes came over her when she had worked at the paper, interviewing witnesses with Tae-kyu. How she would fold away her notepad into her back pocket and walk away from a scene or an interview, and reach the bottom of the stairs feeling as though they had been beaten over the head by a sledgehammer. How they wouldn't be able to articulate what exactly it was until much later.

"I need to go back to the city," Sae said to her mother.

"What's happened?"

She wasn't sure how to say that she was going back for Jae. Even now, she felt the need to protect him. How could she tell her mother that Jae might have been responsible for what happened? As if he hadn't already done enough to their family in her mother's eyes.

"They need me at the paper," she said.

"What about the children?" her mother asked, putting down her spatula. She seemed afraid that Sae was about to take them from her.

Sae looked across the open living room at Hoon-min, sun weary and sucking his thumb in front of the TV. Even as he played with Seung-min in the delights of her mother's garden, she often caught his eyes roaming in search of her. At night his arm was a tentacle, feeling for her in his sleep before rolling into the pit of her arm, his leg heavy on her hip. But he was growing attached to her mother, too. The night before she had watched as her mother had pulled out their long-sleeved pajamas for the boys, rolling the sleeves up to wash their wrists with the patience that Sae had always lacked. The boys would be safe with her.

"I'll be back for them in a week," she said, knowing that she was shameless, realizing that she had intended to do this from the beginning, while convincing herself that she had come here for the boys.

Her mother tucked a strand of Sae's hair behind her ear

before dropping her hand, as if catching herself doing something she shouldn't.

"Do what you want," her mother said, wiping her hands on her apron as she turned away from her. "You always do. How will I stop you?"

ELEVEN DAYS AFTER THE COLLAPSE

Myong-hee dressed herself in a calf-length brown skirt and patterned cotton blouse as she did every Thursday and got on a bus for an hour-long journey to the west side of the city. For years Holt International Children's Services had been housed in a low-rise building with glazed red bricks that glistened like teeth. Now it was a contemporary building—all steel and floor-to-ceiling windows. Adoption, it seemed, was a profitable business.

Her eyes ached in the light—she had not slept at all, tossing and turning, weighing Mr. Li's offer. She had not taken him seriously at first, and had not met him at the airport as he had asked her to, but when he called her from L.A. the evening before, she realized she was tempted by it. Myong-hee lingered for a moment in the courtyard, hesitant as she always was, though she came in once a week, month after month, year after year. Like a woman in search of a severed limb. Inside, the offices smelled of new paint, burned coffee, and plastic. The children's rooms were downstairs, in what remained of the old building. The room enveloped her in its sweet biscuity scent of formula, the hint of vinegar in the sweat of the infants left in their cots for too long. She came as often as she could to hold the newborns, to feed them, change them, trying to remember her own babies' smell.

Washing her hands in the sink, she surveyed the cots, trying to guess which infant had gone the longest without what it craved the most. A purple-faced infant whose cries had become a mewl. The label at the end of the cot had the details: one week old, mother, Shim Ji-won, age sixteen; father, unknown. He was small for a one-week-old, like a feather. Myong-hee was afraid he might float away. She checked his diaper and then mixed a bottle for him, walking around the room with him in the crook of her arm, placing a hand on his small chest as she went from cot to cot to see who she could attend to next.

Even decades later, the act of coming here was mostly one of punishment—circling a room full of infants who could not be satiated, in the center of their layered cries, when she was never enough to comfort them all. But it was also the closest she could get to what she had lost, running her fingers over their cold butter cheeks, waiting for their milk-drunk sighs, to tell them *sorry, sorry*. Most of the time, she was alone in the room—they were always short of volunteers, the few young university students preferring the toddlers. So it was a surprise when the door swung open and a woman with milky skin and an elegant updo came in, tying the strings of her apron behind her back.

She cooed at the infant closest to the door and picked him up, changed him, and then sat down with him. Several chairs had been arranged into a circle at the center of the room, as though those who filled them might talk to one another like recovering addicts.

"You must love babies," the woman said after a moment.

"I wouldn't be here if I didn't," Myong-hee said, though she immediately regretted the impulse to spit venom first, to ward off anyone who came too close. She thought of that room in the pay-by-the-hour inn with a small window that faced out onto the brick wall of another building, the walls so paper thin that she could hear the quickened breaths of the couples next door, the whisper of the man saying he would offer more money for a different position, the weeping of a drunk, the innkeeper chiding a squatter who had stayed hours too long. That inn had housed a world of shame, and yet she had seemed to be the one for whom most of the residents had the most spite. An unwed mother. As though it were the worst of all sins.

She put her feather infant down and hushed another, picking it up and carrying the light bundle, a girl with black hair that stood on end as though full of static. The mother nineteen, father unknown.

"I like to help where I can," Myong-hee said, sitting down beside the woman, in an attempt at reconciliation.

"Are you with the church?"

She shook her head.

"Good, I thought you might be one of those holier-than-thou types," she said with a laugh, covering her mouth with her hand, as though pleased to be able to say something like that aloud. "I have three of my own. It was tough raising them, but they grew up so soon! My husband retired. Old man doesn't know what to do with himself, and now we fight all the time. So I try to clear out of the way. For a while I would go and see my grown-up kids, but it turns out they are too busy with their lives. But you know what? It's not so fun to sit at home feeling like a burden to your kids. What about you?"

"Twins," Myong-hee said with a shaky smile, feeling shy,

finding she could not muster the same careless performance of her basement persona in this room.

"You had your hands full, then."

Over the years the few memories she had of her daughter had lost their color. Whenever she found herself starting to drift in thought about this loss, she would begin walking, or busy herself—tipping out bins full of stained tissues, wiping down the sweat stains from the sofas, mixing soju and water for the girls to drink—and was delivered from the small reel of memories that she carried with her always. Then one day she found that all she had in her memory was an outline, a sense that there was once something she had lost. The ache and chill the only remnants of a broken bone that had long healed over.

At first Myong-hee had believed the adoption agency when they told her that her daughter had been sent to a better place. She practiced the English that she had learned for free at the institutes near the barracks, asking the American soldiers—their bodies large, big boned like a different species—what she might see if she looked out of their windows in their hometown.

The men would tell her about the desert. The mountains. The lakes. The cold. The heat. The plains. Each description rattling loose any certainty that she had held on to. One man told her he had never seen snow before he had come to Korea. Another said that Korean winters were mild compared to the ones he survived in the Midwest. The America she pieced together from their stories was not one place but a land so vast it was many countries. Searching for her child would be like trying to find a sesame seed in an earthenware pot of rice. They had assured her that her child had gone to a place of more opportunities, where hunger was confined to fairy tales or history books. But the more she saw of the men, and felt their hands massage her body like meat on a slab, the starved look that saw right through her, she came to fear that there were many types of hunger, and more than one way her daughter might be starved.

"Only one of them made it," she said, not sure why she was telling this to a stranger. "My daughter's alive."

"Where is she now?" the woman asked after a pause.

"In America."

"Oh? Which part?"

For a moment she said nothing, the vastness of America suddenly overwhelming. Myong-hee was aware that the other woman was looking at her with curiosity. She looked down at her own blouse, the plain skirt, wondering if there was something on her clothes that might betray her. She rose suddenly and put the infant down in her cot, placed her hand on the baby's chest for a moment and then tended to another, annoyed that this woman would bring her shame to life like this.

"I'm sorry, I don't mean to pry. I'm always told I'm too nosy. I only ask because my son took me to San Francisco last year. I've never been so cold! And I was so queasy with all the food. After three days we found ourselves in a Korean restaurant! I don't think I'm one of those traveling types. I'm happy where I am."

Few women spoke to her like this, as though they were old friends. She had avoided befriending women here. Some years before, a group of them had met every three weeks. They were women who had also given up their babies and had changed their minds. Women who had been too poor to care for their infants. They felt they had been tricked into leaving their children, with false promises that they could return for them. They had gathered because they had wanted to do something when they had learned that the orphanage's administrator had tried to fill the orphanages so that they might get more international aid. They met and tried to rally some support from the police and city officials, but no one seemed interested. The officials simply blamed them for having infants in the first place. After a while the meetings became less frequent. The basis for friendship was too painful. To meet was a reminder of an irrevocable past of which they had no path to recourse.

Myong-hee saw that the woman was hardly paying the infant any attention and seemed not to be troubled by the sounds of the other infants mewling. She wondered why she was there. Was she seeking companionship with other volunteers? There was something girlish about her. She seemed to be one of those women who had an active social life, who lived for the excitement of rumors.

Then just as quickly as she had sat down, the woman rose again. "I should be getting back. The old man doesn't cook; he'll starve if I let him. I don't know where the time went."

Myong-hee blinked at this. She had never lived with a man. Did she have what it took to live the domestic life? What did it mean to go handcuffed to a man she hardly knew, with no money? How long before he began asking her about her history with men? Before he handled her like the furniture?

"Maybe I'll see you here again next week?" the woman said.

"I'll be here," Myong-hee said shyly, pulling the bottle from the infant's mouth as she sucked half-heartedly, her eyes rolling back into gentle sleep. Myong-hee set the little girl down, and suddenly she was awake, though silent. When was it that the babies learned not to cry, at least not to call their mothers back to them? The infant's beetle eyes were alert and searching, and Myong-hee felt the need to leave the room, knowing she would disappoint her, too.

Back in the office, Myong-hee lingered at the desk until the assistant could no longer pretend that she did not see her.

"Shim Ji-won's baby. He feels so light. What's her story?" she asked.

"You know we can't tell you that," the assistant said, staring at the computer screen.

"Any news on the Lee Myong-hee file?"

"We know who you are," the employee said without looking up.

"Do you have anything for me?"

"As we've told you every week, we will call you as soon as we receive any communication from the States."

Myong-hee dug her nail into the Styrofoam cup, thinking of the men she had come to know over the years. Men who wanted to mark her body with bruises, men who began to weep as soon as she slid the rice paper door closed, men who wanted her to mother them, men who wanted her only from behind, men who wanted her quiet, and small men who wanted her large and overpowering. She no longer wanted anything to do with these men in the future. And just like that it was decided; she would not go to Mr. Li. When that letter arrived from her daughter, she wanted to be free of her debts. She would find a way to unshackle herself from this existence.

She would find a new life without men like Mr. Li. Become a mother worth finding.

• • •

It began to rain heavily as Sae boarded the night bus back to Seoul. The air-conditioning smelled stale in the humid air. Only two other passengers had settled into their seats and as Sae passed them, they averted their eyes. It was as if she were already marked, her proximity to the disaster visible on her face. Perhaps visible, too, was the dread of the grim task waiting for her in the morgues.

Was it possible that Jae had gone into hiding? He had deserted her once before, but under different circumstances. She recalled the promise he had made to her in the small rooftop studio they had rented shortly after she had found him at the temple. She was in his arms, feeling the warmth of his body behind her, his hand protective over her swollen belly.

"Why aren't you asleep?" Jae had asked.

"You're not sleeping either," she said.

"Are you uncomfortable?"

She smiled at the concern in his voice.

"No," she said, fighting the urge to see what he would do for her if she said she was. She drew the cover over her shoulder, feeling him relax beside her. "I can't believe this place is ours. It doesn't feel like home yet."

"We'll find somewhere bigger soon," he said.

"I didn't mean it like that," she said. After months of hiding him from dorm residents, she felt triumphant, as if they had won a space for themselves in the world.

"We finally have a place," she said, "that's ours."

She sensed that he was worried. Money was tight, and Jae hadn't found a job yet in the city. The paper hardly paid her anything, and after the baby she would have to quit.

"Then let's stay up," he said. "It's not as though you have to smuggle me out in the early hours of the morning. We're free. Just you and me."

"And Bean."

"And Bean," he said, taking in a sharp breath. "You don't think she's going to look like me? I want her to have your nose."

"It could be a boy," she said, shifting the bedding beneath her to remove the pressure on her ribs. "I can't believe I'm so big already. Will you still want me when I'm so big I can't walk anymore?"

"Of course," he said, without missing a beat. But she felt him stiffen behind her. "Does that happen?"

"No," she said. "I don't know."

"Seems like it's the kind of thing we should know. We live at the top of four flights of stairs."

"We have a little time," she laughed. "You could practice carrying several sacks of rice up the stairs. Get some muscle on those legs."

"You sound like my drill sergeant in the army," he said. He ran his hands over her belly. "You're perfect."

He lifted her T-shirt and leaned over her, putting his lips to her hip bone. The act made her feel strangely powerful. Since she had found him, they had frantically searched for a place to live and a way they might forge a life together. The initial relief of finding him had masked the anxiety she felt now—that she had impelled him, that he was beholden to her. She did not know whether she could trust this gesture of worship. Hadn't he made her feel this way before? And still he was capable of desertion, of absence.

"Do you love me?"

"You know I do," he said, unbothered by the question, his breath hot in her ear.

She held his hand as he reached for her breast.

"Why did you leave me at the inn?" she asked. It was the first time she had felt brave enough to ask him.

He buried his face in her hair, saying nothing. She became afraid he would not answer. That this would become another one of those deep silences forming a gulf between them. There were things that she sensed she could not ask him. About the interrogations. She had heard the stories of students who had been changed by torture. Who spoke of the loneliness they couldn't shake off, their altered sense of time. When they were not receiving the electric volts to their genitals, or being held underwater, they were kept in windowless rooms where guards delivered their meals at irregular intervals so they lost all sense of time. She was afraid of pushing him away with her questions.

"I didn't want to become a disappointment to you," he said after a while. "I don't want you to give up anything for me. Don't stop working at the paper. I don't want your life to become something less because you met someone like me."

This felt like a reluctance to be part of her life, but it also felt like a warning. That he could disappear again.

The streetlamp outside gave them a sliver of light. She moved to look at him, feeling the gravity of her belly shift as she turned, and put her hand on his face, feeling the light bristle on his cheek. He no longer seemed as boyish as he had been when they first met.

"I chose you; I came to find you," she said. "I want you to remember that."

He nodded. "I know."

"Will you promise me something?" she asked.

He stroked her hair, and she brought his palm to her mouth to kiss it.

"Promise me you won't disappear like that again."

"I promise."

TWELVE DAYS AFTER THE COLLAPSE

The morgue attendant pulled back the sheet. Sae looked at the floor, catching a glimpse of a flattened skull, unsure whether she was ready to cross the threshold into a world without Jae in it. She forced herself to look. Tufts of hair were embedded in the remains of the corpse's forehead. Half of his face was missing. She surveyed the rest of the body: the sinewy purplish torso and dark nipples, then on the left side, a visibly shattered limb that looked more like an elephant's trunk than an arm.

"It's not him," she said, recovering her breath.

"How old did you say your husband was?" the morgue attendant asked her. His scalp glistened with grease. The flickering light above them gave the impression that he was swaying slightly.

"Thirty," she said.

"There are two bodies about that age, around the height you described, though there are others you might want to look at, just to be sure. If he has any siblings, you could ask for a DNA test."

"He was an orphan," she said. "But one of my sons could give a sample."

She felt his eyes on her.

"I didn't think to ask; you must have had them young."

She felt a strange compulsion to laugh and thought she might save it to tell Jae later. *The morgue attendant was hitting on me when I was looking for you.* He rolled out another body and lifted the sheet. The fist in her stomach tightened.

"You see this?" he said, sliding his hand under the corpse's hand and lifting it up to reveal red abrasions. "He has no fingerprints, they're rubbed raw. I'm guessing he was trying to claw his way out. See this discoloration here? Nicotine stains. Was your husband a smoker?"

She shook her head. They were not his hands. Jae's hands were slimmer, thicker around the knuckles. She thought of the dorm room she had as a student. The length of his body in the shadows in that room where no words were exchanged between them. Where anything above a whisper was audible in the rooms surrounding them. Male students were forbidden from the women's dormitories, but sometimes when she was able to smuggle him in, they would wake in the early hours of the morning to the sound of a lone voice and an acoustic guitar from three doors down, followed by the click of the tape player as it ran its course. That room of hers that they could cross in three paces. So much of their early time had been spent in rooms where they could not speak or divulge their secrets, the walls surrounding them porous to the occupants next door. In that room there was no talking, only what could be communicated with a glance and a touch. In that room, they came to know each other's bodies, and found scars whose histories remained silent, like symbols painted by their ancestors on cave walls. Give her any small patch of Jae's skin, she thought, and she would know it.

Disappointed, the morgue attendant closed the freezer door before moving on to the next one.

"Were there any visible marks on your husband's body?"

"He had a birthmark over his heart. It looked like a rabbit's foot," she said.

The morgue attendant nodded noncommittally and made note of this. "Anything else? Any previously broken bones?"

"None that I know of."

Whatever they had done to him in prison all those years ago had not left a mark. When Jae came back to her, the damage was invisible; the greatest scars seemed to be in his mind.

An acrid and slightly sweet tang of rotting chicken accompanied the third body. It was clear from the corpse's height that it was not Jae.

"It's not him."

"Have you checked the other morgues?"

"This is the first one."

She looked back at the row of bodies yet to be put back in the freezer. These bodies that had once been washed lovingly by a mother, caressed and held, who had felt the warm touch of another and yet now lay so alone. Where was Jae? Where was he without his boys crawling over his limbs, the warmth of her hand on his back as he slept?

Seeing the expression on Sae's face, the attendant gave her a sympathetic look and said, "It gets a little easier, if that's any consolation. I'll keep an eye out for the rabbit foot. Why don't you leave me your pager number?"

Tae-kyu was waiting for her in the lobby of the hospital, upstairs from the morgue. She hated to cry in front of him but could not stop. He led her by the arm to the bench, away from the hospital entrance and out of view of the curious glances of those standing by.

"I told you to wait," Tae-kyu said, angry. "I told you I would wait with you. Why would you go in there alone?"

"What am I missing here? Tell me I'm missing something," she said, ignoring his question. She wanted, more than anything, to see Jae's face, to hear from him that he had been looking for her, that there had been a mistake, that he was not involved in any of this. Just as quickly she knew his omissions would needle her, puncture any certainty she had about him. She needed to know what had happened. She was determined to find the answers, even if it meant digging it out of the earth with her bare hands. She closed her eyes, feeling the heat in her swollen eyelids. "They can't be responsible for this, can they?" she said.

The humid heat began nosing itself into her clothes, expelling the chill of the morgue.

"Jae said they were cutting corners. He was unhappy," she said. "But I still can't believe it. How am I going to face all of those families?"

"Well," Tae-kyu said, leaning his elbows on his knees. "You don't have to worry about that for now. They've only named Mr. Bae. No one is going to be knocking down your door just yet."

Sae froze. "You don't think that's strange?"

"Do you want an angry mob at your door?"

"No," she said. "But why wouldn't they name Jae as well?"

Tae-kyu shrugged. "Mr. Bae was the head of the company. The families only want to know who was in charge. It's not as though they need the names of everyone who . . . What is it? Hey, where are you going?"

• • •

In the disorientation and confusion of the first few days after the Tower's collapse, Sae had been so focused on looking for Jae and then, later, Mr. Bae, that she had not considered broadening the scope of her search to include others she might know. After the morgue, Sae went through the newspaper archive. Every day after the collapse the paper had printed the names of those who had been killed alongside a list of survivors.

In revisiting the list, she spotted a familiar name: Lim Hae-soo. Hae-soo was a common name, but it was also the same name as the overworked administrator—the only other permanent employee who worked in the office with Jae and Mr. Bae. It seemed to be too much of a coincidence that another person of the same name should be on the list. They had worked in a tiny office where a begrudging intimacy was inevitable—Sae hoped that Hae-soo would be able to tell her what frustrations Jae wrestled with in working in the Tower.

Hae-soo was difficult to track down, and her mother was cagey on the phone, speaking only of her financial troubles and worries for her daughter, but Sae had been able to piece together that Hae-soo was still recovering in Ansan hospital.

The hospital was new with gleaming white marble floors and a modern-looking reception area. Sae approached a receptionist wearing bright red lipstick.

"I'm here to visit Lim Hae-soo," Sae said.

The receptionist typed something into her computer before glancing briefly at Sae.

"Room 401," she said. "You can take the elevator on the other side of this wall."

On the fourth floor, the afternoon light revealed a throng of patients communing in a narrow ward. Hae-soo's mother had given Sae the impression that their family had been struggling financially, so the private room was a surprise. A small sofa area where presumably visitors could rest was partitioned by a low wall. A large bouquet of lilies and roses took up most of the bedside table.

Hae-soo was asleep, her bandaged arm resting awkwardly across her stomach. Her long hair looked waxy and unwashed. Sae was unsure how long she sat there before Hae-soo opened her eyes.

"Hi," she rasped, wide-eyed. Sae was uncertain whether Hae-soo recognized her. "Could I have some water?"

Sae rose and filled a glass with the barley tea from the jug that had been standing on the cabinet.

"How are you feeling?" Sae asked, grasping her hand.

"I don't know." Hae-soo gave a weak smile. "I've been sleeping a lot . . ."

"Are you in pain?" Sae gestured at her arm. "That's one heck of a bandage."

"Is it? I guess it is," she said, as if unsure of what she was doing there. Then, after a moment, she seemed to find her footing. "At school there was a girl who broke her arm, and everyone signed her cast leaving her sweet notes. I was kind of envious; for a while I wanted one too."

"I know what you mean. Maybe I can be the first to sign your cast."

Hae-soo's smile contorted into a wince as she shifted in the bed. "Are you okay?" Sae asked.

"It's the bruising in my ribs. It hurts to laugh."

"I'll hold off on the jokes, then," Sae said.

"I was watching this comedy show the other night. It's the only thing I want to watch, and I had to turn it off. I was cracking up. It was this gag where—"

Hae-soo continued describing the comedian's performance in great detail and then abruptly recalled her high school days. She spoke continuously, as though afraid of silence. Sae waited for an appropriate moment to enter the conversation, but after a while Sae sensed Hae-soo's stream of consciousness was a form of self-protection.

It was only when a nurse came in to check on the IV fluid that Hae-soo stopped speaking, her mouth clamped shut.

Sae sensed an opening. "I don't know if you've heard, but I've been unable to find Jae. I was hoping—"

"You know what I've been craving?" Hae-soo said, interrupting her abruptly. She seemed terrified by what Sae might say. "This shrimp and cream pasta from the restaurant downstairs. Sometimes I'd skip lunch for the whole week to save up and then go and have a whole dish for myself."

Sae was taken aback by this turn in the conversation and was unsure of how to respond. "Would you like me to get you something from downstairs?"

"No, at the office, I mean. Is it strange that I wanted to eat by myself? I never ate with anyone."

"Everyone needs a break sometimes," Sae said at last.

"Mr. Bae was always asking me to do things, sometimes things that I had no idea how to do. He was always leaving me notes with tasks I had to complete. It was overwhelming."

Sae nodded, urging her to continue.

"I was thinking about quitting. I wasn't even supposed to be in the Tower. Usually I'm in Buam-dong; they rarely need me on-site. But Mr. Bae asked me to pick up an envelope to be couriered over. I was at the atrium. There was a perfume shop by the café. I was going to treat myself. So I was there," she said. The glass in her hand was shaking. "And then there was this sound; I can still hear it in my head now. Like this long moan."

Sae's ears pricked at the mention of Buam-dong, a sleepy residential neighborhood. Before Sae could ask her more about it, Hae-soo continued.

"They say the bone is shattered," she said. "I can't remember how many screws the surgeon said he put in it. It could have been a lot worse. They think a column fell over me. They had to cut me out of there."

"I'm sorry, I realize this must be hard for you," Sae said, the imagined scene seamlessly merging with her memories of the rubble as she looked for Jae. "I don't think you were alone in being unhappy," she began cautiously. "Jae didn't think the project at Aspiration Tower was going as it should."

Hae-soo fidgeted with a piece of loose thread on her blanket and fought back the tears. Their eyes met briefly, and Hae-soo looked away.

"There was the usual stuff," she said with a shrug. She seemed to sense that this wasn't enough. "A tight deadline. Worries about money. We had to move because one of their projects fell through. The investors ran out of money. There was a problem with the building that made it tough."

"A problem? When you say 'building,' do you mean Aspiration Tower?"

Hae-soo's eyes grew wide, as though she realized she had made a mistake. "I don't know the details."

Sae decided not to push Hae-soo. "Was there anyone Jae was working with that he was in conflict with?"

"I don't know, I don't think so," Hae-soo said quickly.

They sat in silence for a few minutes.

"They're saying that the building collapsed because of a miscalculation made by L&S. Do you think that could be true?"

Hae-soo shook her head vigorously. "I wasn't supposed to speak to anyone," she said softly.

"What do you mean?" Sae asked. "Did Mr. Bae ask you not to talk to me?"

Hae-soo looked nervous. "I'm sorry," she said. "I think you should leave."

At the nurses' station outside the room, Sae caught the attention of a young nurse with a large mole on the side of her nose.

"Can I ask you something?" Sae asked. "It's about Lim Hae-soo in 401. Does she have many visitors? A boyfriend?"

The nurse shrugged. "Why do you ask?"

"I saw those expensive flowers," Sae said, trying to sound as casual as she could. "I've been trying to set her up for years, but she's always turned me down. I wondered if she already has someone."

The nurse seemed to relax. "I don't think so. She just had one visitor. Young man, corporate type. I had the feeling it was work related."

"Thanks," Sae said, placing her hands in her pockets so the nurse would not see that they were trembling. She wanted to ask her who was paying for the private room, but knew she was unlikely to get an answer.

She took the stairwell instead of the lift and walked into the heat, thinking of the office Hae-soo spoke of in Buam-dong. It was an unusual place for an office. For the first time in days she felt calm. Finally she had something to work with, a trail uncovered in the rough. Sae found a phone booth on the street and held the receiver in her hand until she knew how she would conduct the call.

Buam-dong was nestled at the base of Inwangsan Mountain, at the end of a military checkpoint that had recently been opened to the public. The neighborhood was filled with large single-family homes behind imposing gates. The only dim lights on the narrow strip of the main street came from a hole-in-the-wall corner store—the kind that was slowly being replaced by fluorescent 7-Elevens. The few other businesses—a coffee shop and small restaurant—were closed for the night. Sae slowed as she reached a realtor's office at the end of the street, where a portly man sat with his ankle on his knee, reading the day's paper.

"We're closed," he said, without taking his eyes off the paper. "I'm waiting for someone."

"I've come on behalf of L&S Engineering. I called you earlier," she said, forcing a smile. "I'm Hae-soo's cousin. She just wanted me to do her this favor. She said you would have a spare key for the office."

"Ah, yes . . ." he said, patting his shirt pockets, unconcerned. "I haven't seen Mr. Bae in a while; he must be busy. He's always standing out by the alley, smoking, pacing like he's waiting for bad news."

The implication that Sae was unlikely to encounter Mr. Bae in the office did little to calm her. She was sure that some sort of confrontation was inevitable—whether it was in the form of evidence, or more clues to where Jae might be.

"He's working on a contract out of town," she said quickly. It was clear that the man had no idea about L&S and what they did, or that they were somehow connected to the Tower.

The last hurdle was finding the office itself, though her conversation with Hae-soo had given her a clue. Sae was familiar with small neighborhood businesses like this—the way information would circulate easily like a light wind. She had to be careful not to rouse suspicion. She thanked the man before pretending to remember something. "Is there an Italian restaurant here at all? I promised my son I would bring home some pasta."

The office was on the second floor, in a residential studio just above an Italian restaurant, which had closed early. Sae paused at the top of the stairs, placing her ear lightly on the door, and heard nothing more than her quickened heartbeat. After several moments, she opened the door to find a small room with two narrow desks. A stale smell hung in the air. The small kitchenette was not in use and several boxes were piled high in the sink. A large ashtray filled with cigarette butts lay on the windowsill. She looked for signs that someone might have been living at the office, but there was no bedding or evidence of any meals. It was clear that neither Mr. Bae nor Jae had used this office as a place of refuge.

Sae immediately recognized one of the desks as most likely belonging to Hae-soo—it was neatly organized, and a wilting flower hung its head in a jar marked with water stains.

On the other desk, Sae found a calendar with Jae's neat handwriting on it. The sight of it brought him to life in the room and filled her with a desperate feeling—a sense that she had to find him urgently, the fear that this might be all that remained of him.

Sae looked around her, eyeing the drawers and papers on the desk. Somewhere, she thought, she would find a vital clue or detail that would lead her to him. She opened the drawers and rifled through the papers, looking for a contract that might detail the work that L&S Engineering had agreed to do, or even an invoice or agreement with the name of a contact at Taehan Group.

After trying to pick at a locked drawer with a paper clip, Sae gave up and sat at Hae-soo's desk going over a book of accounts, running her finger over transactions that meant little to her. Moments later she slammed the binder shut and crossed the room to rifle through the papers that were scattered on the other desk. Buried under several manuals, Sae found a large orange envelope with a set of blueprints and felt her heart quicken as she unfolded them, recognizing them as the structural sketches of Aspiration Tower. She flicked through the pages several times, trying to decipher the notes and calculations, more aware than ever that she would struggle to do this alone.

TWENTY-ONE DAYS AFTER THE COLLAPSE

"I'll have another," Yung said, setting his glass down on the table. Myong-hee paused before reaching for the empty bottle of whiskey in front of her, surprised. He had never been much of a drinker; he was disciplined about his two-whiskey limit. Over the years, she had marveled at his restraint—the way he would drain his glass or switch it for an empty one on the table while his business partners were distracted. He was a man who maintained absolute control in his dealings, even personal ones; he was vulnerable with no one.

"More of the same?"

He nodded.

She left the room to get another bottle, diluting it to stretch out the evening. With his generous forehead and receding hairline, Yung did not resemble the Chairman, but he could conjure his father into the room with a gesture, and serving him was a point of ambivalence for Myong-hee. She set down a plate of fruit and dried cuttlefish on the table and reached for his glass to pour him another.

"Before I forget, there was one meeting that I meant to tell you about," she said. "The head of corporate loans at Nara Bank came in with Mr. Jo of Sangmyong Electronics. They were talking about the acquisition of a company called Onha Tech. They seem to have developed a special technology—"

Yung raised his hand. "Not now. I can't."

Myong-hee nodded, though the response was unexpected. She had assumed that he had come in for her reports, not because he had nowhere else to drink. The recent announcement about the third-party vendor's assumed responsibility for the Tower's collapse had quickly been followed by rumors that Taehan Group could still be held liable. The realization that the disaster posed a real threat to Taehan Group filled her with a strange tingly feeling that she could not place.

"They said on the news that it was the swimming pool," she said, calmly smoothing her skirt. She suspected that even if the public were forgiving, the Chairman would not be. "How is the old man taking it?"

"I couldn't tell you," Yung said with a smirk. "I don't know where the old man is." Yung raised the glass to his lips. "I can't seem to keep track of anyone these days. Mr. Bae, the incompetent little shit. I asked only one thing of him. How difficult is it to find someone?"

He leaned forward to place his elbows on his knees. "Mr. Li was in here all the time. Did he tell you where he was going?"

"I wish I could tell you," she said, lowering her gaze, afraid her eyes would give her away. Though she saw she did not need to worry. Yung was not looking at her.

"I'm kidding. Of course he wouldn't tell you. I don't know why I said that." Yung was slurring now and spilled the remainder of his whiskey on his shirt. He seemed not to notice. Instead he began to laugh. "Maybe Father is right. I'm not as meticulous, or as paranoid as him. Father used to take us all on a tour of his factories. He wanted us to know that he knew every department, every section of the production line like the back of his hand. Then afterward he'd take us to the top of Namsan and point to every building he'd ever built. Not because it was our inheritance, but because he wanted us to know what he had built from nothing. A reminder that we will never achieve as much as he has."

It was Myong-hee's turn to reach for a drink, unhappy with the turn in conversation. All she wanted was a drop to burn her tongue, just to take the edge off, though she was rarely able to stop it there, especially if what Yung wanted was to divulge the past. She explored the margin between her sense of gratitude to him and the mounting resentment that he had long abused their exchanges. Over the years, she had shared with Yung any information that had passed through the rooms that would give Taehan Group a competitive advantage—rumors of company mergers, news of investments being made by foreign companies, details of products being developed by small companies that Taehan Group could make even better. In exchange, she had had a channel to Geun-ye. At first she had lived for the details. *Was he colicky? Who was holding him when he fussed?* But as the years progressed it seemed to her easier not to know. Just as Yung did not want the scraps of information she had gathered for him over the past few weeks, she no longer wanted to hear him talk about Geun-ye. There was, after all, only so much the heart could take.

"The next chairman has to be the guardian of his work," he was saying. "There isn't any room for mistakes."

"You think your position as the next chairman is in jeopardy?" she asked, and when she felt the tingle return, she realized she was excited that Taehan Group was in real danger.

He sneered at this. "Are you kidding me? This is the ultimate test. Father wants me to prove I can get Taehan Group out of the crisis. I think that was his plan all along. And I will fix it. I will. He'll see that he should have had me in mind for the chairmanship all along. What did he see in Geun-ye anyway? It was always Geun-ye, Geun-ye, Geun-ye. It always comes back to him, doesn't it?"

"I think you've had enough," she said, gently removing the glass from his hand. She was shocked by the bitterness in Yung's voice. Years had passed since his younger brother's death, and it still hurt Myong-hee to hear his name. "Let's not talk about Geun-ye now."

For several weeks there had been a palpable sense of shock as a result of the Tower's collapse, but now business was picking up again; the men were resuming their routines.

Earlier that evening, Myong-hee had had to deal with a girl who had drunk too much and had fallen asleep while entertaining a group of men, had consoled a young junior employee at a shipping firm who sat weeping for an ex-girlfriend, and had turned a group away because all of her rooms were occupied.

Now a man pretended to have lost his wallet and credit cards and had become argumentative when Myong-hee insisted that he would have to find a way to pay.

"Frankly," the red-faced man was saying, his breath thick and acidic, "I think you should waive the fee. Do you know who I am?"

Myong-hee smiled tightly. "With all due respect, all clients who—"

"I said, do you know who I am?" he shouted, as if the source of the confusion had its roots in how loudly he had said it. "I'm a manager, do you understand? At a major company." He slurred as he tried to hold his head up in his palm, his elbow resting shakily on the counter.

"I've plenty of money," he said. "But you know, I think one of your girls took my wallet. I knew I shouldn't have trusted them. A bunch of flower snakes the lot of you!"

"Mr. Lee," Myong-hee said. "If you need to make a call to someone who can pick up the tab for you, I'd be happy to—"

"I'll take care of this," a deep voice said from behind. It belonged to a tall man with wet-looking, neatly combed hair and a side part. He looked to be in his late thirties, and his smooth, unlined face was vaguely familiar.

"I'm sorry for the inconvenience," he said, setting down his credit card on the counter. He was wearing a gold Rolex and elegant cuff links.

"And who are you?" Mr. Lee demanded to know.

"Why don't I show you to a cab?" the tall man said, taking Mr. Lee by the shoulders.

By the time the tall man returned for his credit card a short while later, most of the rooms had emptied, and Myong-hee found herself feeling weary and eager for bed.

"I don't know why people come here when they know they can't afford it," he said, slightly breathless as if he had run back to see her.

"It happens more often than you'd think," she replied, charmed. "Let me get you a drink, on the house, of course."

As Myong-hee stepped behind the bar to pour him a whiskey, she remembered him as the accompanying member of a group of bankers who had come in shortly after the Tower had collapsed.

"How is Mr. Shim?" she asked. "You were with him the other evening. Are you also at Nara Bank?"

"No," he said, reaching into his pocket before pulling out a crisp business card.

BYUN SANG-HOON

"I'm not with the bank. I'm in private wealth management for a few high-net-worth individuals."

"That can't be an easy job," she offered. "In my experience those clients tend to be the most difficult. Here," she said, setting the drink on the bar between them.

Mr. Byun took a leisurely sip of the whiskey. He seemed to be a man who had an appreciation of life's finer offerings; Myong-hee sensed that he was good at what he did.

"My clients don't give me a hard time," he said. "The trick is to know more than most. By the time the analysts at banks have written their reports to advise their institutional investors, it's already too late. It helps to know a company's secrets before they know them themselves."

"What do you mean?" she asked, feigning ignorance, though inwardly she was attentive, suddenly, to the possibility that he could be undercover police investigating her arrangement with Yung. Her eyes stalked him in search of other clues, but she was quick to dismiss the idea; her intuition told her that he was moneyed and was telling her the truth.

"Well, imagine," he said. "If there's a trial and Taehan Group is found guilty, there won't be a company left! It will dissolve all the contracts Taehan Group has got around the world, and all of the company's assets will be sold off to compensate the victims' families. If I were an investor, I would want to know now, rather than later." He picked up his drink and took a large gulp without taking his eyes off hers. She realized that he wanted something. The tingling sensation from earlier in the evening returned, and she shifted to lean against the bar behind her. For years she had been preoccupied by her debts and her own survival. There had never been space to dream that the Chairman might get a taste of what he deserved.

"Rumor has it that the president of Taehan Group comes in now and then. I'd pay a lot to be a fly on that wall," he said, placing the glass back on the counter.

"What makes you think a man of his position would have the time to come to a place like this at the height of a crisis?" she asked. This defense of Yung was habitual. She didn't know enough about Mr. Byun to give anything away.

"I'd have a difficult time upholding Myongwolgwan's reputation if my customers thought the walls were listening," she said without taking her eyes off his. "It could really impact my business."

"You would be compensated, of course. Think about it," he said, taking the last of his drink.

Myong-hee watched him leave, thinking of the memo that Mr. Li mentioned, the evidence that he claimed to have destroyed. There was certainly more to the crisis than Taehan Group was letting on to the public, but was it enough to bring down the company? She was not sure. A titan like the Chairman did not topple easily. She wiped down the counter and took stock of the liquor, aware that over the course of the evening, her mood had lifted. The intermittent tingling she felt, she realized, was not excitement but something dangerously close to hope.

5:30 P.M., October 30, 2016
Chairman's residence, Gugi District, Seoul

Since Geun-ye's death I have often reflected on the relationship between fathers and sons. It seems to me that fathers may know their sons intimately without understanding them, and vice versa. Even now, so many years later, I still find that my earliest, happiest memories are with my father. My love for him was simple, uncomplicated. I will never forget the wobble of his topknot when he laughed, the ripple of muscle under his thin, wrinkled skin as he sat waiting for a raccoon to walk into the traps that we built.

He was a man of few words, but he loved a great performance. In the winter when we huddled together in our small hut against the cold, he would delight us with his impersonations of the bears and beasts of the stories he would begin but never finish. In the mornings my siblings and I would try to remember the last part of the story we had heard before falling asleep and would always fall short of an ending.

I worshipped him, but he did not understand what I was trying to do for our family. The first job I was able to find after leaving my family was as a delivery person, wheeling vegetables and rice from the market to the wealthy Japanese homes in the village. On my first delivery I was conscious of my howling stomach. I imagined the ache in my siblings' bellies. I looked over my shoulder at the busy merchants. I was invisible to them. It would be easy, I thought, to slip away with the food and retreat onto the mountain path. I could feel the swell of saliva at the thought, but also knew that it was shortsighted. We would have enough food for perhaps a month at most, but then what? No, I would not give in to what I wanted most in the moment at the cost of what I needed in the long term.

The delivery was for a wealthy Japanese family. I peered into the property from the gate and admired the large grounds, the stillness of the pond with carp swimming in it. It emboldened me. It was possible to live like this, I thought, if I worked hard. So I ran back to the market, eager for the next delivery. I made myself visible to the merchants, familiarized myself with the shortest routes through the back alleys from the market to the wealthier neighborhoods. Every night I fell asleep as soon as my head hit the sack of rice I used as a pillow. I had an agreement with a restaurant owner who had found his inventory stolen several times in the night. I slept on the restaurant's hearth and guarded the inventory, nestled in the smell of rotting fish and occasionally waking to the pinch of a rat's teeth on my toes.

Over the course of several months, the merchants nicknamed me "Lightning." If ever anyone needed something delivered in a hurry, they would call on me. One afternoon, I arrived at a home with golden gates to find a finely dressed gentleman shouting at his staff. He had a narrow face and a small mustache that hid a row of large, overlapping teeth. I hung back and listened. He was in a rage because his driver had not shown up to make an important delivery. He then noticed me and asked me if I could drive.

I nodded yes, and he asked me to come to the cement factory he owned so that I could make a delivery overnight. I said I would. The only hurdle to overcome was the small matter of not knowing how to drive. I rushed to find my friend Won-san, who worked at the home of a wealthy Korean man who had a car, and asked him if he could teach me. It just so happened that the Korean businessman and owner of the car was away in Japan, and his chauffeur took pride in showing me how to switch gears in his four-door sedan.

By nighttime I felt confident that I could get from one place to another. I thought that I would be driving a sedan, but when Mr. Oshida took me behind the warehouse, he led me to a large cargo truck about five times the size of the sedan. I looked around the leather interior of the carriage. Much of the machinery looked the same. I started the engine. The steering wheel felt heavier, the stick shift did not move as I expected it to, but I managed to get the truck rolling. The man sitting next to me was incredulous as I swerved on the road and asked me if I had ever driven before. Even so, I managed to get us there.

I was off to a shaky start, but this was an important lesson for me that one doesn't always have to know everything about a business or operation; it is possible to learn things as you go along. After I proved myself as a driver, Mr. Oshida kept me around at the factory to do odd jobs as a handyman, loading up the trucks and making deliveries.

"You never stop asking questions, do you, Lightning? If I didn't know better, I'd say you were being insubordinate," he said one day. It is true that I was curious about all aspects of the business. I also asked a lot of questions so that I could improve processes where I could. If things could be done faster, after all, more could be achieved. I suppose I caught Mr. Oshida's attention with all my questions, and he invited me into his office one day. He said that he was impressed with the way that I thought and wanted me to learn the books. I had no idea what he meant by "learning the books," but I said I would do it anyway. After several months working in accounting, I was a confident bookkeeper.

I went home as much as I could over the next ten years—taking sackfuls of rice as well as new clothes for my brothers and sisters. They were always ecstatic to see me. We would all eat together and they would eagerly feed on my descriptions of city life. My father would often withdraw during these stories. He didn't like the fact that I didn't live at home. On this particular occasion I had come home to tell my father something. Just days before, I had overheard Mr. Oshida speaking on the phone and had the first hint that Japan was losing the war. In the wake of all this uncertainty, I went home to my father to discuss whether I should get a loan and offer to purchase Mr. Oshida's company. My father was against it.

"You've done so much to support us," he said, not looking at me. "Your brothers and sisters are thriving."

"I'm glad, I—"

"But don't give up on this land. Once the Japanese leave the peninsula we will have control over our land again. We need more labor. It's getting easier with your brothers getting older, but we need your help here. You've had your adventures and now I want you to come back home."

"What are you saying?" I said. "I'm working away from home so that we can survive here."

It was as though he hadn't heard me. "If you said you wanted to leave us because you want to become a scholar, then I would understand. But an entrepreneur? It's not an honorable profession."

"And how would I feed our family if I were to become a scholar?" I said. "Can I fill our stomachs with ideas? We will be reduced to eating paper."

He turned away from me. "The city has changed you already. You are only thinking of yourself, of becoming wealthy. You've lost sight of your family."

"I am only thinking of our family! I can't stand to see you living like this."

"How can you raise your voice at your own father? I don't know who you are anymore."

My heart was beating fast. I could not understand my father's thinking. How could he be so blind to our poverty?

I went back to Seoul, my heart heavy after the disagreement with my father. Several days later, the Japanese surrendered to the Allied forces. Shortly after, on the day that Korea was liberated from Japan, I entered Mr. Oshida's office and found that he had shot himself.

A month later, I secured a loan and offered the money to Mr. Oshida's widow. I purchased the cement factory. You see, I had a dream. And that was that I would save enough money to purchase a house in Seoul big enough for my family. Then, perhaps, Father would finally see what I had been trying to achieve. I did not know that a war was gathering like a tidal wave on the horizon. I was not to know what would happen to our great country.

I learned a great deal about construction in being a supplier, and soon I was not content simply to be only one part of the process. At first, I was merely a subcontractor to more established construction firms and took whatever business I could get. The presence of the Americans created a great deal of projects, and by 1950 I had established a reputation as a reliable and efficient construction company. Taehan Group had grown considerably, and I had a workforce of almost seventy men. There had been talk of war in those days; it was always a possibility, but one morning I woke to the sound of an explosion.

I went out onto the street to see a crowd fleeing in one direction.

I stopped a man and he said that the bridge between the north and south sections of the city had been bombed as the North Koreans were advancing. I had no choice but to abandon my construction sites, close my shop, and gather all the cash I had. We all became refugees, crossing three hundred kilometers from Seoul to Pusan.

In Pusan, I was restless and worried for my family. I befriended a U.S. Army lieutenant named Henry MacMan. He was a short man with hair the color of dust, who compensated for his height with incredibly lean mass. I begged him to allow me passage to the North. He advised me that it was not safe. It was torture not to have any news of my family. Every night I returned to the lieutenant's tent and asked if there was any way for me to get to the northernmost tip of the peninsula. I overheard the general making plans through the thin canvas tent and came up with one of my own. I had left everything behind in Seoul and had only an oxcart, but by the next morning I had hired several workers and offered my services to the army. I suggested that they would need help with construction sites as they advanced north, and I put forward my services.

The night before I was due to leave with the army, I felt a hand on my arm and turned to see a familiar face. It was So-nyuh, a girl whom I had grown up with in my village. Her hair was cut short in a bob; the meager food rations had taken the youthfulness from her cheeks. I held on to her arms, hope building in me that if she had come to the South then there was hope that my family had somehow fled, too. But it emerged that she had been in Seoul several months before the invasion visiting her relatives there. We walked to the makeshift settlement where many had set up huts pieced together from straw matting, discarded boxes, and flattened metal cans. As I walked her home, I remembered that our families had often joked when we were very young that we would marry. Joke or not, I decided then and there that after I got back from the North, I would honor my family's wishes.

Over the next two years, I assisted the American army as they established their bases. During those days, I had gradually trained myself to sleep less and less every night. It has become a lifelong habit to sleep only four hours a night. Now, with my medication, I am forced into sleeping the days away. As a young man this sort of thing would have driven me insane. When I am not working, I am restless, settling into a feeling of uselessness and futility. I am a man who needs to keep his hands busy. Staying close to the Americans was lucrative, because I learned things ahead of most, and I was able to use this information to my advantage. And so it was that I was able to discover plans of the American army, to be at the right place at the right time. What they needed more than anything was labor as they set up their bases and established more permanent quarters in the middle of the city.

Soon I was able to round up a group of hardworking men who would gather at the foundations of the army base in exchange for food and a day's payment of only a few won. Once the war was over, there was no shortage of work. An entire city—no, a country—had to be rebuilt. That's how my construction business began. At first, selling information about the army's movements was more lucrative than my construction projects. Anyone wanting to start a business came to me, because I knew what the Americans were doing. Soon aspiring politicians came to my door, asking what they could do to better their chance of winning the hearts of the Americans, because they all knew that this was their only way of succeeding in politics.

I never was able to get back to my hometown of Yongchonggun, but I honored my father's wishes by marrying So-nyuh. Over the years I have paid brokers to make inquiries about my family's whereabouts but without much success. As I began rebuilding our country, I thought that if I could not find them, then at least I should make it easy for them to find me. It was important, more than anything, for me and my work to be visible. I thought if I built something big enough, then somehow we would be reunited. I had no choice but to force the success of Taehan Group—it was my flare shot out in the dark, a light that would guide my family on their path back to me.

TWENTY-TWO DAYS AFTER THE COLLAPSE

It had been less than a year since Sae had quit her job at *The Seoul Daily,* but in that time the offices seemed to have fallen into disrepair. She was disheartened to see several cubicles sitting empty, the desks collecting dust. It was hard not to feel that the paper had lost its ambition in speaking truth to power, or perhaps had exhausted itself in attempting to do so. The coffee table at the center of the news floor was overrun with remnants of late nights—napkins drowning in empty ramen containers, abandoned paper coffee cups and wooden chopsticks. It was early but she had come in to wait for Tae-kyu rather than go back to her empty apartment, which was eerily quiet without the children. To her surprise, the editor was not yet in the office, and she found Tae-kyu asleep on the sofa with one arm over his eyes. She picked up the empty soju bottle on the floor and shook him.

He woke with a start, blinking several times before reaching for his glasses under the cushions.

"What time is it?"

"Six-thirty," she said.

He rubbed his face and turned onto his side. "What are you doing here?"

"Couldn't sleep," she said. "How long have you been sleeping here?"

Hoisting himself up heavily, he smoothed the back of his hair, resigning reluctantly from the idea of sleep.

"A while. Even before the Tower."

"I'll make us some coffee," she said, maneuvering between a narrow aisle of boxes toward the kettle. The sink was overflowing with dirty mugs.

"Where is everyone?" Sae asked, setting two paper cups on the table between them, looking around in dismay.

"This isn't going to cut it," Tae-kyu said after a sip, willfully ignoring her question. "I'm going to need some broth. Why don't we grab some breakfast?"

"Are you going to answer my question?" Sae asked, as they waited for their soup.

"Are you going to tell me why you've got that look about you?"

"What look?"

"That coyote look. You've found a scent somewhere; you're hungry for prey."

"You first," she said.

"It's just me and Reporter Kang now," he said.

A waitress with a pale face and painfully red lips came and set their bubbling soups on the table.

"Lim went to the *Times*, Lee quit after a run-in with the new editor. Neither of them were replaced because of budget cuts." He spooned more soup in his mouth. "Your turn."

"Taehan Group is covering something up about the Tower," she said.

Tae-kyu continued sipping the broth, unaffected by this. "Based on what?"

"I found Hae-soo in a private hospital room. She had been instructed not to talk to anyone, it seems, about what L&S was doing in the Tower. But I managed to find their new offices, and I found this," she said, setting the book of accounts on the table.

"You've been busy," he said, without surprise. "What's that?"

"L&S Engineering's accounts," she said. "What do you think?"

Tae-kyu wiped his mouth with a tissue and balled it up in his hand before taking the binder. After a while the pale-faced woman returned and asked them if they were finished. She seemed eager for them to leave and gathered up the banchan dishes to clear the table.

Sae watched Tae-kyu as he read the invoices, trying to gauge whether he was noticing the same thing that she had.

"Assessment of storm damage of a rural corner shop," he said. "The renovation of a small apartment, an addition . . ." He cleared his throat, as he often did when he came across an incongruous fact. "These guys are small fry. They've never done anything as large in scale as work in the Tower."

"Exactly," she said. "Why would Taehan Group hire an inexperienced team for such a big job?" Sae asked.

Tae-kyu closed the binder and rubbed his cheeks, contemplating this.

"They might have been the cheapest," he said.

"Except there's no evidence that there was a bidding process for the project either. They didn't shop around."

"There's something else that's worrying you," he said after a moment.

"I never thought to ask Jae about it. It never occurred to me," she said. "It bothers me that I didn't think to ask six months ago."

Tae-kyu gave her a wry smile. "Don't be so hard on yourself. Sometimes we don't see the people closest to us."

"Well, look who it is." Suh, the editor, a pudgy man with skinny limbs, stood up with some effort as Tae-kyu and Sae walked into the office. "You've got that look in your eye," he said jovially. "If I didn't know better I'd say you think you're on assignment. How are the kids?"

"I'd like to help Tae-kyu with a story," she said. "Investigating what L&S Engineering was doing in Aspiration Tower."

He gave a hearty, phlegmy laugh. "Haven't changed a bit, then. How about saying hello? I thought it's already public knowledge, isn't it? L&S made a mistake, and they collapsed the Tower?"

Sae and Tae-kyu exchanged looks and Sae said, "No one has even heard of L&S Engineering in the industry. It seems suspicious that they would be given such a big project without a bidding process."

Suh seemed unmoved. "This country was built on cronyism. I don't think that's suspicious."

The editor's lack of curiosity seemed to explain why the other reporters had left and the sad state of the paper that she had given so much to.

"What readers want to read are the stories of those who have lost loved ones. Human interest stories. Death sells. The readers can't look away. It wouldn't be right to turn on Taehan Group right now; this is a devastating tragedy. Our national symbol of success, in a pile of ruins."

Sae shot Tae-kyu a look, but he did not meet her eye.

"That's the kind of thing the *Times* writes. *The Seoul Daily* has always investigated cronyism and injustice and—"

"It wouldn't take too much time to make a few calls to ask about who L&S Engineering had partnered with," Tae-kyu said gently. "Or who was responsible for operating the leisure center once the pool was opened." Sae found his restraint difficult to understand and gritted her teeth to keep herself from shouting.

Suh looked from Tae-kyu to Sae as though realizing they were colluding against him. "Fine, make a few calls, but I also want the human interest stories by the end of the day. Got that?"

Later that afternoon, Tae-kyu drove her back to the L&S offices, and she ran with her jacket over her head against the downpour to the stairwell, pausing at the door after she had unlocked it, searching for signs that someone had been there since her last visit. Everything was as she had left it.

When Tae-kyu entered the office, his glasses steamed up and he looked around the small studio blindly before wiping them clean.

"It certainly is a small operation, isn't it?" he remarked. "I guess some companies celebrate their humble origins. Isn't there some legend about the chairman of Taehan Group operating out of an insect-infested shoebox just after the war?"

She shrugged, disinterested, already absorbed in the papers on the desk. Earlier that day, they had made some calls and discovered that a company called SM Health had put in a bid to run the leisure center at the top of Aspiration Tower after the pool had been completed. But further inquiries into SM Health revealed no previous projects or operations. Sae wanted to see if she could find any references or agreements between SM Health and L&S Engineering.

When she looked up again, she saw that hours had passed. Neither of them had moved.

"So you're really not expected at home at some point?" she asked Tae-kyu after a while.

Tae-kyu let out a soft laugh. "They stopped expecting me at home years ago. I've been told not to come back."

"What did you do?" she asked, trying to be lighthearted. Immediately she regretted this, recalling how Jae had chided her tendency to interrogate others, burrowing into places of their pain to satisfy her own curiosity.

"It's as I was saying before. I stopped paying attention. We pay the least attention to those closest to us. I was focused on all the wrong things. I neglected my family. I regret it now."

Sae felt her cheek grow warm at this unexpected openness in Tae-kyu. He had struck her as a man who was without regret, who had the wisdom to never take a misstep.

"I'm sorry," she said.

"How are the boys?" he asked.

"They're fine," she said, brushing him off, trying to mask the fact that in truth she had not allowed herself to think truly of how they were. It was easier to dive headfirst into the investigation, to keep a sense of forward momentum if she didn't think about them or, worse, think about how she might tell them of Jae's disappearance.

"It's important to be there with them, I think," he said. "It's not that you can't relate to them later; it's more that you don't know what questions to ask them after a certain point. You don't know what's relevant to them anymore."

Sae thought of how assured Jae was as a parent in knowing what they needed. At times, his assurance about what was best for the boys, his bond with them, had filled her with jealousy. She remembered coming home after interviewing survivors of the Gwangju massacre for a commemorative piece, and being unable to fully shed the darkness of those stories at the front door. It was as though she had returned a stranger to her life. Jae and the boys seemed encased in self-sufficiency; her presence seemed superfluous. Jae seemed to notice that she had been quiet and laid his hand on her shoulder.

"Is it the interviews?" he asked.

"No," she said, shaking her head. "I'm just tired."

She felt his thumb on the back of her neck and leaned into it to show him that it wasn't him that she was angry with.

"Do you need more time off?" he asked gently. "Is it the kids?"

"No," she said. "If anything, I want more time with them."

She could not bring herself to tell him that she was jealous. How could she? She knew that she was the envy of every mother in the country. When she had told a friend that Jae was staying home with the children, her friend had seemed incredulous.

"What if I stopped working for a while?" she said, hardly able to face him as she said it. "And stayed home? Maybe you could find work?"

She felt his hand tense behind her back.

"What would I do?" he asked. "After all this time off?"

"It's not going to get any better, is it? The longer you wait. You said you wanted to finish your degree."

"What is it that you want? More money?"

"No," she said, surprised by the question.

"Do you see me as less because I am staying home with the kids?"

"Where did you even?" The suggestion made her angry. It seemed to her that he wanted to start a fight. "Why can't I have some of the goodness in life? Why do I have to be the one staring down at the dead bodies? What if I want to be the one staying home to hold them and feed them?"

"I thought you wanted to continue the work we started in college," he said, the anger dissipating from his voice. "I didn't want you to sacrifice anything because of me."

She hated it when he spoke like this. The way he would make himself small in their marriage. As if he hadn't changed her life for the better. It had felt, at times, like a form of hiding.

"I'm just so tired," she said, leaning her head against his chest.

Shortly afterward he came home and told her that he had found a job with Mr. Bae.

"I'm going to get some fresh air," she said, rising to her feet. "Coffee isn't working for me anymore."

She walked to the phone booth at the end of the street and called her mother. No sooner had she heard the boys' voices than she was overcome with an urge to put the phone down again. It was easier to have them at a distance than to find that her love for them was no longer an easy, uncomplicated thing, but something that had begun to pain her.

* * *

Some hours later, Tae-kyu rose to leave.

"When's the last time you got more than four hours' sleep?" he asked.

"I can't remember," she said.

"Try tonight, if you can," he said.

As he moved toward the door, Sae became aware of what was missing.

"I've just realized something," she said.

"Hmmm?" Tae-kyu stepped back into the room.

"Wouldn't you expect to find some samples somewhere?"

"Samples?"

"If you're building a pool. Wouldn't you have an invoice for some tiles? Or samples of tiles that line the pool?"

She had his full attention.

"When I met Mrs. Bae, she seemed confused when I asked her about the pool. What if . . ." Sae said. "What if there wasn't a pool at all?"

Tae-kyu walked over to the desk and ran his fingers over the notes written on the blueprints. "I'm no expert, but there are some calculations here of the weight bearings on the rest of the structure. We should talk to someone who can decipher this for us."

She nodded.

"Aim for six hours," he said. "I mean it."

She murmured that she would try, already lost in reexamining the invoices.

She was unsure of how much time had passed when she heard a sound at the bottom of the stairs.

"Did you forget something?" she asked. Tae-kyu was famous

for his forgetfulness and had a penchant for leaving his most prized possessions scattered in spaces he had inhabited. She became aware of the halting of movement; she had startled whoever was down there.

She crossed the room toward the door, hardly able to hear anything other than the sound of her hammering heart. She flung open the door, unable to see more than a silhouette as her eyes adjusted to the darkness.

"Jae?" she asked.

The figure at the bottom of the stairs froze. In the shadows she could make out the faint outline of a man.

"Jae?" she asked again. In her haste to follow him, she slid down several steps and landed awkwardly on her ankle. Holding on to the wall, she hopped down a couple of steps before testing her weight on it. Hot flares of pain shot up her leg, radiating up her calf.

By the time she reached the bottom of the stairs and stepped onto the sidewalk, the figure was emerging from the phone booth on the main street. Hobbling toward him, she saw that he was stockier than Jae. As he stepped into the lamplight, she recognized the familiar outline as belonging to Mr. Bae. Even at a distance she could see that he had lost weight since the last time she had seen him; the meat of his cheeks sagged and his hair looked wiry and thin.

As she drew closer he raised his arm to flag down a cab. Sae called out to him and ran through the searing pain in her ankle. Before she could get close, Mr. Bae had disappeared into the taxi, which was now nearing the traffic lights less than fifty yards away.

It was near midnight and there were few cars passing through the residential neighborhood, but luckily another cab appeared after several moments, and she asked the driver to follow the only other car on the road ahead.

Mr. Bae's taxi pulled into a narrow alley in the busy streets of Gangnam. Thumbing over some notes to the driver, Sae got out of the cab and into the blast of the sights and sounds of the unsleeping city. Office workers in suits walked haphazardly in the middle of the road. Music blared from underground bars and karaoke rooms. Mr. Bae entered a dimly lit building. A small sign glowed in red with the word MYONGWOLGWAN. A karaoke room for men. A place she could not enter discreetly. What was he doing here? It was odd that he would come to a place like this alone. Room salons were places where men went as a group.

Standing in the middle of the street, she stepped back to survey her options before approaching the edge of the building. Light beckoned at the end of the alleyway. The back entrance to the club allowed men to exit with women without the risk of being seen by any passersby. The passage and door were in the safety of shadows. The smothering smells of a urinal had her holding her breath until she found a set of steps leading down to a narrow, empty corridor.

A line of small lights illuminated the floor. The larger breaks between them signaled doors. She heard one opening and closing some distance away. She did not know much about room salons, but it appeared to be a high-end establishment. Sae crept toward the sound of muffled conversation, careful not to put too much weight on her ankle. What was Mr. Bae doing here? The idea of a man wanted for criminal negligence joining a party seemed unlikely. Had he called Mrs. Bae to tell her that he was going to be late? No, that didn't seem right, either. She moved along the corridor and pressed her ear against the door. She heard a low murmur of somber conversation. The more she listened, the more she was sure that it was Mr. Bae's voice. There was another burst of noise from a room nearby, and for a moment all she could hear were the sounds of crashing tambourines over easy conversation. Sae put her hand on the door, ready to enter, when she heard a new voice talking with Mr. Bae. The familiarity in it made her freeze.

TWENTY-THREE DAYS AFTER THE COLLAPSE

Myong-hee locked the door behind her and leaned with her back against it, pausing to take a deep breath. All evening she had been fighting her way to her office and all evening she had had to contend with disgruntled customers. One client had been expelled from the club because of his disturbing and salacious requests.

Since her encounter with Mr. Byun, she had been thinking of the equipment she had in the small closet at the back of her office. The recording equipment had been a holdover from the dictatorship, when the national intelligence service had insisted on recording the rooms to monitor conversations of a pro-communist or anti-government nature. After the withdrawal of the intelligence agents some years before, the equipment had mostly sat collecting dust. Eight months ago, Myong-hee had experimented with recording the rooms for herself. She'd had the idea that she could use some of the information exchanged in the rooms for her own gain. Initially she had been hopeful that this material could be used to help her erase her debts. However, she quickly found that even with Song-mi's help there was never enough time to fully review the hours of recordings generated at the end of the evening and stay on top of all she needed to manage her business. More recently she had taken to only recording the rooms when there were meetings between important figures that she knew of in advance.

Mr. Byun's offer, and the promise of compensation, had made her reconsider. It was not difficult for her to imagine why investors would want to know about the future of Taehan Group—the company's stock had taken a dive since the crisis, and there were rumors that the company could be taken to trial on civil and criminal charges.

She slid the bookcase and opened the door behind it. The windowless space was just big enough for a person to sit in front of a narrow desk. Two walls were covered with cassette holders emptied by the intelligence agents as they left. The third wall held Myong-hee's recordings that she had marked by date.

Myong-hee wiped down the buttons of the recording equipment with a rag and was about to conduct an audio test when she heard a knock.

"What is it?" Myong-hee asked.

"It's Song-mi," Min-hye's muffled voice said from the other side of the door. "She's had too much to drink."

Myong-hee followed Min-hye down the halls and found Song-mi in one of the empty rooms reserved for unusually large parties. She lay with an arm over her eyes, unmoving on the sofa.

"You know you can't sleep here," Myong-hee said, sitting beside her. "You should be in the waiting room."

Song-mi sat up slowly, as though the act of sitting upright was a feat of great strength. Her hair looked flat and dull, her eyes puffy as though she had been crying.

"I would," she said. "I just can't stand the smell in there."

"How much have you had to drink?" Myong-hee asked.

"I haven't been drinking." Song-mi seemed surprised by Myong-hee's tone. They all knew they would be fired if they lost control of their ability to hold a drink. "Or no more than I had to. I'm just tired."

Song-mi looked pale and frail, a sparrow with a broken wing. Was it Myong-hee's imagination or had she lost weight? She put a hand on the girl's forehead. It was cool to the touch. She wanted to feed Song-mi something warm and nourishing.

Instead, she said: "Go home and get some rest. You're no good to anybody like this."

"I just need a minute," Song-mi said, propping herself onto her elbows.

Myong-hee could see the dark circles under her eyes. "You'll have to touch up your makeup if you're serious about getting back in there."

"I don't know, I think some of the men dig it," she said with a sudden bright grin. "They love that frail, demure, and tired schoolgirl act. I think they like to fantasize that I need sex as a break from studying for exams. Forget sleep, gentlemen, I need to feel you inside me!"

Myong-hee laughed, though the pleasure of seeing Song-mi's sense of bright humor return was tinged with concern that it seemed forced.

There was the sound of the bell, alerting them to the arrival of new customers. At the reception desk, they greeted a man with oily hair and an unnaturally flat-looking nose. There was a panicked urgency in his manner, and he seemed to be vibrating with nerves as he told her he had come to meet Kim Yung.

"Song-mi will take you to the room," she said. Yung had not

told her he was coming. She noted with interest that in recent weeks he had taken to using the club as an office.

As Song-mi looped her arm in the stiff figure of this man, she shot Myong-hee a look, and Myong-hee gestured to her ear. Song-mi winked before leading him away to a room.

Myong-hee went into the kitchen to fix a tray of snacks—salted peanuts and dried cuttlefish—taking her time, safe in the knowledge that Song-mi would be her eyes and ears in the room. When she entered the room, it was to see that Yung had arrived. In the lamplight, the nervous man seemed strangely familiar. After setting down the tray for the men, Myong-hee graciously slipped out of the room. A woman leapt back from the door and into the corridor.

"What are you doing there?" Myong-hee asked.

"I'm looking for someone," the woman replied.

Myong-hee felt a tremor in her chest. In the darkness, she could only see the woman's bobbed hair, the silhouette of her simple T-shirt and jeans. Myong-hee wished to pull her into better light, to examine her for a resemblance, though what did thirty years do to a face? It was another punishment of adoption that a mother could pass her own child decades later without recognition.

"I have to see who he's meeting with," the woman said, placing her hand on the door handle.

It took several moments for Myong-hee to register that the woman had not come looking for her. Myong-hee held the woman's wrist, more forcefully than she intended, annoyed at how close to the surface her hope was.

"I can't let you in there," Myong-hee said. "What are you doing here?"

"I'm looking for my husband."

"Save your domestic disputes for when he comes home," she said, feeling her disappointment start to dissolve into a general weariness.

"He's not . . ." she began, her eyes roaming, her attention pulled to the sound of the voices coming from the other side of the door. "The man in the room, he's my husband's business partner—"

"The same goes for financial disputes," Myong-hee said, her hand firmly on the woman's shoulder, leading her down the corridor. "I can't have you hanging around here. It's bad for business."

"It's not about money," she said. She stopped walking and appealed to Myong-hee. "My husband's been missing since the Tower collapsed."

"Aspiration Tower?"

"He's an engineer." The woman paused, turning her face toward the room. "I need to know where he is."

Myong-hee felt herself soften. "He's with the president of Taehan Group, Kim Yung."

"I could have sworn . . . his voice . . . it's just the two of them?" the woman said, her face falling. "The president of Taehan Group?"

"That's more than I should have told you," Myong-hee said, motioning for the woman to keep moving.

"L&S meets with Taehan Group," she murmured to herself, as she absentmindedly fingered a bubble of air in the wallpaper.

"L&S?" Myong-hee tried to think why the name was familiar to her. It took her several moments to remember that it was the name of the company announced to be responsible for the collapse of the Tower. Myong-hee's fatigue was replaced by a growing interest in the woman. There was an educated, professional quality about her, and an unusual bravery too. She seemed more concerned with putting these pieces together than about the consequences of being in a place most women would not enter.

Curiosity aside, Myong-hee needed to get her out of the hallway, before anyone saw her. "Let's find a place to talk."

The woman followed her, still brooding on some private disturbance. In the stark, unsentimental light of her office, Myong-hee examined the woman's face for her daughter's own. She seemed to be about the right age, late twenties perhaps. She had delicate features—small eyes and nose, and she wore no makeup. Myong-hee's gaze fell on the woman's neck in search of the birthmark that had once been so prominent at the base of her daughter's ear. What would that birthmark look like now?

She was so engrossed by this thought that she did not realize her mistake until it was too late. The woman moved toward the bookcase and the half-open closet door behind it.

She looked from the equipment to Myong-hee, searching it with interest. "You're recording the rooms?"

"That's none of your—"

The woman picked up one of the tapes and ran her hand over the recording equipment, as though fascinated by what she saw.

"This is expensive stuff, it's government-grade equipment. . . ."

The fact that the woman knew this alarmed her. "Are you with the police?"

"My name's Sae. I'm not with anyone. Like I said, I'm looking for my husband," she said, pressing the record button before stopping it again. "The man who's meeting with Kim Yung, have you seen him here before?"

There was a moment of silence as Myong-hee contemplated the implications of this. "Was your husband working with him?"

Sae nodded.

There was a determination about her. Myong-hee had a sense that the woman before her did not easily conform or follow the rules. It seemed to Myong-hee that Sae was just the kind of person she needed.

"Do you think I could take a look at these?" the woman asked, already poring over the dated tapes on the shelves. "I won't ask why you're recording the men."

Sae chewed on her nail, the phone receiver wedged between her ear and shoulder, watching the cars sitting idly on the highway.

"So let me get this straight. The man responsible for the collapse of the Tower goes to meet the president of Taehan Group at a room salon after seeing you?" said Tae-kyu. "The same Taehan Group that is now in legal proceedings against L&S Engineering?"

"My guess is that they think a room salon is inconspicuous," she said, biting a thin thread of nail between her front teeth.

"Sounds like you haven't heard the news."

"What now?"

"Mr. Bae turned himself in to the police this morning."

Sae bit down hard and felt the warm, bitter salt of her blood on her tongue. She squinted into the morning light, confounded by this news.

"There's definitely something here, but I'm strapped for time today," he said. "Suh is hounding me for human interest stories. My engineer contact has said he can meet us tomorrow to discuss the blueprints. He's out of town today."

Sae felt impatient with Tae-kyu's lack of urgency.

"I've been thinking that there must be others we can interview, laborers who L&S must have hired to do the construction who can tell us more," she said.

There was a pause on the other end of the line.

"Assuming they are alive. Many of them are day laborers who come and go on construction sites without a contract. These people might be difficult to track down."

She had an idea. "I know someone who might be able to help. My friend used to be a documentary maker; he filmed laborers during the—"

"Sae," Tae-kyu said. "Be careful. If Taehan Group is intent on covering this up, they will spare no resources to silence you."

"I'll see you tomorrow," she said, before hanging up the phone. It was not like Tae-kyu to be dictated by fear.

Moments later, she lifted the receiver and dialed Il-hyung's number.

"Hi, it's me," she said when he answered. There was a pleasure in hearing his voice, a feeling of coming home. But then she heard the pause, the uncertainty on the other end of the line, and she remembered that they were not on such intimate terms anymore. "It's Sae. I have a favor to ask. It's important. When can I see you?"

By the time Sae approached the front door of her apartment it was past lunchtime. Il-hyung had agreed to meet her the following afternoon. A dull bone tiredness had set in, and she knew she would not return to the office in Buam-dong. There was nothing to do but concede to sleep.

Passing the front window, she saw that the light was on inside. Hesitant in the corridor, she was alert and awake, her heart knocking at her chest, expectant. If Mr. Bae and Kim Yung had been alerted to her investigative efforts, perhaps so had Jae? Could it be Jae waiting for her?

Then she heard the sound of a child's giggle and felt the tension fall away, weary of feeling for Jae everywhere.

She opened the door.

"Seung-min? Hoon-min?"

"Where have you been? It's early," her mother said. "Your neighbor had to let us in."

Hoon-min wrapped his arms around her and squeezed her thighs. As she kissed the top of his head, the smell of sand and sweat flooded her with longing. Seung-min hung on the back of the sofa, jumping, uncertain of her until he had buried his face in her soft belly.

"You should have called to say you were coming," Sae said.

"I did, but you weren't home," her mother said, removing large Tupperware boxes of side dishes from black plastic bags and placing them in the fridge. "What have you been eating? You haven't touched anything in here."

The boys flattened themselves on the floor, rediscovering their toy cars, and Sae felt her heart lighten—her missing them had been like a heavy weight. Yet as the afternoon wore on, a fresh burden gnawed at her. Something Tae-kyu had said to her earlier in the morning was bothering her, but it refused to be pinned down. She was moved by her mother's gesture—coming to the home Sae had shared with a man she had refused to accept—to support her. But even in the cloud of warmth, something nagged at her. It occurred to her only later as she unstuck Hoon-min's sweaty cheek from her arm while he napped and saw her mother asleep on the sofa why she was not happier to have them here. In her mother's home, the cocoon of Mallipo, the boys were at a safe distance; they were untouchable there. In this apartment they were too close, within arm's reach. They were breakable.

TWENTY-FOUR DAYS AFTER THE COLLAPSE

Il-hyung was waiting for her at the corner of Jongno-4-ga, wearing the same pair of oversized, wire-rimmed glasses that he had worn since college. The weight that he had put on over the years looked good on him. The sight of him gave Sae a sense of returning to a long-forgotten childhood home. She could not remember how it was that they had grown distant from each other.

"It's been a while," he said. He looked past her shoulder, a habit of shyness Sae had forgotten.

"Too long," she said with a warm smile.

"We should get going," he said gruffly.

As they walked, Il-hyung told her he kept in touch with the laborers he had interviewed for his last documentary. They met once a month as union members at the basement of a church in Myeong-dong. Someone, he thought, might be able to share something about the construction of the pool in the Tower, or better yet, know someone who had recently worked there. They walked through the avenue of stalls on the wide street, the chorus of sounds—the hawkers calling, missionaries demanding repentance, songs serenading first loves lost and buried. They pushed past tourists, uniformed students reluctantly pulled to their after-school cram sessions.

They arrived in the middle of an impassioned speech after which the men queued for a meal around large foil trays of rice and bulgogi laid out on a table. Il-hyung was something of a celebrity among them as someone who had cared enough to document their stories. Sae sensed that they trusted him. Il-hyung asked the senior members of the union for information about anyone who might have worked at Aspiration Tower. A hush descended on the room, and those who had spoken jovially grew visibly uncomfortable. Several men rose from their seats and lingered by the food.

At last, an unshaven man with salt-and-pepper hair leaned over to Il-hyung and whispered to them both.

"Most of the men here won't talk about it. You know we tried to talk about it years ago but no one listened. But give this guy a call; he's crippled, so all he does is talk. Give him a chance and he'll talk your ears off," he said, pressing a piece of paper into Sae's hand.

There was a warm wind in the air as they stepped out of the church basement. Il-hyung walked a few steps ahead of Sae with his hands in his pockets before turning, as if he had only just remembered that she was there.

"Mr. Han sounds like a good lead," Il-hyung offered. He seemed apologetic that the meeting hadn't led to more information. "Do you want a drink?" he asked uncertainly. "I guess you need to get back."

"How about here?" she asked, pointing to the orange carts on the street—the moonlighting restaurants for those too sad or reluctant to go home.

As they shared a bottle of rice wine, Sae told him about

what she had learned in the days after the Tower's collapse. At the meeting she'd had the watchfulness of a guard dog sensing movement on the periphery of its territory. Now the tension was beginning to ebb, and Sae was not sure if it was the flush of wine or the comfort of an old friend's company.

He only seemed to be half listening to what she was telling him. Over the years Il-hyung became most at ease addressing a large crowd and increasingly uncomfortable in intimate exchanges. To those who did not know him well, he appeared standoffish and disinterested, but Sae knew better. It was difficult to remember how they had grown distant. It began to bother her that she could not remember the last time they had spoken.

She reached for the bottle when he stopped her.

"Don't you think you should slow down?"

"I can hold my drink better than I could in college."

"Anyone can hold their drink better than you could in college," he muttered, taking the bottle himself.

"Do you really think that Jae might be out there," he asked, "in hiding?"

"It's what I'm hoping," she said, thinking of his previous disappearance. "It's possible that he's afraid; maybe he's protecting us."

Il-hyung looked into his drink, as if deliberating whether to tell her something.

An uncomfortable sensation came over her, a memory dredged up from the silt.

"Are you okay?" he asked.

"I'll be right back," she said, steadying herself as she asked the vendor for the key to the toilet in the nearest building.

She stood over the sink, clutching the edges of it. The raw stink of the toilets beckoned the memory into her throat. She pressed her forehead against the cool mirror, waiting for the nausea to pass.

It was winter, six months before the announcement of the democratic elections. They had finished printing their newspapers and flyers that they were going to pin up all over campus. It was a task that Sae had enjoyed doing with Il-hyung when she had first joined the movement, as it involved taking a long walk from one end of campus to the other, giving them ample time to talk. It was the only time that they spent together alone. But that afternoon, Il-hyung was irritable.

"Where were you last night?" he asked, after pinning one of the flyers to the notice board outside of the law school.

"They barricaded the street. The police were stopping to search everyone. I had all our materials in my bag. I had to turn back."

Il-hyung said nothing as they walked inside the next building, making her feel as though she had done something wrong. After pinning the flyer to the notice board, he paused to look down the corridor as if expecting someone. Sae had started to feel annoyed. What did he expect her to do? Circle the borders of the city to get to the meeting?

"I came to your place after the meeting. I was worried about you," he said. "They said you weren't home."

Sae felt her cheeks burning. She and Jae had taken a walk in the snow, marveling in the crunch of it under their shoes, the silence that seemed to blanket the city.

"I went out for a walk," she said.

Il-hyung looked at her directly for the first time since they had begun walking through campus.

"Someone's been writing reports on us for the cops," he said.

"You think it could be someone in our group?"

He dropped his gaze then, and she was immediately angry.

"I don't have to report to you where I am at night," she said. "Just because I don't turn up for one meeting doesn't mean that I'm suddenly ratting you all out to the police." She knew he didn't really believe it was her. It was a provocation to get her to admit she had been with Jae.

He grabbed her arm to stop her from walking away. "I'm not accusing you. I know you wouldn't do that."

She hadn't expected him to concede so easily. "Then what . . . ?"

"You said Jae is on scholarship. But you didn't say which kind."

"I never asked," she said, shrugging. "You think the police are paying him?"

He raised his eyebrows.

She shook him off. "I recruited him; he didn't know anything about us until I approached him."

"Sure," he said. "But you don't think it's weird, how he figured out how to forge those employee numbers? It took Yu-jun months to infiltrate those factories."

Until now she had not been aware of his jealousy, but now she saw it plainly.

"That doesn't mean he's working for the police." She pushed the stack of papers in her hands into his chest. "You can't stand that he's turned into a hero, can you? That he figured out a way for us to make progress in the factories. He grew up in one, okay? That's how he knows so much about them."

"I think you're letting your feelings for him cloud your vision of who he really is."

She wanted to slap him. She was sick of his intellectualizing, his pretension that everything he did was rational.

"You know, at least I admit that I have feelings. I don't hide behind ideology all the time. You never own anything you feel; you're like a machine or a robot. It's exhausting."

Il-hyung pushed his glasses up the bridge of his nose, a nervous habit that she had observed whenever he did not know what to say. He seemed stunned that she had turned on him.

"Sae," he said after a long pause.

She didn't want to hear it. He had stepped out of the bounds of their friendship. She would not be controlled. She took off her denim jacket and wrapped it around her fist, smashing the glass on the wall to reach the fire alarm. It was time to gather the students for the protest, and they would need help getting out of their classes.

"I saw him talking to—"

She pulled on the lever, his words drowned out in the high-pitched shriek of the alarm.

Sae felt more sober by the time she returned to the orange cart.

"There was something you were going to tell me," she said, clearing her throat again. "All those years ago, about Jae."

He opened his mouth but said nothing for a while and tapped the table in front of him, as if unsure of where to start.

"It's something I wanted to tell you earlier," he said. "When you were telling me about what happened at the Tower."

Sae waited for him to continue.

"I saw him getting into one of those executive sedans after

one of our meetings all those years ago. He was with a man in an expensive-looking suit. They seemed to know each other well. The man in the suit was scolding Jae."

"A sedan? What are you saying?" What he was implying was unthinkable. "That he was a police informant?"

"That's what worried me at the time," he said. "I did some snooping around. I knew he was a scholarship student, and there were rumors flying around that the police were paying students' tuition in exchange for information."

Sae froze. Afraid of what he might say next.

"I never found any evidence that he was an informant."

She let out an exasperated laugh. "I don't know what I would have done if—"

"I never got to the bottom of it until recently."

"Recently?" Sae snapped her head up, meeting Il-hyung's eyes.

"After the disaster at the Tower, I saw him on the news. The man that Jae had met outside in the sedan." He picked up his glass and took a sip, before continuing. "It was Kim Yung, the president of Taehan Group."

2:30 P.M., November 5, 2016
Chairman's residence, Gugi District, Seoul

Did I sacrifice my family life with So-nyuh in service of the family I left behind in the North? It is true that after the war I was often on the road and was only home sporadically. But my family life has been harmonious because I have been a strong role model for my children—they knew that my absence was in service of something great for our country.

After the war, we began to rebuild what was left of our country. They say that over five million people lost their lives in the conflict. I had survived by stalking the Americans, providing them with labor in establishing their bases. Afterward, when the contracting work for the American military began to dry up, I sold whatever I could by repurposing the dregs of what was left to us. The uniforms the Americans discarded, for example, could be dyed and restitched to be fashioned into suits. My first automobile was made from the shell and armor of an American jeep whose engine I replaced with whatever scrap metal I could find. My time working for the Americans served me well—I learned a great deal from them—and Taehan Group was on the front lines rebuilding the housing, roads, and bridges that had been destroyed during the war.

My success in these projects brought me to the attention of the new president, Park Chung-hee. The man was a visionary. A man of my generation. He was handsome. Hair cut very short, a flattish nose, and a whole-belly laugh that could halt at any moment before he struck his subordinates in the face. I liked him immediately. We understood each other. He was exactly what our country needed—a leader who would motivate the workforce with a clear vision for our country.

You bristle at this characterization of him. Perhaps you, too, thought he was a dictator. What your generation doesn't understand is that material prosperity is impossible without a central organizing force. Confucius once said that people must be first taken care of materially before they can prosper spiritually.

I was called to the Blue House, a government building built on the gardens of the royals. The stone bridge that led to the reception area, the vast halls filled with chandeliers and red carpets—all of it seemed to foretell a prosperous future. In his office, President Park stood by the window and told me about his vision.

"For generations our countrymen have been told what to do. First by the ruling elite of the Yi dynasty, then by the Japanese. How can we expect the people of our country to be organized? They've never had to think for themselves!"

He offered me a glass of the finest American whiskey.

"Imported, of course," he said, closing his eyes, his eyebrows furrowed in concentration, as if it were the only way to appreciate its taste. "You see this, right here, this is the problem. We rely on importation. If we are going to lift ourselves out of poverty, we need foreign currency. We need—"

"To export," I said, finishing his sentence. I was one step ahead of him. He nodded.

"The Americans are worried about communist movements in Thailand," he said. "They want to help the local governments to build roads there to police the North. I think we should put in a bid to help them. I can offer you a loan on any equipment you need."

I knew nothing of the treacheries of those foreign climates then and the possibilities for Taehan Group with an influx of American dollars was impossible to turn down. Success in Thailand would pave the roads for Taehan Group to establish itself in other places—Vietnam and, later, the Middle East and beyond.

That evening, after meeting with President Park, I returned to my home to look at my sleeping sons. They would be inspired by my hand in the country's reconstruction, in my allying with figures as powerful as the president. But how did I keep them hungry so that they would work as hard as I had in the pursuit of their own ambitions?

I remembered an incident with my father when I was young, when he had caught me spying on him as he chopped firewood in the yard. He had called me over and pressed some chestnuts into my hand, winking at me that I should not tell my siblings about this special treat he had set aside for me.

I was so proud and delighted by this secret attention that I returned to the task of splitting the husks of corn from the cob with renewed energy. That is, until a spill from my sister's pocket revealed she also had the same special treatment. I watched her in disbelief, feeling disappointed. His word was the law. We looked up to him and longed for his approval. But there was something else, too. I wanted to be seen by him, to feel indispensable among my six other siblings, to be valuable.

And so, I learned from this that children always benefit from a healthy dose of competition. Some might think it too harsh, and So-nyuh often wanted to intervene, but I never let my sons know how proud of them I was. I wanted to instill in them a hunger to continue to strive to be better. To never be complacent because they felt that they belonged to a wealthy family.

I am aware that I may have fanned the flames of competition

between Yung and Geun-ye. I thought this would fuel their ambition. Between my trips abroad, I would gather the family for dinner and expound my views that I thought it outdated that a role should be handed in the order of birth; rather, I would favor merit. I know that it is an unusual thing to select one's youngest son as successor, but for a long time Geun-ye had shown himself worthy of the chairmanship.

You see, Geun-ye was a questioner. He was never satisfied with a response given by an authority. Even as a child, it was never enough for him to be told that he would be burned by the fire; he had to touch the flames to know what it meant to be scorched. In a hierarchical society such as ours, some might see this as insubordinate, but I recognized his determination, his doggedness to get things done his way. That, of course, is the mark of a leader.

But I believe that he was later misled by the workers at the cement factory. You see, what I had not accounted for was the fact that he was far too emotional. Giving too much weight to one's feelings as a leader is dangerous, akin to putting a weapon in your hands that you will turn on yourself.

TWENTY-SIX DAYS AFTER THE COLLAPSE

"I thought you were asleep," Sae said, rising from the toilet seat. "Is the light bothering you?"

Seung-min shook his head.

She flushed and led him back to the futon. Since the boys had returned, their sleep had been fitful—their legs and hands restless and clawing for her in the darkness. Her mother had said that her late meeting with Il-hyung had unsettled them, with them anxiously waiting by the window for her to return.

"What is it?" Sae said, putting her hand on his forehead. No fever. "It's late. Go back to sleep."

She lay down beside him.

"I thought I heard Appa come home," he said.

"It's just Grandma in the other room," she said, when she could speak evenly. She didn't want Seung-min to detect any uncertainty in her voice. She was still digesting what Il-hyung had told her. She had assumed that L&S Engineering had won the contract at Aspiration Tower because of Mr. Bae's contacts, but Il-hyung had opened the possibility that Jae had been the one to win the project for them. But what was the nature of Jae's relationship to Kim Yung so many years ago?

Seung-min pulled the blanket over his shoulder, despite the heat.

"How long is Grandma staying?" he asked.

"I don't know," she said. "For a while."

"Until Appa comes back?"

Sae said nothing.

"I was scared you weren't going to come back to get us. That you weren't going to come back. Like Appa."

There it was. A knock on a door she kept locked from them. Jae would have known exactly what to say if it were Sae who had not come home. But she did not know how to make his absence small, or dumb it down, make it sting any less. It was better not to speak of hypotheticals at all.

"I'll always come back, I promise."

"Will Appa come back?"

"You should sleep now," she said, unable to answer. "Or you'll be tired in the morning."

She held out her arm and he rolled into her, his head resting on her shoulder. She lay for a long time, listening to the softer, slower breathing of his sleep. Il-hyung had told her he was suspicious of Jae from the beginning. What was it that he had seen that she had not? What had she buried within herself about Jae, the way that she had buried her memory of her last exchange with Il-hyung?

Seung-min's question rang around the room. She didn't know if he was coming back. She was beginning to think that she didn't know who Appa was.

THIRTY-THREE DAYS AFTER THE COLLAPSE

Under the sober strip lights the club was less luxurious, the scuffed floors and wooden furniture looked tired and stripped of polish. Yet even in this harsh light the madam's professional pride was evident in the thoughtful touches, the fresh flowers at the entrance and the organized rows of liquor in the bar.

The madam took off her glasses and put the newspaper down on her desk as Sae entered the office.

"Back again so soon? Has anyone told you you're a hard worker?"

"There's a lot of material to sift through here," Sae said, taking off her thin jacket. Over the course of several days, Sae had sat through hours of footage searching for a face that she recognized. The madam had said that she vaguely remembered having seen Mr. Bae before the Tower's collapse some months ago, though she did not remember the exact date. Sae hoped finding this recording of him in conversation with Kim Yung might tell her more about what had happened at the Tower. Il-hyung's revelation weighed heavily on her, and she hoped, too, that she might learn something of the nature of Yung's relationship with Jae.

She felt the madam's eyes on her, studying her as she settled in the narrow recording room and switched on the monitor.

"You could be really pretty, you know," the madam said, throwing her glasses on the table. "With a little makeup. Some nice clothes. But you don't care, do you?"

"Not really," Sae said.

"You don't really care what others think of you," she said, smiling faintly. "Perhaps you're freer than most of us."

Sae placed a tape into the player, unsure of how to respond. The scenes seemed to loop in their repetitiveness. Men being shown in. Served drinks. Undressing. Dancing. Singing. Limping out of the room on the arm of one of the girls.

Sae did not know how long she had been sitting there when she felt a hand on her shoulder and a cup of tea was set down beside her. Sae glanced up at the madam; this small act of thoughtfulness brought the sting of tears to her eyes.

"Have you found anything yet?" the madam asked.

"Nothing," Sae said, pressing her eyes with the palms of her hands.

"You should take a break now and then," she said.

Sae swiveled in her chair to face the madam and took a sip of her tea. In her silk blouse and jeans, there was a timeless elegance to the madam's appearance. She was a quiet, powerful presence. Sae had the sense that the madam read everyone in the room as she entered it. She seemed to know what Sae was thinking.

"You get used to it after a while," the madam offered. "The way the men behave."

"And to think that their wives know nothing," Sae said.

"Some of them know. Many turn a blind eye to it. I think

some pretend their husbands are the ones who sit awkwardly tolerating what happens around them in these rooms. Never the willing participant. Never the one to go upstairs."

Sae glanced at the monitor. Had Jae ever been in one of these rooms? The recently uncovered facts—Jae's relationship with the president of Taehan Group and the office move—hinted that there could be many more things she didn't know about him. It was possible that these were inconsequential secrets. Yet it was the fact of the omission itself that troubled her. Were lies and evasions necessary to the survival of every marriage? Did relationships survive because of the tacit agreement not to pry open doors that had been closed to the other?

"Were you ever married?" Sae asked, suddenly curious.

"Would you marry, if you worked at a place like this?"

"I don't have any assumptions about the women who work here."

"You would be the first."

"But I am curious how you got here."

The madam was silent for a moment. "Single motherhood was, and still is, like social death. People think I deserved what had happened to me. No one wanted to help me. I did what I could. I used to have long hair down to my waist—I cut that off and sold it. Sold anything else that was of any value. It was hard to find work. There were factory jobs, but I didn't last there—they wouldn't let me take breaks to feed the baby, and at the end of the month I was in no better place financially. I ran out of money. We were going to starve to death."

The madam brushed off a small piece of lint from her jeans and leaned forward on the sofa, her elbows on her knees.

"I took the baby to her father's house and begged him to

take her. He threw a fistful of bills in my direction and told me to get lost. A baby girl was of no interest. He only wanted sons." The madam paused before continuing. "I took her to the orphanage as her father had suggested. I told myself it was just for a few weeks. I found a job at a department store and made enough to get set up. At least for a little while. But when I went back for her I walked through the children's rooms and couldn't see her. She had already been adopted."

All of this was said lightly, meant to be a sanitized version of the past. Sae didn't know what to say—it was too bone-close and raw, even as it had been washed of pain.

"I started at the American military barracks. I thought it was the best way to earn money fast and in dollars, too. Believe it or not, the government encouraged women like me to do that kind of work; anything that would bring in American dollars. We were such a poor country then. I learned a little English then, too. I thought that would help me later, when I had enough to go to America. Back then I was determined to find her. But after a while I realized I wasn't going to earn enough that way. Every hour I wasn't with her was an hour too long. I couldn't wait the years it was going to take me to earn money working like that. I wanted to open a bar, I thought running a business would help me to make more money more quickly. But who was going to lend me money? The bank? Only moneylenders who were married to the mob. When the first bar I ran flopped, the moneylenders told me I could run a different business that would help me pay off my debts. I hated the idea at first but then I thought, what choice do I have? Better for me to run it than some sadist."

Their silence was broken by the competing sounds of clattering heels and laughter as the girls arrived for the evening. She expected the madam to rise and attend to them, but she remained on the sofa.

"Do you have children?" the madam asked at last.

"I had my sons very young," Sae said tentatively. "It's always been like waging a war—work and children, I wanted to know what it would be like for my head not to be so busy. I quit my job so I could be with them. I was missing so much, and now with everything that's happened, I don't know how to be in the same room as them."

Sae had said more than she intended. She wondered whether this was a particular talent that the madam had, drawing out a person's most intimate thoughts. When she looked up, it was to see a stricken look on the madam's face, as if Sae's distance from the boys pained her. The madam pointed to the frozen screen.

"See Junior here? You can still see the baby fat in his cheeks. Not long out of the barracks, I bet. He should be used to this kind of team building after the army, but you can see it here, he's still not comfortable. He practically jumped out of his skin when Song-mi came to sit with him. He probably grew up with sisters, maybe the only son in the family. Still sees her as human." She reached across Sae and pressed play. "Just wait and watch what happens after a few drinks. He'll speak up, have a rant at his superiors, say all the things he's been wanting to say. It's the lubricant that keeps this well-oiled economy running. Give the juniors a space to air their grievances, soothe them with a few drinks so they can whip him and work him hard the next morning."

The madam rose to leave the room and paused at the door.

"You should do what you have to, to find your way back to your sons."

"Thank you . . ." Sae said. She opened her mouth to say more, and the madam paused at the door. "I don't know how to address you."

"You can call me onni," the madam said.

Sae was warmed by the idea, the proximity of having a woman such as the madam as an older sister. But just as quickly she seemed to retract this offer of intimacy.

"Or call me Myong-hee, *American style,*" she said with a wink.

What seemed like hours later, Sae heard a voice from behind her.

"I'm sorry," she said. "I didn't know anyone was in here."

Sae turned around to see a young woman leaning her head against the bookcase. It was Song-mi, a woman she recognized from the tapes.

"It's all right, you can come in," Sae said, shifting in her seat.

"This is the only room in this place that doesn't stink of cigarette smoke. It's weird; I just can't stand the smell anymore."

Sae nodded and pointed to the chair, inviting her to sit down. For more than five minutes she had been staring at a paused screen, a furious scurrying in her mind. Frustrated that she had not made much progress in looking through older material, Sae had tried a more recent tape in the machine. Her heart had nearly stopped when she found footage of Kim Yung sitting with Mr. Bae, berating him. The audio quality was compromised, and Sae could only pick out fragments, but she was able to piece together that Mr. Bae had failed in his efforts to find a person named Geun-ye. Sae was disappointed. There was no mention of Jae.

Song-mi slumped into the leather armchair, with one leg over the armrest. There was still something of a teenager about her.

"You've been in these rooms for a while," Sae began. "Have you ever heard of this person, Geun-ye?"

Song-mi came over to the screen and watched some of the footage, rubbing her stomach gently. Song-mi put her hand over her mouth and paused and then let out a soft burp and seemed to relax. "Yung was talking to Mr. Bae about Geun?"

"Why? Who is he?"

"I'm not sure, exactly," she said. "I've heard the boss and Yung talk about him. If I didn't know any better, I'd think that it was their love child."

"The boss? You mean Myong-hee onni?" Sae asked. "How do you know Geun isn't their love child?"

Song-mi smiled and leaned forward conspiratorially. "Let's just say Yung has no interest in women. Rumor has it that he paid an employee to impregnate his wife, you know, like the impotent kings of history."

Sae drew back, fascinated. "Could Geun be a lover?"

Song-mi shrugged, delighted by the question. "Maybe."

"But you've never seen him here?"

Song-mi shook her head. "Why do you ask?"

"They're looking for him. He disappeared when the Tower fell."

Song-mi shrugged and leaned suddenly toward Sae. "You smell of nectarines. Great," she said, moving away and slumping back into her chair. "Now I'm going to be craving nectarines until I finish my shift."

Sae raised her wrist to her nose, puzzled. The smell was faint, barely perceptible. It took her moments to remember cutting nectarines for Hoon-min before she left.

The realization came to her. "How far along are you?"

"Can you tell?" Song-mi froze, gathering her legs to sit upright. She flattened her dress against her stomach. "I'm not showing yet, am I?"

"No," Sae said. "Do you know who the father is?"

Song-mi shrugged. "Does it matter? I would have been happy enough with just one parent."

Just then the door opened and Myong-hee came in.

"Anything?" she said, then, noticing Song-mi: "What are you doing here?"

The concern that passed over Myong-hee's face was not that of an employer but the distressed look of a mother who could not feed her child. Sae sensed Myong-hee's desire to touch Song-mi and her inability to do so.

"Just taking a break," Song-mi said, her face contorted as though she were in discomfort, or perhaps nauseous.

"Try having some rice porridge every couple of hours," Sae said to Song-mi, squeezing her shoulder. "Hunger only makes it worse. Trust me I know; I had the worst morning sickness with my second."

"Is it true?" Myong-hee asked Song-mi later, after Sae had left. Myong-hee had the sense that Song-mi had been avoiding her all evening. "Is that what's making you sick?"

Song-mi placed her bag on the table and stood stiffly in front of her, like a child being scolded by a schoolteacher. Myong-hee sank back into the sofa. How had she not seen the signs?

"What are you going to do?" Myong-hee asked.

"I want to keep it," she said, her lips downturned with worry.

"Save yourself the heartache," she said sharply. The girl's face fell.

"It would be the only family I have in the world. I just want the chance." Song-mi looked down at her hands as though ashamed of this. "I want to know what it's like to have a family."

Myong-hee's heart ached at this. Was this how her daughter felt? The agency had assured her that she had gone to a loving family who could care for her. They had described the scenes Myong-hee later discovered were from Hollywood films—women with curled light hair wearing dresses that were nipped at the waist, who baked cakes and served their children. But why was it that when she pictured her daughter, she pictured her alone? The member of the family left behind as a sedan pulled away, the one who was always last to be served at the dinner table. It wasn't because of her daughter, she knew, but because of her son.

"Please don't fire me," Song-mi said. "I have nowhere to go."

Myong-hee looked up at Song-mi's face pleading with her and remembered her own pleading.

"Have you thought about how you're going to do this? How are you going to support yourself? You can't work here once the baby arrives." Myong-hee wanted to know that Song-mi had a plan. Myong-hee had been too naïve, trusting that she would be taken care of.

Song-mi looked blankly into space. For now it seemed all Song-mi had was the will to do whatever it took to hang on to the child.

"Let's go," Myong-hee said, gently tugging on Song-mi's sleeve.

"No, please," Song-mi said, pleading still. "At least let me stay until I start showing."

"Pack your things," Myong-hee said. If there was ever going to be a chance that she could do it, Song-mi would need someone. "You're coming home with me," she said.

Myong-hee thought often of the sex education classes that were given at the maternity center—a small building that reminded Myong-hee of the workers' dormitories attached to the factories she had walked past every day near the home where she had lived with her father before they had moved to the city. It had a communal shower and a large canteen. Most of the girls were all in their late teens or early twenties. All ready to be reeducated and rehabilitated to become dutiful citizens. Their stay was paid for on the understanding that their infants would be given over for adoption. For a better life, they were promised, in America.

On Myong-hee's first day, she had been horrified to sit next to a girl who whispered to her that it was her second time in the home.

Myong-hee was disgusted that she could be so reckless.

"You judge me now, but you'll see, at least this way I know I have a roof over my head and three meals a day."

They were offered sex education classes that gave them advice such as:

Keep your legs together.
Do not walk about late in the night.
Don't dress provocatively.
Never drink; keep your wits about you.

Keep your conversations with men at a minimum; do not say anything that may be construed as flirting.
If you are tempted to sleep with a man, think of your parents.
If you are tempted to sleep with a man, consider whether you would like a career as a prostitute.

During this time Myong-hee kept to herself. Her situation was different from the other girls', she told herself, because she knew she would give the child to the Chairman. It was a comfort, she had told herself, because at least she would know that the child would grow up in good hands.

No one told her about, and never did she imagine in her wildest nightmares, the possibility of twins.

Song-mi stepped into Myong-hee's apartment, her eyes sweeping the corners of it. Myong-hee, too, cast a critical eye over her living room—the mother-of-pearl dressing table seemed out of fashion, the walls too white and clinical, the orchids she cherished for their reliable bloom suddenly garish. She never had visitors. To allow anyone in her apartment felt more intimate than undressing in front of them.

"You can have the room over there," she said, pointing to the room opposite the kitchenette, and put her bag down.

"Just for me?" Song-mi asked, looking surprised, a protective arm around her belly.

"You didn't think we'd be sharing a room, did you? I'll still need to sleep, after the baby comes. You should unpack," she said. "Don't feel you have to do anything. You should rest."

"After the baby comes . . . ?"

"That's right." Myong-hee laughed at the stunned way that Song-mi said this. "You do know that's what happens at the end of this?"

But Song-mi was not laughing. When Myong-hee looked up it was to see her standing with the back of her hand covering her mouth, weeping.

"You mean I can stay?"

"As long or as little as you like," she said, as lightly as she could. Uncertain of what to do to console her, Myong-hee busied herself by shuffling through her spare cupboards for something they might eat. Opting for the curry cubes over the instant noodles, she chopped half of an onion, a soft carrot, and a potato and set them to boil. Tomorrow, she thought, she would go to the big supermarket rather than the corner store and fill up the fridge.

A little while later, Song-mi was still fighting back tears as she sat down to eat. "Are you sure about this?"

"Yes," Myong-hee said, a little impatiently. "Now, this isn't going to be any good if it gets cold."

Song-mi nodded but did not touch her spoon. "When I was five or six, I was taken to this huge house with a big grass garden and mountains all around. It was a really fancy neighborhood. The woman who wanted to adopt me was so pretty. She had perfect skin. I was on my best behavior because I wanted them to like me. I was so excited to be her daughter. I was so sure when they dropped me off that I would see them again. But then the next day, the couple came back to 'try out' another girl, and they chose her instead. I just want to make sure this is for real. No one has ever done anything like this for me. I mean," she said, searching Myong-hee's face for clues. "Why are you doing this for me?"

She thought of the day after she had given birth to the twins, the way Secretary Gong had handed her an envelope full of cash. When she had asked what she should do with the girl, he responded immediately, as if it was something that had come up before. *There's an organization,* he said, *called Holt International.*

"I'm offering you," Myong-hee began, setting down her spoon, no longer hungry, "something that I never had."

THIRTY-SIX DAYS AFTER THE COLLAPSE

Sae left Myongwolgwan feeling empty and exhausted. After hours of reviewing footage, she still had not found what she was looking for. Mr. Han, whose details she and Il-hyung had been given, had left her a message that she was welcome to drop by whenever she had time and that he was happy to talk to her. She looked at her watch, knowing that she should go home to allay the boys' worries, but instead she found herself on a bus across town, heading toward the university campus. For the moment, what troubled her the most was this relationship between Yung and Jae. Yung was at least fifteen years Jae's senior, with an engineering degree from the same university. Had he been a mentor?

The university campus was as Sae remembered it, with its long, majestic driveway and distinctive triangular gate, the carefully clipped hedges, the leafy spaces between buildings. The few students visible on campus moved in the leisure afforded to them by the summer holidays. It was a different atmosphere from when Sae was a student and everyone had been on edge, ready to clear off at the first sign of a protest.

In the library, Sae walked between the empty rows between bookshelves. It was in these silent spaces that Sae and Jae had forged a place for themselves. In that time there had been few places for them to be alone, their intimacy often broken by the appearance of others. There were hidden corners of campus that were theirs—the abandoned chemistry lab, the empty wings overlooking the stage in the music hall. Eventually Sae became bolder, smuggling him into the women's dormitory. There they sat on the floor, formally, forced into silence by the thin walls. Sae lit a candle and turned on a fan, turning the volume up on her radio so they might whisper. She picked up the pencil on her desk and wrote, *You have to be quiet. If they hear you, I'll have to find a new place to live.*

He smiled, taking the notepad. *It's ok, we can sit in silence and just stare at each other.*

She slapped him lightly on the arm, her hand over her mouth to stop herself from laughing out loud. He shrugged and put on a face of mock confusion, making her laugh even harder.

Stop it. You have to help, I can't stop giggling.

She pressed a pillow against his face. He caught her hand and drew her closer. Then kissed her, and the hunger sprang up from inside her.

It was always her place, never his. Whenever she had complained about the few places they could be together, he would find another abandoned space on the campus. He had never offered his place.

"I'm sick of hiding and sneaking around all the time," she declared one night. "I want us to be out in the open."

The next day, Jae arrived at the dorm early and knocked at the door, acting like a formal guest or visitor.

"What's going on?" she asked.

"You're coming with me," he said, grinning. "I'm taking you out of town. Do you trust me or not?"

"I didn't know this was a test of trust; you told me it was going to be fun," she said, as she took another step on the mountain path. "My legs hurt. How much longer?"

"We're almost there," he said. "I thought this would be easy for you. I've seen you running like hell during the protests."

"Let's say I'm more of a sprinter," she said, catching her breath. "I hate stairs."

"You can't stand it, can you?" he said. "You hate not knowing. We're almost there. See that pavilion over there? That's where we're headed."

She smiled at him, touched. "Race you to the top?"

He grinned, sprinting ahead. She laughed, hardly able to breathe while running, and reached out, catching his backpack, tripping him over, until they were both on the ground, laughing. She couldn't remember the last time she had laughed so hard.

At the top of the mountain, her breath was taken away at the sight of vast stretches of farmland in the valley below.

"I come here sometimes when I need to clear my head."

They sat away from the trail and gazed at the square rice paddies below. It was a windless day, and a perfect silence settled between them. They had become inhabitants of sound, awakened by the sound of sweeping broken glass in the early mornings after a riot. Here, it was as if they were in another country. A peaceful one. Sae rested her head on his shoulder, and Jae put his arm around her. Here, looking below at the reddened maple leaves, happiness crept in. Whenever they were in the women's dormitories, or sneaking away from meetings, she had felt guarded, guilt gnawing at the edge of her pleasure. Was she allowed this when there were girls younger than her working without sleep, earning less than was necessary to sustain them? What gave her the right to be happy when students were arrested for speaking out against the government and were raped in interrogation cells, or when the poor were deemed unsightly, and were rounded up and driven to another city before being released? The more happiness she felt with Jae in these moments, the more she promised herself she would double down and work hard for those who were suffering.

"You look so serious," he said.

"I'm happy," she said. "Is that allowed? Doesn't it sometimes feel that way? Like it's illegal somehow?"

"Well," he said, putting his arm around her. "That must make me a fucking outlaw."

The yearbooks in the engineering department were riddled with missing photographs. This was the era when many wished to remain invisible to the police. She ran her fingers over the pictureless names. One of them made her falter, the words catching like fabric on a nail. Kim Geun-ye. Where had she heard the name before?

Turning the pages, she ran her fingers down the rows of faces. She thumbed quickly to another section of the yearbook, a quickening in her chest. Then, dropping it, she pulled out another year, the sound of the pages beneath her thumb like a zipper ripping, exposing something contained but ripe for the picking.

The year was 1986, and there was no entry in the engineering department for Kim Jae-geun, no photograph of that focused expression anywhere. Pulling out another year, she flipped through its pages looking for his name, his familiar face, and found none. Sae held on to the bookcase as she rose, trying to regain sensation in her feet. Each step that she took away from this absence had a muffled quality; her hearing seemed to have dulled. As she walked to the administrative office, she had the sensation that the corridors around her were leaning.

Even before the assistant at the administrative office returned from the filing room, she knew what the answer would be.

Kim Jae-geun had never been enrolled at the university.

By 1986, it was clear to everyone that protests alone were not enough to topple the government.

"We aren't going to bring about democracy through protest," Il-hyung announced one evening. "For fundamental change, we need to become workers ourselves." It was during a rare mountainside retreat, where several senior students had introduced themselves to the most committed juniors.

There was a charge in the room. Someone knocked over a bottle, and the clink of it hitting the floor brought attention to the sudden silence that intruded among them. Sae looked at the others, guessing who would stay and who would bow out. Abandoning their education to work in a factory was a commitment to the movement that would divide the room. It was one thing to participate in a protest, another to lay down one's future.

"It's only through getting to know the workers themselves that we can learn how to help them. We need to infiltrate the factories and ally with the workers. That's how we are going to bring about revolution," a senior member of the movement, a man with high cheekbones who looked too old to be a student, told them.

There was a thick silence. No one seemed to want to speak. The upperclassmen shot one another meaningful looks before calling a break.

"Why don't we have a few drinks?" one of them said, shaking a bottle of soju. Some of the women appeared from the kitchens with snacks. There was a shift in atmosphere as everyone began to relax. Sae noticed that Jae didn't touch his drink. When he stood up to leave, she followed him out of the room.

In the darkness, the woods were electric with the sound of crickets, the air cut by the sound of hissing reeds. The day had cooled, and the temperature was now pleasant.

"I didn't mean to scare you," she said, when he turned abruptly.

"I was afraid it was someone else," he said with a relieved smile.

"A walk?"

They strolled through a narrow avenue of birch trees whose silvery bodies seemed naked in the moonlight.

"You're worried about what the seniors said," she began, to fill the silence between them. "I don't think they mean that we have to drop out of college completely. There's always the summer and—"

"It's not that," he said. "I know how we can get around the screening process. In the factories, I mean. It would be easy to forge identity numbers. So that they wouldn't know that we're students."

She stopped walking and watched him move into the fold of darkness. Over the weeks that had passed, Sae had seen the transfer of his unbroken concentration to the words of the upperclassmen. She had been surprised by the intensity of his commitment and also, she realized, disappointed. She felt her cheeks burning at the thought that she wanted him to look at her, if only once, with that look of attentiveness.

"Getting the job will be the easy part," he continued, reappearing in the light, hardly noticing that she had stopped walking. "But how do we befriend the workers? Convince them that we're genuine? They might be resistant to us. How do you drop into the conversation that you want to start a revolution?"

He turned, finally, to see her smiling.

"How do you know so much about factories?" she said.

"I spent my childhood in one," he said. He looked down at the ground and wiped the sole of his shoe on the grass, as if he were trying to rid himself of the fact. It seemed to be a strange thing to be ashamed of in light of all of their debates. She wanted him to look at her so she could see what he was feeling. Just as abruptly he began walking again and jumped up onto a large rock on the edge of the path. He helped her up. Below them, the river glistened under the flood of moonlight.

"You never talk about where you grew up or went to school," she said, wrapping her arms around her knees.

He leaned over the edge of the rock, as though considering a leap into the water below.

"The less we know about each other, the better, isn't that right?"

"Nice try," she said, smiling. "I'm not letting you off that easily. You never seem intimidated. When the upperclassmen speak matter-of-factly about being arrested for all of this, you never seem fazed by it."

He pulled off a leaf from a low-hanging branch.

"I've seen you at the protests," she said. She had observed his calmness, the way he was willing to throw himself between a student on the ground and the riot police, as if his life was weightless. She had moments of paralyzing fear of torture, of her suspicion that it wouldn't take much for her to surrender. She felt herself to be fraudulent. It was one thing to throw Molotov cocktails, to say that she believed in change, but she did not trust herself, thought that perhaps even before the interrogators touched her she would betray the other students.

"You don't seem scared of anything," she said.

"I'm scared all the time," he said.

"But not of the police," she said. "You don't seem afraid of the future."

"You're right. I'm not," he said.

"Then what are you afraid of?" she asked.

"Of being found out, I guess," he said, after a long pause, his eyes meeting hers. The look startled her. He seemed to know her own suspicions of herself as a coward. Just as she was about to ask him more about this, they heard footsteps in the long grass behind them. Il-hyung appeared with the older upperclassman.

"Good man," the older student said, grinning, slapping Jae on the back. "It's always the quiet ones who get the girls, am I right? Who's coming for a swim?"

Back at the offices of *The Seoul Daily,* Sae sat by the microfiche, poring over the archives, searching for anything she could find on Taehan Group and its president Kim Yung around the time that Il-hyung might have seen him with Jae. It was in searching through these articles that she came across a small article about the death of the Chairman's youngest son in a car accident. Kim Geun-ye. Now she knew why the name had leapt out at her when she had seen it in the yearbook. She remembered hearing the announcement as she waited anxiously for news of Jae's whereabouts shortly after he had been arrested.

If Geun-ye had been a student in the engineering department, then was it possible that Jae had known him? Was Geun-ye the link between Jae and Kim Yung? Sae rose from the desk and looked out at the city slick with rain. Opening the window she gathered the rain in her palms and wet her face, trying to quiet the shrieking crosscurrents of thoughts, the fever rising to her cheeks.

8:30 A.M., November 15, 2016
Chairman's residence, Gugi District, Seoul

One morning at breakfast I saw my youngest son, Geun-ye, gazing out of the dining room window, having hardly touched his soup or rice. At first, I was furious. How spoiled and ungrateful my sons had become. Decades before, my siblings and I would have diluted our soup with tears of gratitude, believing ourselves to be feasting with a king at the sight of even half of the side dishes my sons were given. I was already in a foul mood. The manager of my shipyard had called to report that he had fallen short of his production number. The workers had begun pulling stunts—all clocking out early at the same time so that output at the factories had slowed to a halt. There were rumblings that the workers wished to form a union. I knew that if I entered into conversation with them about wages it would only encourage more demands. I refused to negotiate with them. The workers would start to want a say in how my company was run. Next they would have opinions about how profits should be distributed, or on processes by which men should be hired!

I could see by Geun-ye's downcast expression that something was troubling him. He had been subdued during breakfast, volunteering little when it was his turn to speak. I waited until the others had left to talk to him.

"If you're worried about your exams, you should double down on your efforts instead of worrying about them. Don't waste your time on feeling when you can memorize another theorem," I said.

"Father," he began. "Am I capable of doing the things that you've done?"

The question caught me off guard. I was unaware that my ambitions for him had become transparent. Of course, we are all plagued by doubt occasionally, but I didn't like his lack of confidence.

"Why wouldn't you be? You're my son."

This seemed to crystallize something for him. There was a shift in his expression, a resolve growing in him.

"I'd like to learn more about the business," he said. "I want to take some time on the factory floor to know how things work there. I'd like to take some time off from university."

For a moment I was stunned and did not know what to say. I had often taken Geun-ye as a child to the factories so that he might understand some of his responsibilities later in life. But this seemed to have had an adverse reaction in him, and he grew up to become the child who was the least interested in the business. So this new development lifted my mood immediately. The workers were becoming more difficult to motivate, and it occurred to me that Geun-ye could report to me everything that he saw. I had also begun to suspect that a group of communists was radicalizing my workers, putting ideas such as unions in their heads. If Geun-ye were working in the factory, I thought, he could help to identify them and expunge them from the business.

I expressed my delight at the suggestion. Some time off from his studies in service of an education of a different kind was not a bad idea. I gave it no further thought, for I was in danger of running late for a meeting with President Chun.

After I had proved Taehan Group to be an asset to the nation with my projects overseas, President Park Chung-hee had given me cheap loans and state-owned assets that he needed fixed—

shipyards, steelworks, heavy machinery plants. I spent time in these facilities, identified problems, and made them productive again. By the end of the 1970s, I was no longer just in the construction business but had become the chairman of a conglomerate of businesses.

In 1979, President Park Chung-hee was assassinated by his very own right-hand man—a man he trusted—and replaced by a military man who I did not fully trust. President Chun Doo-hwan had a shiny pate, flat cheeks, and a strong jaw. When he smiled, you saw how large his mouth was. It was so large as to be otherworldly, like a demon. I had heard rumors about him. Sick things. Sadistic things. I was wary of him.

When I walked into his office, he had several other advisers with him. They had already broken open a bottle of whiskey, though it was not yet noon. They were discussing the forthcoming Olympics, to be held the following year. Over the years it had become evident that the bid for the Olympics had been ambitious, wishful thinking, the desperate punt of a nation wishing to be recognized as a member of the industrialized world. They were lamenting the fact that the mayor was a spineless politician who was now trying to bow out of his commitments in preparing for the Olympics.

"As if that wasn't enough, this," President Chun said, tossing a magazine onto the table, "is what I have to contend with."

I picked up the magazine to see a photograph of a student protester running with a Molotov cocktail in his hand.

"It's like a virus—the students are infecting everyone. Tenant farmers are asking for a raise. Taxi drivers are on strike. Even fucking office workers are taking to the streets, calling themselves the necktie brigade! I have the ambassador to the United States asking me what we're doing to handle the situation, and the mayor, the chickenshit, saying there needs to be a different committee organizing the affairs. All the while, the foreign press are publishing stories like this on the front cover."

I nodded. It was true that such images reflected poorly on our country. It was proving bad for business. I began to feel weary, unsure of why I had been summoned.

"We need to clean up this city, make it sparkle. What have you got in the works?" he asked me.

"A residential building in Gangnam. We're repairing a bridge on the west side of the city; there's also the—"

"There's nothing impressive about a residential building," he said. "I want sparkles. We need something bigger, brighter, stately. Something to make those Olympic tourists realize that they're not touring the third world. Something fucking modern. We need our own version of the Empire State Building."

There was a pregnant pause in the room. When I did not immediately respond, the president threw his glass at the wall.

"Have I got to spell it out for you? I'm telling you to make it happen. Do you understand? Something tall, the tallest building in Asia! I want that to be on the front of a fucking newspaper, do you understand?"

The tallest building in Asia in less than a year, to be completed before our dear city hosted the Olympics—this was a challenge that intimidated even me. But as I have told you before, it is not in my character to claim that such a thing is impossible. I resolved that Taehan Group would break another record on the world stage. This thought quieted any fear I had. And lo and behold, I kept my promise to the president. Aspiration Tower was completed two days before the opening ceremony.

THIRTY-EIGHT DAYS AFTER THE COLLAPSE

Sae stood waiting for Tae-kyu in the square outside *The Seoul Daily* offices, a place of purgatory where office workers whiled away their working day, smoking, postponing their inevitable return to their desks. Earlier that day, Sae had met with Mr. Han, the laborer that the union leader had referred her to. She had been told to look for a cinder block wall covered in ivy. Mr. Han's house was at the top of a hill in a haphazard neighborhood at the edge of a slum. She moved through the sounds of this unforgiving place—a voice scolding a field full of students over loudspeaker, the solemn sermon from a rust-stained church tower. At the top of roughly cut concrete steps, there was the majestic view of the skyscrapers downtown, a vision of a city that seemed to belong to a different country.

A thin man sitting with a cigarette rose to his feet as she approached him.

"You must be Miss Kim," he said with a smile. "I'm Han Sun-kyu; come in. My brother, Sun-jin, and I have been waiting for you. Can I get you something? Some powdered coffee? It's sweet but gives me a nice kick."

"Coffee is fine," she said, smiling.

He led her through a stone kitchen to a small room. Sun-jin seemed to be in his mid-forties, though his beard made him look older. Sitting with his back against the wall, he raised his eyes from the TV, set aside a large ashtray full of cigarette butts, and rearranged the acrylic tiger-print blanket covering his legs so she would have room to sit. His brother had told her on the phone that he had been in an accident on a construction site some years before but had not gone into detail. Sun-jin caught her staring at the outlines of his childlike shins, and she looked away, at the calendar hung on a rusty nail on the wall. It was marked AUGUST 1989. A woman posed in a bikini, her hair wild like a black lion's mane.

Sun-jin smoothed the blanket in front of him.

"Falling three stories will do that to you," he said, aware of her discomfort. "The doctors say I was lucky to survive. It could've been my neck. I could have ended up unable to move at all from the head down."

"That would've saved us some money with our phone bills," Mr. Han joked, reentering the room with a tray with three steaming paper cups. "He likes to talk on the phone. All day long. I don't even know who he's talking to. It's either that or the TV."

Sae forced a smile, taking the warm cup in her hands, afraid her pity was palpable. In all of her years of protesting, the workers' suffering had remained an abstraction. Now she saw that it was a life sentence for many.

"So you're Il-hyung's lady friend? Are you helping him make another documentary?"

"No," she said. "I'm a journalist."

"We tried to talk to you lot years ago when he had his accident, but it never went anywhere."

"What happened?"

"Third floor. By the atrium," Sun-jin said.

"Those sons of bitches just handed over a few notes at the hospital and that was it. When I went back asking for compensation, they said they had no record of him working on the site," Mr. Han said, kissing his teeth, the edges of his ears glowing red.

"Why are you surprised? We've worked on sites where accidents happened, and bodies were set aside so people could get back to work. We were never people to those managers, just bits of defective machinery," Sun-jin said, throwing back what was left in his cup and then crushing it in his hands. "Anyway, I was going to tell them about what was happening at the Tower, but the papers weren't interested. There was too much other news in the lead-up to the Olympics."

"What was happening at the Tower?" Sae asked, suddenly impatient.

"A string of disasters!" he said. "Every few months there would be a new team overseeing the construction. New teams of subcontractors. First the plans were for a low-rise apartment block. It was almost completed when the Chairman changed his mind, saying he wanted to convert it to a high-rise commercial center. The contractors who said that they needed to redo the foundation were fired. He was a man who hated to hear that what he wanted was impossible. The Chairman had a deadline, and he wouldn't tolerate any delays. He kept hiring and firing anyone who disagreed with him, until he found a team who would get the job done."

Sae thought of the blueprints that she had found in the studio in Buam-dong and wished she had brought them with her.

"So you're saying that the foundation of the Tower wasn't sufficient for its revised height?"

Sun-Jin nodded. "As the plans for the building kept changing, some of the support columns were cut away. Add a pool to the mix, and of course it's going to collapse."

She set down the cup in her hands. She wanted to be clear that she understood correctly. "So you're saying that Taehan Group was at fault to begin with?"

"He said that the markings on the blueprint highlighted load-bearing beams," Tae-kyu said, a few steps ahead of her. Sae had asked him to meet his engineer contact without her. "And that the calculations on the margins showed they were aware of the problems in the structure."

Sae bit her lip. The day had been sapped of its humidity, and leaves had begun to droop from the trees, but she felt the beads of sweat begin to tickle her neck.

"So where does that leave us?" she asked.

Tae-kyu stopped walking and turned to face her. "He also suggested that no engineer in their right mind would venture to increase the load without fortifying the structural foundations." He paused to think, running his hand over the bristle on his cheek. "How long do we think they were working on this?"

Sae thought back to the documents she had seen. Jae had come home with news of the project in the winter.

"Six months," she said, remembering something she had noticed in the office. "What if they hadn't been building a pool in the first place?" she said. "There were no tiles, no plans for the pool itself."

"But if they weren't building a pool, what were they doing in there?" Tae-kyu surveyed the office workers. "That would be at the crux of everything. We could go to city hall and see the planning permits they submitted, maybe that would help."

Sae threw her coffee cup in the overflowing bin.

"I can call them this afternoon."

"I should get back," Tae-kyu said. "Are you going to be okay?"

"Fine," Sae said, wiping the palms of her hands on her jeans. Then she remembered. "The name Kim Geun-ye, does that ring a bell to you?"

"You mean the chairman of Taehan Group's youngest son? They said it was a car accident, right? No other parties involved. Naturally everyone assumed it was suicide. Why do you ask?"

Tae-kyu brought out a packet of cigarettes from his front pocket, and Sae held her hand out for one. "A funny coincidence. The name came up recently, that's all."

Tae-kyu put a cigarette in his mouth and offered her the lighter. "I remember Reporter Kang and I joked about the timing of it, like it was meant to deflect attention from the labor unrest at the Chairman's cement factory. The Chairman is capable of a lot of things, but no one thinks he would drive his own son off a cliff to highjack the news."

FORTY DAYS AFTER THE COLLAPSE

In late October, there was a softening in the autumnal weather, the march toward winter slowing to a languid crawl. Song-mi's presence in Myong-hee's apartment brought with it, it seemed, additional sunlight. Myong-hee loved the sound of the noises of another human going about their daily routines in the next room. Happiness presented itself like an unexpected visit from a long-lost friend.

Myong-hee had suggested that Song-mi should rest rather than overexert herself by working in the smoky rooms. In return, she would wake to find Song-mi fixing them something to eat—steamed eggs, spicy pork and kimchi stew, fried rice, or marinated beef.

"I didn't know you knew how to cook," Myong-hee said to her, eagerly spooning the broth into her mouth.

"I just do what they do on TV."

The soup was delicious. When Myong-hee lived alone, there were days when she forced herself to have a second meal. She set down her spoon, careful not to eat too fast.

"You mean you taught yourself to cook by watching a show?"

Song-mi shrugged and looked out of the window, turning her face as she tried, and failed, to suppress a smile.

"I was bored and I had a craving for kimchi jjigae," she said, though Myong-hee noticed that Song-mi had hardly touched her bowl.

"Are you sure you don't want me to come in and work for a few hours?" Song-mi asked.

"Do you really want to?" Myong-hee said.

"I just want to help," she said. "Maybe I could help Sae onni with the tapes."

The mention of Myongwolgwan, and Mr. Byun's offer of payment for information about what had happened at Aspiration Tower, dampened her mood. Myong-hee held the image suddenly of a toddler running across her living room, playing hide-and-seek, and then disappearing into one of the dark karaoke rooms of Myongwolgwan. No, that was no place for a child. There was something of a shock in seeing this specter of a future child; until recently she had been haunted by fragments of the past.

Since Song-mi had moved in with her, Myong-hee had begun to notice people laughing in conversation as they walked leisurely through her neighborhood, the majesty of the street littered with yellowed gingko leaves. The world seemed more colorful, alive to her. For once she noticed the small gestures of love around her, the young man who gave up his seat for an elderly passenger, the generosity of strangers in rushing to help an unsteady child on the stairs leading to the subway. The light seemed to dance differently on the river as Myong-hee looked out on her way to the club. Even her debt seemed less like an impossible incline to be treaded for the rest of her life. Mr. Byun's offer seemed to dangle new possibilities for her future. There might be a way, she thought, to build a more secure future for all of them.

Until now Myong-hee had not done more than keep a cursory eye on Sae's examination of her tapes. Now she was determined to help her—there was a possibility, after all, that something on those tapes might be just what Mr. Byun was looking for. When Myong-hee arrived at Myongwolgwan in the evening, Sae was already waiting for her at the entrance. As the sun began to recede behind the low-rise buildings in the alley, the air had taken on a damp chill. Sae's overcoat looked threadbare, and Myong-hee turned her back on her growing sense of pity for her. As they stepped into the club, her newfound optimism nudged her with a thought: Maybe they would find something on the tapes that would free them all.

FORTY-TWO DAYS AFTER THE COLLAPSE

Hoon-min leapt with delight as she opened the door and rushed forward toward her with raised arms. Seeing the bright blue Super Sentai figurine in his hands, Sae asked him what he had been up to.

"Uncle gave it to me."

"Who?" she asked.

Stepping out of her shoes and into the living room, she saw Il-hyung sitting on the floor with her mother. The low table between them held a crowd of colorful side dishes around a bubbling bowl of tofu soup.

"When did you make all this?" Sae asked, ripping off her scarf.

"Il-hyung called, and I told him to come here. He was waiting at the bus stop. Why didn't you invite him here, Sae? Were you really going to make him wait outside?"

"I didn't think I was going to be so late."

"Didn't you think I would want to see him? How long has it been? Ten years?"

"More than that," he replied, his ears flushing pink at her mother's fawning of him.

"Il-hyung has been telling me that his mother hates living in her apartment. Can you believe it? Living in a high-rise was all she talked about when we were living in Mallipo," she said.

Her mother was talkative, always happiest in a group of people. For a moment it felt as though the mother of her childhood had been returned to her.

"Why haven't you eaten until now?" Sae asked, unsettled, without knowing why, that Il-hyung should be here.

"I hate eating alone," he said as her mother placed several pieces of beef on his rice, as though he were a treasured son. "Most nights, I don't bother unless my work crew goes out as a team."

"Our Il-hyung is so nice-looking," her mother said, shooting Sae a meaningful look. "It's about time you got married, isn't it? Is it young people these days or this city? Why are they waiting so long to get hitched? I don't understand."

"Leave him alone," Sae said, refusing to look at either of them. "I'm sure he has his reasons." His hair fell into his eyes; he was in need of a haircut. He was fiercely loyal, hardworking, and loved by everyone. His bachelorhood was a choice. He was not the kind of person to marry just because he had stepped into a decade when marriage was part of the social contract, as many of their other friends had done. He would never agree to being set up by his parents. She picked up her chopsticks. She was not hungry but could not resist her mother's cooking.

Seung-min sat at the table, unusually still, watching Il-hyung, hanging on to his every word, while Hoon-min circled them, his Super Sentai figurine in flight.

"This radish kimchi is delicious," Il-hyung said.

"Let me get you some more," her mother said, palming the

side dish and rising with one hand on her knee to raise herself to standing.

"Don't get up," Sae said, mindful of her mother's bad knee. "I'll do it."

Sae had not seen her mother animated like this in years, attentive to Il-hyung's every mouthful and moving the side dishes on her side of the table so that they might be closer to him. Having refilled the plate and cut the radishes into smaller pieces with scissors, she stood by the sink and watched the happy domestic scene. To an outsider looking through their window, they would appear to be an ordinary family. It rose slowly, a deep sea creature toward the surface of light, a longing that she did not know she had. The ache of an absence that had been there since before Jae's disappearance. There had been no meals like this with Jae and her family.

After clearing the dishes, Il-hyung watched Seung-min pick some rice off the cuff of Hoon-min's trousers.

"They're good, these boys," he said.

Her mother nodded in agreement, pausing for a moment as she peeled a Chinese pear in her hands.

"You were a good kid, too," her mother said to Sae, smiling a little sadly. "A little too good. You couldn't bear to see anyone suffer. Couldn't let anything go. And so you had to get involved with all of those protests."

The idea that her mother still saw some good in her brought a prickle of emotion to Sae's nose. She had no idea her mother had understood why she had been unable to stand by the sidelines. For years she had carried around the guilt, the weight of her mother's grasp on her jeans when she found out that she had been to a demonstration. When she had won her place at university, the village had put up a banner to announce the news, just as they had when Il-hyung had been accepted the year before. She was the golden child. Proof that poverty was no shackle. That after the pillage of history—the occupation, the war, the dictatorship—at least the next generation could be stable, have material success. In the villagers' eyes, she held all the promise of rising to a better future. To join the student movement was to risk that future, to lead to a fate worse than living in poverty. She remembered her mother begging her not to get involved.

"You were led down the wrong path by that boy—"

"Omma, please," Sae said. It stung to have her talk about Jae this way. "Don't."

Sae could feel Il-hyung's eyes on her, but she did not look up to meet them, feigning great concern over an old cut on Hoon-min's arm.

Later, as Il-hyung stood up to leave, Hoon-min swung from his hand, trying to tug him back to the ground.

"I want you to stay!"

"I'll come back another night," Il-hyung said.

"I'll walk out with you," Sae said. Her mother disappeared into the kitchen and returned with a large bag full of food. She thrust it into Il-hyung's hands. "Make sure you eat. You can come back for more if you run out."

Il-hyung made a show of protesting the food but seemed pleased to be taken care of. They walked down the stairwell in silence. It was only when they reached the street level that Il-hyung stopped to face her.

"Your mother doesn't know that I took you to the first meeting?"

Sae shook her head.

"You let her believe that Jae led you to join the movement. Why?"

"You saw how she is with you. You're like a son to her. Jae was an orphan. There wouldn't have been anything I could've told her to redeem him." She saw another question gathering in his eyes, so she kept speaking. "You said you found something."

They found a narrow booth in a chicken and beer restaurant. Sitting across from Il-hyung, she saw that he had been masking worry all evening.

"What was it that you didn't want to tell me on the phone?"

She saw him hesitate, looking into his beer before deciding to take a sip.

"Is it true?" she said. "Was Jae an informant?"

He licked his lower lip and touched the rim of his glass with his finger.

"I went to see my guy. He's retired and living in Ansan now. He was never political, but he didn't like being in the police either. It was just a job for him. He helped us out when we had students on the inside. Getting them little luxuries, handing them letters from the outside world, that sort of thing."

Picking up the glass, he took a sip before continuing.

"My guy was working at the front office, in intake on the night of the factory arrests. He said he remembered Jae coming in because there was some confusion. The warden wasn't happy about some aspect of the paperwork. My guy said he had other things to do and didn't worry about it too much. But later that night a sedan pulled up outside and a man came in carrying a box of apples."

"Apples?"

"A gift for the warden."

Sae shrugged. "So what?"

Il-hyung let out a soft laugh.

"That's what I was thinking. Which makes us both naïve," he said, stroking his forearms, as if trying to comfort himself. "The box, it turns out, was lined with cash. Later, when he went around to check on the protesters, Jae was missing."

"Could it have been a different division of the police? The anti-communism bureau?" Even as she asked the question, she realized that if that were the case, no money would have changed hands. "Do you think it could have been Kim Yung?"

"I don't know," Il-hyung said. "I wish I could tell you."

After Jae's return from the temple, Sae thought of him as a man who had returned from the front lines with a war still raging inside him.

One night she had awoken with a jolt, the baby kicking her in the ribs. Seung-min had rolled off the futon and was sleeping with his head on the laminate floor. Jae was not beside her. He was pacing the living room like a patient in agony waiting for relief from pain.

She had seen him like this before and went to him, putting her hands on him, pulling his face to hers so that their foreheads were touching.

"It's okay, it's okay," she said. "You're not there anymore. They can't hurt you."

"You don't understand," he said. "It was nothing."

He was silent, as though trying to gather the right words to describe what he had endured.

"Nothing happened to me there. And to think that for some others it was so—so . . ." he stammered, unable to finish the words.

"Don't do that," she said. "You don't have to compare."

"Sae," he began. "I hate this. I hate that I'm like this. You should leave me, Sae."

"Don't start."

It was as though he wanted to know how hard he could push her before she would leave him. In his world, everyone was leaving him or beating him. He did not speak of his childhood often, but when he shared fragments of his memories, she understood that for him, what was meant to be love was really pain. The experience of torture, she knew, had only further unraveled him.

She put her hands over his. Tried to comfort him.

"I'm not going anywhere."

He punched the wall. She didn't flinch, and that upset him. Her trust in him not to harm her seemed to scare him.

"Your mother was right. I'm no good."

"I'm not going anywhere."

He grew quiet. Her large belly pressed against him, and the baby kicked them both.

"Listen, even Sprout here is trying to tell you it's okay. We love you, we're family."

Now Sae recalled this memory, deeply unsettled. She had assumed that torture had been his undoing, but if what Il-hyung had discovered was true, she no longer knew about the nature of the war raging inside him.

• • •

As she put on her jacket to leave she saw a fine rain had begun to come down outside. Il-hyung brought out an umbrella and opened it.

"Take it," he said, "I haven't got far to go. I'll call you tomorrow."

She felt his trembling hand beneath hers as he gave her the umbrella. When she looked at his face in surprise, she saw his cheeks were flushed.

Il-hyung looked down at the wet pavement. "I should have said something all those years ago. You wrote me all of those letters, and still I . . . I somehow never had the courage."

She wanted to thank him for what he had done, or to apologize for the dissolution of their friendship. Instead she said, "I never meant to hurt you."

He gave a little laugh and nodded, still not daring to meet her eye. "I hope you get to the bottom of this and find him. I mean that, even though I don't think he ever deserved you."

He pulled his jacket over his head and stepped onto the road and into the rain, disappearing into the storm.

FORTY-FIVE DAYS AFTER THE COLLAPSE

Sae was able to narrow down the dates of Yung's visits by sifting through Myong-hee's collection of receipts. It helped to know there was a system for culling extraneous recorded material, but after hours of trawling through irrelevant conversations, she was beginning to feel discouraged. Sitting with her chin in her hand, Sae felt her eyelids grow heavy. The sachets of instant coffee offered more of a sugar rush than a caffeine boost. After a while the images all seemed to appear the same, so she was already several moments into the exchange when she saw Mr. Bae receive a drink from Kim Yung. She pressed pause and then rewound the tape to start at the beginning of the exchange, cross-checking the date—it was six months before the collapse of the Tower.

Mr. Bae sat stiffly across from Yung with the posture of a man who was at the mercy of another. There was no sign of the arrogant, greasy man Sae had known. At first it was difficult to hear what was being said—someone was sitting on one of the mics in the room—and all she could do was read the movement of Mr. Bae's expressions as they swung from forced politeness to panic and fear.

There was the sound of shifting material on the mic, and then the sounds of the conversation were unmuffled. Mr. Bae moved forward in his seat, leaning toward Yung.

"I understand your predicament, but even a few days of closure could—"

"Father won't allow it. Operations must continue; sales must continue."

"But the risk of collapse is—"

"So fix it. And quietly."

Mr. Bae seemed almost in pain at this. "Just give us a week to secure some of the columns. You're asking us to sneak around, to work around the occupants in the building. We can't work fast enough."

"It's like my father says: 'Impossible' is a mindset. Geun-ye owes me. Aren't I paying you a fortune to get this done in the way we agreed?"

"What if we were to close the building once a week?" Mr. Bae said carefully.

"Do you know what the turnover is in one day in that building? Do you understand what it will cost us?"

Sae let the video play to static. Finally, it was clear to her. The simplest explanation of all. L&S Engineering was there to try to fix the shoddy work, to rectify a fundamental instability in the building's structure.

She pressed eject and heard the click of the released tape when Myong-hee appeared at the door.

"What is it? Have you found him?"

Sae glanced at the tape in her hands. "There was never any swimming pool."

Myong-hee came over and pushed the tape back in and replayed it. She paused after Mr. Bae and Yung's conversation came to an end and then rewound it. She was about to play the tape again when the door opened and Song-mi appeared.

"I thought I told you to stay home."

"I got bored. Hey! I know that guy," she said, pointing to the image of Mr. Bae on the screen. "What happened to him?"

"Mr. Bae," Sae replied, staring at Song-mi. "He turned himself in to the police."

"Right!" Song-mi said excitedly. "He was with me just before that; he was pissed, saying he did everything his boss wanted him to, but now they were asking him to take the fall for him too."

"Everything they wanted him to . . . ?"

"Yeah, he was talking about some body they were looking for at the morgue."

Myong-hee and Sae exchanged glances. "A body?"

"He didn't mention who it was?"

Song-mi shook her head. She sat swinging her legs under the table. "No, but he did show me his bank book. He got *paid*, that's for sure!"

Sae jumped to her feet. "I have to take this to the paper."

"You can't leave with this," Myong-hee said softly, but firmly. "I wanted to help you find your husband, not to help you become a whistleblower."

"This is evidence," Sae said. "I have to clear his name. They're trying to frame L&S Engineering for something they didn't do, falsifying—"

"This isn't evidence; this is private property," Myong-hee said. Her face had hardened, taking on a gray, stony pallor. "I have a business to protect."

The warmth that Sae had observed in the hours she had spent with Myong-hee had dissipated, and there was a sting in the realization that they were not friends.

"I can protect you as a source," Sae said evenly, fighting a rising panic that she might not be able to take the evidence beyond these rooms. "The paper only has to say that it has evidence. I don't want to expose you."

"You need to go."

The panic filtered into anguish. Worst of all was the fear that this meant, somehow, that she would be unable to find Jae. "This might be the only way that I can find him."

"If there's one thing I've learned it's that if someone is hiding it is most likely that they don't want to be found. He's allowed you to believe that he might be dead. Don't you think that's message enough?"

There was a stunned silence in the newsroom.

"We can't run this," Suh, the editor, said after a long moment. "We don't have any evidence."

"Then we'll find some." Sae shot Tae-kyu a look, trying to catch his eye. "Of course we can run the story. We have to. It's everything this paper stands for."

Sae grabbed Tae-kyu's sleeve. "They went to huge lengths to conceal what they did. This is murder. They could have closed the building. The Chairman refused on the grounds that he didn't want to lose revenue."

Tae-kyu refused to meet her eye. It seemed he was already aware that nothing would be done.

"I don't understand. Running the paper, telling our citizens the truth—that's what we are about."

"You're right," Suh said. "That's what *The Seoul Daily* stood for once. But we've been struggling for years. Our subscribers have gone down. The perception is that things have improved. The dictatorship is over."

"So . . . this is the story that's going to save the paper," she said, unclenching her teeth. Her mouth felt dry and she placed her hands on her cheeks to release the tension in her jaw.

Suh and Tae-kyu exchanged looks.

"We've been acquired," the editor said, clearing his throat. "By another news group. They made us an offer we couldn't refuse."

Several ashtrays were piled on top of one another on the editor's desk, and the keyboard near the large computer monitor was buried under stacks of papers. The idea that another news group wanted to invest in the paper was laughable to her.

"Another news group?" she said. "Why don't you just come out and say Taehan Group is buying the paper? Purchasing your silence?"

"They've promised us some independence," the editor said. "It was either that or fold entirely."

"You're complicit, you know that? You're complicit in murder."

Tae-kyu followed her out onto the street but Sae waved him off. The edges of her vision were shaky with rage.

"I suspected Suh for a while, but I didn't know it was Taehan Group, I swear it."

"I respected you," she said. "Have you actually been trying to help, or have you been reporting back to your new owner about our line of investigation? Whose side are you on?"

When Tae-kyu spoke it was with a paternal patience that further enraged her.

"The timing is difficult, I give you that. But if we wait a little while—"

"They're only acquiring the paper now because they are afraid of what evidence will surface if they go to trial. I don't need you. I can do this on my own," she said. "Maybe you can tell your superiors that."

Sae got out of the taxi and ran up the steep concrete staircase toward Sun-jin's house. In the darkness the badly lit streets felt hazardous. Sae forced herself to slow down. The work she had ahead of her was already substantial. How long would it take? Months perhaps? If she could get a statement from Sun-jin, if she could get the statements of all the laborers who had worked at Aspiration Tower, then she would be able to get the evidence that she needed. She would need Il-hyung's support, and perhaps Sun-jin would be able to help her get in touch with other people who had worked there. She didn't need the paper. Or Tae-kyu's empty promise of help. Or video evidence from Myongwolgwan.

At the top of the hill, large bags of waste were visible by the front gate. Large pieces of furniture were among the piles of refuse. The house had been culled of most items—there was no phone, no calendar hanging on the wall. Gone, too, was the acrylic blanket, exposing a large worn circle of linoleum.

Turning back to the street she saw Sun-jin's brother, Mr. Han, making his way back up the hill, his step faltering on seeing her.

"Ah, you're back," he said overly brightly. "I didn't know you were coming."

"Where's Sun-jin?" she asked. "Is he okay?"

Mr. Han lowered his gaze. "He's fine. I thought it was easier for him to go first; he was never going to be much help with the move."

"You didn't mention you were moving," she said.

He stared at a piece of wire, part of the landline, in the small concrete yard. "We've found a nice place across town. A place where Sun-jin can get some help. It's been a struggle for all these years, you know, trying to make ends meet and trying to look after him as well. All that worry. It would be nice to be free of that."

Sae understood immediately. "Taehan came to you, didn't they? Made you sign something? Some kind of nondisclosure agreement?"

His eyes met hers briefly before swimming away. All that was offered was a slight nod. "I appreciate what you were trying to do. When the accident first happened we were desperate for someone to listen to what we had to say. But they made us an offer we couldn't refuse. What happened was terrible . . ." He sighed deeply. "We talked about it a lot. Sun-jin didn't want to take the money, but I persuaded him to agree. See, the thing is, after a while it just struck me that maybe truth and justice, all of those things, feel like a luxury for those who can afford it."

Sae felt her pager vibrating in her pocket. It was probably Tae-kyu offering some useless apology. Mr. Han moved past her with his head bowed, and she let him go.

"There must be someone else who would be willing to talk to me about what happened," she said, calling out to him, but he did not turn around.

Everything was stacked against her. The paper would not run the story, Taehan Group would coax witnesses out of their words and memories with the offer of a more comfortable life. Myong-hee had the only piece of damning evidence against them. It was no longer 1987. There was no movement rallying to support her. She was on her own.

As soon as Sae arrived back home, she opened the fridge and pulled out a beer. She sensed her mother's eyes on her from across the room.

"What is it?" Sae asked.

Her mother handed her a message from the landlord informing her that she was behind on the rent.

"It might not be a bad idea . . ." her mother trailed off, carefully searching her face. "To move, I mean."

Sae folded the note and placed it on the table. Even now, she hoped that Jae might walk in. To move felt like an acceptance of his absence.

"The other day I found Seung-min on the stairwell, and when I asked him where he was going, he said he was looking for his dad. I understand you don't want to talk about it with them, but maybe a change of scenery would do everyone some good."

"I'll find the money," she said.

In the bedroom, she found the boys locked in sleep, their heads touching as if in quiet communion. She thought how protective she had been of Jae, how heavily she had carried the burden of looking after him, his rehabilitation, how she still thought it was her fault he had been arrested, that their lives had taken this turn. Her mother had been right not to trust him. And perhaps Il-hyung had been right after all about romance. Jae had simply been an idea, a fiction that she had assembled from the pages of his notes. She sank to the floor beside the boys. Drawing up the blanket over Seung-min, she saw that he was holding on to a fistful of one of Jae's shirts, as though tugging his father back to him from under the skin of his sleep.

There was a buzzing in her pocket, and she remembered the message on her pager. It had been left by an unfamiliar number. Reluctantly she got up again and punched in the number to retrieve her messages.

"Hi. It's Oh Jung-hoon, from the morgue? You probably don't want to hear from me. It's not great news. Uh . . . I think you might want to come down here in the morning. I may have found the rabbit foot."

FORTY-SIX DAYS AFTER THE COLLAPSE (A.M.)

Even before the morgue attendant had folded the sheet past the forehead, Sae knew. Even in death he was as she had loved him, she recognized the cliff of his cheekbones, the thickness of his eyebrows, the dip of his clavicle. She wanted to see the rise of his chest, to see the ghost of his breath but there was only stillness. His lips had grown dark and there were bruises on his chest. There were no other clues, no visible marks. For once she did not wish to burrow for more, or to know how it had happened.

"What I don't understand is why the body was kept here, with all the other unidentified bodies. And it's odd that the names don't match. I came across it by chance when I was looking for someone else. I remembered the rabbit foot. Thought I should check it with you," the morgue attendant said, oblivious to her recognition.

Sae did not respond. Instead, she leaned over Jae and murmured his name, as if trying to rouse him gently from a deep sleep. She still believed that she could call him back to her, as she had done before, with a can of cold beer on a too-hot day. She was willing to surrender her anger, she would forgive anything, she thought, if he would open his eyes and allow her to see, once more, that look of intent attention. She wanted to touch him, to comfort him, but there was nothing, he was not there. It was she alone who wept for them both.

When had she last seen him? In the morning, on the day the Tower collapsed. Jae was trying to tell her something, but Sae was not looking at him. She was on the phone, looking for a pen, her day without him had already begun.

"I have to go," he mouthed when their eyes met across the room. She smiled at him, raising a finger, and then, moments later, hung up.

"My love—" he began to say. He looked as though there was something he wanted to tell her.

"Appa, you're a bad guy, pew pew," Seung-min said, pointing a chopstick at him.

A genuine look of hurt passed over his face before Jae registered the role he was expected to play. Jae clutched his chest, pretending to fall backward. "My own son!"

"Stop pointing things at your appa," Sae said gently, picking up the receiver again, her mind on other things. "We'll see you tonight."

She circled the memory again. What had he been about to say? *Look up,* she wanted to tell herself. *Memorize those thick wild eyebrows, the shy gaze of adolescence in his warm eyes.* Over time their love had become a quiet, unspoken thing that lived in stolen looks. As though the spell would be broken if declared openly. There was something he had wanted to tell her that morning. If she had only looked up, not in such a hurry to start her day, she would have seen it. His hesitation to leave. Something hanging unsaid between them.

Look up, she wanted to tell herself, *and ask him not to go.*

* * *

She didn't know how long she sat there with the body; her thoughts seemed to swim through her aimlessly. In death, as in life, he had evaded her curious hunger to know him. But wasn't this also what she had loved? It was the mystery of him that had beckoned her toward him that first moment in the library.

So it was not the evasion, so much as the desertion that she could not forgive. Hadn't she seen them in her mind's eye, one fragile being helping another into their old age?

"Traitor," she said. "Why did you stop talking to me? We were supposed to be a refuge for each other. How could you leave me like this? Traitor." And then she was holding on to him and sobbing. "I don't know who you are, but I don't know how to do this without you."

After what felt like hours, she rose. What she wanted more than anything was to wrap her arms around Seung-min and Hoon-min. To rest her head against the base of their necks and smell them, to feel their hearts beating against her own chest. She needed this more than any historical fact. Their warmth, their safety, was more important than any ambiguous truth.

"I'm sorry about the mix-up," the morgue assistant said.

"You said earlier the names don't match," she said, bone weary.

"Oh that," he said. "I don't know what happened there."

Sae's eyes fell on the clipboard. "What was the name on the body?"

He looked at his notes. "Kim Geun-ye."

2 P.M., November 27, 2016
Chairman's residence, Gugi District, Seoul

I will admit that the president's demand consumed me. When workers on the Tower fell behind on their deadlines, I slept in shipping containers on-site, to make sure that they would keep on task, that we would be completed before the Olympics.

Here I ask that you turn that off. Let's speak plainly. Off the record. A dying man deserves to offload one confession, after all. It is true that I was not as attentive as I could have been to what was happening at home. I was not aware of Geun-ye's miseducation. By the time I understood what was happening, it was too late. He had become radicalized.

I was never concerned about the student protesters. They were never any threat. All they did was make a lot of noise about nothing—they wanted the American military gone, they didn't like American investments and the interests they represented, they said we needed to be liberated from U.S. colonial rule. What nonsense! What an ungrateful generation! Without the American military we would be a nation of communist beggars. What would we survive on? The crumbs of aid thrown at us by the rest of the world?

There were rumors that the students were trying to infiltrate factories to incite the workers. One morning after breakfast Yung followed me into my office.

"Father," he said. "It's Geun-ye. He's joined a radical group, and he's trying to mobilize the workers at the cement factory."

It was true that strikes were beginning to intensify. Cities around the country were taken hostage by the demands of hostile citizens who had no sense of gratitude for how far we had come as a nation. Productivity came to a standstill in my factories. Worse, during the strikes the workers had begun damaging my property. Despite these facts, I would not believe that my favorite child could have any hand in this. I had faith in his intention to be a persuasive force, the leader that Taehan Group needed to inspire the workers to look beyond their daily quibbles and work hard for their future.

All I could see was Yung's jealousy, his efforts to turn me against Geun-ye. I lashed out at him.

"Do you think I'm so out of touch with what's happening in my factories, with my own flesh and blood, that I would believe your foolhardy accusations? Geun-ye has twice the potential you'll ever have as a leader. He's a stabilizing force there. How can you not see that?"

I threw him out and went about my business, trying to shake off the poison of his jealousy. To satisfy myself that there was nothing to worry about, I went to visit the cement factory in question and checked on Geun-ye. He was more subdued than usual, but everything appeared to be in order.

It was sometime later that it happened. Mr. Gong came in, sweating, twitching and uneasy in his suit. He told me that there had been a fire at the cement factory. The riot police had to be called in. As I entered the scene each of my employees lowered his eyes. There was something they weren't telling me.

The police informed me that they had removed the charred remains of an employee who they had yet to identify. I cursed. The last thing Taehan Group needed was more negative press attention. I could not face the foreign newspapers publishing photos of the scene. At one of my factories! I retired to a makeshift container office to call my secretary when Yung came in.

We had not spoken since our argument some weeks before.

"What is it?" I asked him.

"Father," he said. His voice broke off for a moment. "It's Geun-ye."

"What about Geun-ye?"

He told me that the fire had begun when Geun-ye had set himself alight. In protest of my factory conditions. The workers had seen him light himself in flames. They said Geun-ye ran through the factory grounds, fire blazing. I refused to believe it. I demanded to see him immediately, storming into the storeroom where they had set aside his body. I lifted the cover. He was unrecognizable to me. His body was smaller than I remembered. The face of my child, too distorted to look at.

I will admit that I hardened. I threw the tarp over the charred remains. I left the room and locked myself in the container. I was seething with rage. Feeble-minded child, he had been brainwashed by communists. I told myself there was nothing to mourn, no great loss if he was so simpleminded. I shut off any feelings of love, before they could soften me. This was no child of mine. There were practicalities to oversee—I would have to manage the crisis. I would not have this incident setting an example for others.

In a crisis one must be quick thinking. Immediately an opportunity presented itself. We would deflect attention away from this incident by making our family tragedy public. This is the only time I inverted the truth.

Tell them it was a car accident, I told Yung.

FORTY-SIX DAYS AFTER THE COLLAPSE (P.M.)

Sae did not believe in secrets. Exposing the truth was what she had campaigned for as a student, in her professional life. But now she wanted to impress upon the woman who had stepped into the morgue some hours ago, to implore her to turn back, to return home to her children, to live richer for having unambiguous memories. Now no memory would remain unturned. His ignorance about the students' intentions in the library. His familiarity with the factory's processes. His unwillingness to talk about his family life. Even as she suspected that it was Yung who had helped to get Jae out of prison, she had not allowed herself to see it. He had hidden at the temple, not from the police but from her.

There was so much she did not know. How heavily did the secret weigh on him? Was it so deeply buried in him that he was not conscious of the lie moment to moment, or was it a weight that burdened him constantly?

She thought of the nights he paced in the moonlight, unable to sleep. He had been his own torturer. In turning a blind eye to the gaps in their history, in not interrogating it, she had also been complicit. It was as Il-hyung had said: When it came to Jae she no longer wished to be curious.

She staggered out of the crowded hospital lobby and strangers eyed her warily as she bumped into them. Outside, the sun hurt her eyes and she stood in the dwindling late afternoon warmth, knowing where she had to go but unable to decide how to get there.

There was so much she did not understand, but she no longer trusted herself to do the guesswork, in her ability to interpret his actions. To know him was to seek those who had known him in a life he had lived without her.

An hour later, Sae arrived at Taehan Group headquarters, where a small group of journalists stood idly waiting like bored schoolchildren. They did not notice her as she hurried up the steps to the lobby. It was only as she approached the elevators that a thin security guard stopped her.

"I need to see Kim Yung," she said breathlessly.

The guard had a faint smile on his lips, as though this request amused him. "And you are?"

"Tell his secretary that I've come to him about Geun-ye," she said, feeling the guard's dismissive gaze on her scuffed shoes and worn jeans.

The guard reached for the phone, unhurried, and murmured something she could not hear to the person on the other end of the line. Shock had altered her sense of time, and the call seemed to extend for what felt like hours. The gleaming lights of the empty lobby seemed to taunt her. After a long while, he put down the receiver and led her to the elevator.

A young secretary in a navy suit was waiting for her when the doors opened, and motioned for Sae to follow her. At the end of the long corridor a panoramic window framed a view of the majestic mountains standing guard over the old royal palaces. A view reserved only for the privileged few. The secretary opened the door to a conference room. Kim Yung sat at the end of a long table, his hands gathered together in a gesture of patience. The media presented him as a soft-spoken man with a tentative manner. There had been concerns that he would not be the incisive decision-maker the Chairman was, and a risky choice for the position of successor. But in person, he was a formidable presence. He had an intimidating gravity about him that in another context, she realized, could be construed as charismatic. She stole a glance at his face, searching for Jae's features in his before forcing herself to look away.

"I think you know who I am," she said quietly.

"Why, your reputation at the paper precedes you . . ." he said, almost pleasantly. "You're quite the dedicated journalist, even working off the clock."

The resemblance was not in any feature as much as it was in his voice. It was Yung she had heard the first night she had been at Myongwolgwan. To be in a room with the ghost of Jae's voice struck her more forcefully than sitting with his body.

"I've just come from the morgue," she said quietly.

"Ah," he said, the sound dying a soft death in his throat.

He did not offer any more. When she could trust that she could speak evenly, she continued, "I'm hoping you can tell me why the body of my husband, Jae, is labeled as your dead brother?"

Yung sank back in his chair, his eyes never wavering from hers. He seemed undecided about whether there was still a way to turn her out of the room. He wiped the table in front of him and leaned forward with gathered hands. "Why do you think? Sometimes it's the simplest answer. He was my brother. The thorn in my side. Full of surprises. Even his arrival in the world was a surprise. He was a half brother—a fledgling picked up at the front gate, left by some careless mistress. He was my father's favorite, you know. Until he arrived, we thought Father was incapable of love. Those of us who actually cared about the family business, it sickened us. I'm the eldest son. The obvious heir to the business. But Father only had eyes for Geun-ye."

"You were threatened by him," she said.

There was a pause. Kim Yung looked across the table as though someone was seated there.

"Jealous? Maybe. Threatened, no. Geun-ye never showed any interest in the family business. He was a quiet kid, doodling in his sketchbooks. But he did like to ask questions. I think Father enjoyed being challenged by him."

This image of Jae bent over his notebooks, his hair falling in his eyes, the hint of his tongue at the corner of his mouth, brought tears to her eyes. In the absence of family, it had felt as though Jae had belonged wholly to her. To hear him described so intimately by a stranger was jarring.

"Then suddenly I saw a change in him that began to concern me. He started to ask my father questions about his factories. Geun-ye said he wanted to learn more about Taehan Group's operations. Father was having trouble with his workforce at the time. There was talk of unionizing. Geun-ye offered to help, said he would try to understand the perspectives of the workers so he could advise Father on how he might lead them. It took us all by surprise. My father the most. You should have seen his face. He seemed ready to give Geun-ye the whole company there and then. My father's worst fear was that we would never experience adversity, that we would be spoiled. No one would believe who we were based on how we dressed. That was Father back then. Austere. He wanted us to know about poverty. So imagine his delight when Geun-ye volunteered to work on the production lines, saying he wanted to learn the business from the bottom up, giving himself a different name so that no one would suspect who he was. Father loved the idea and reveled in the fact that he had a spy in his rebellious workforce."

Sae remembered Jae's discomfort on seeing her at the factory when the Chairman had visited him there, and his desertion of her after the fact. Other memories quickly followed, him grinning at the station on seeing her after a week's separation, the light in his eyes after a day's monotonous work. Sae wanted to believe the love was real, even if nothing else had been. Her hunger for the truth wrestled with her desire to leave. The truth was a flame she wanted to curl away from.

"Did you believe him?" she asked.

"It seemed so sudden, I was immediately suspicious. I wanted to know about Geun-ye's intentions. I planted some contacts at the university to find out what he was up to. It wasn't difficult. So many poor students willing to rat out their fellow classmates. Imagine my relief when I found out that Geun-ye had joined the student movement. It was a better outcome than I could have ever wished for. I wanted to tell Father immediately—to expose his son as trying to wreak havoc and revolution in his own factory. But Father was never going to take it from me. It was better to wait and allow things to play out on their own."

"You wanted him to be arrested, for the Chairman to learn of his activities that way," she guessed.

"Something like that," he said, smiling faintly. "I figured it was only a matter of time. But there was no plan. I certainly didn't expect some idiot to set fire to himself in protest at the factory. On the evening of the fire, my father was in another city, overseeing a building project across the country. I was called to attend to the situation. They led me to the body of the worker. There was some confusion as to who he was. As I stared at his charred remains an idea came to me. Geun-ye had been arrested, along with a handful of other workers who had participated in the protest. I visited the prison where Geun-ye was being held. He was in isolation, afraid. No one had touched him. No one suspected who he was. He was weeping. He had no idea that I had been following his advancement into the student protests. He thought that I had only just uncovered what he was up to. It was a pathetic sight. He was pleading with me. What he was most afraid of in that moment was being found out. No one in the movement, he said, knew who he was. He was ashamed of Father's empire. Of who he was. If only Father could hear it! His favorite son, his intended heir, wanted to disavow all of it when all I had ever wanted was a fraction of the time Father gave to him. I wanted to leave him there to rot. I wanted him gone. So I proposed a deal. I would arrange for his release if he disappeared. He could live as he wanted, as someone who had been excised from the family. And I would tell Father that it was Geun-ye who had died in the fire."

Sae sat stunned by this act of audacity. "But the news . . . it was announced that Geun-ye had died in a car accident?"

"That was decided sometime later for the sake of the press. After all, could you imagine the message that would send? Imagine the headlines: *The Chairman's son self-immolates in protest over working conditions!* The shame of it. No, Father wouldn't accept that. So a car accident was fabricated. No one inquired or interrogated the facts too closely. And privately our family gathered to mourn over some unnamed worker's body. I had cut Geun-ye loose and secured my place. Father would never know, and I was assured that he would see me then, that I was to step into my position as heir."

Sae wanted to rise and return to that cold body in the morgue, to shake it. Why had he concealed who he was? She would have respected his bravery in challenging not only the system but the values of his own family. What was it that he did not trust? Himself or her?

"You knew about us," she said.

He shrugged. "When I found out about you, I knew he was never going to be a threat to our family or my father's business. He was just another man who had lost his mind and his principles to his pants."

This assessment of Jae's commitment to the movement was as repulsive to her as the way he had said it. This was the man who had presided over their marriage.

"So why involve him in the Tower?" she said after a while.

He scoffed at this. "You look at me like I'm a monster, but he came to me. For years I heard nothing from him. He kept his side of the bargain, lived a quiet life. Then one day he reemerged, asking for work. He was desperate, he said, and he had a family to support now. I offered him money, but he was too full of pride to be paid off. So I introduced him to Mr. Bae, an ambitious employee of mine who had been clamoring for a promotion. Created a company that did the dregs of the construction work that wasn't worth Taehan Group's time. It was easier to keep him close and have someone to keep an eye on him."

The large glass windows in the conference room were sealed and the room felt airless. It was a claustrophobic feeling to realize how small Jae's world had been. How controlled. She understood, too, that she was treading on something else.

"And then when you discovered the structural problems with the Tower, you hired them to fix the building under the cover of constructing a swimming pool," she said.

There was a stalled silence, and Kim Yung leaned back in his chair and eyed her wearily.

"You threatened him," she said, suddenly realizing. "Jae wouldn't have done this. He wouldn't have put all of those lives at risk."

Yung laughed. "You say that as someone who knew him so well."

He seemed to enjoy the sight of her face falling and tapped the table with his finger as if to emphasize his point.

"Did you know what a coward he was? He was terrified. It wasn't difficult at all to make him see why he had to participate in our little renovation. After everything I had done for him—I saved him from prison, I allowed the two of you to have the life of poverty that you so wished to have! If it were me, I would have taken the money!"

This description of their life together, as a permitted, controlled arrangement, was so diminishing that for a moment it felt as if he had squeezed the breath out of her. She looked away. This, she understood, was a diversion. When she felt able to control her voice, she said in a low voice, "You inherited the Tower. Your father oversaw its construction. The failures of structural integrity are all his. Why do all of this?" Then, before he could answer, she realized. "You wanted to prove yourself to the Chairman."

Yung scoffed. "Clever. And yet you claim you didn't know about Geun-ye? Or maybe you did know. And you were waiting for the right moment to exploit the family connection."

"You're disgusting," she said, rising to her feet. "A thousand people have died, who knows how many more are still lying under that rubble? The public is going to find out about this."

"You seem to forget that I'm a man of considerable resources."

"I know about your bid for the paper. But you can't buy every newspaper in the country, or pay off every witness."

"Can't I? I've found that people are easily persuaded by money," he said with a faint smile.

"You're wrong about Jae. He believed in what we were fighting for." She had crossed the room to the door when Yung spoke again.

"Seung-min and Hoon-min," he began. "My own nephews and I've never even met them. I'd like to. I hear they enjoy the preschool by your apartment, though they probably loved your mother's place in Mallipo even more. These wide-open spaces, they're so great for the kids. The city is just so filthy—"

Every fiber of her body seemed to shudder in response to the knowledge that he had been watching them.

Yung gave her a lopsided smile. He was a man who was used to getting what he wanted, and Sae could see it satisfied him that he had cornered her. "I find the city a very unsafe place to be. Don't you agree? So much traffic on these narrow alleyways. Why, just the other day I read this terrible story about some hit-and-run driver who knocked down a mother in front of her kindergartner. The world is such a scary place, don't you think?"

FORTY-SEVEN DAYS AFTER THE COLLAPSE

Myong-hee set the tape on the table. "I want to talk to you about what's on this tape."

Sprawled lazily on the sofa, Yung looked unmoved at the sight of it.

"I'm not interested in what other companies are doing right now. I'm just trying to keep my own house in order. I told you that," he said irritably.

"This is about your house."

"Go on," he said, pressing his chin against his chest as he lit a cigarette.

"There was never any swimming pool, was there? You set L&S Engineering up."

"This whole detective bit." Yung gave her a lopsided smile, as if amused by this turn in conversation. "It suits you."

Myong-hee ignored this. "You knew the building was unstable. You asked Mr. Bae to fix the building, but you knew there was a chance that it might collapse. It's all here, on this tape."

He sat up, leaning over to tap the ashes away from his cigarette, widely missing the ashtray. Sitting with his elbows on his knees, he wiped his face with his hand. "So what?"

"All these years, I've been handing you information. I've

watched you sabotage small companies, stealing their ideas before they have a chance to grow, interrupting deals, undercutting prices. Taehan Group is bigger than ever, and I'm still here."

Myong-hee saw the tension in his jaw and realized she was finally getting to him. Yung nodded rapidly as if in agreement with some internal thought. "You want money, is that it?"

"This tape implicates the Chairman. You say on it that he knew about the instability in the Tower. This tape could be the end of Taehan Group."

Yung began to laugh. "Are you blackmailing me?"

"Without what I've done for you all these years, Taehan Group wouldn't be where it is today. I want to be paid what I deserve."

The smile disappeared from his face. "How much, exactly, do you want?"

Sae walked through the crowd of protesters, toward the shrine honoring the lives of those who had perished in the Tower. Since she had left Kim Yung's office, she had been unable to eat or sleep, wondering if she was still a believer. In all of those years she'd been in dogged pursuit of truth, she had never considered what one did with it. Had never considered the weight of it. Of its capacity to strip people of their lives. Of their hope. Of their faith in a God. In justice. In the goodness of others.

Those still hoping to find the remains of their loved ones pitched tents on the land from which the Tower rose, cooking on hot plates and using portable toilets. As she walked past these tents she saw the placards that told the stories of the lives cut short: the cigarette vendor who had gone in for only a moment to use the Tower's restroom, the retiree who had gone to buy an anniversary present, the hundreds of workers who had worked in the offices on the upper floors.

And now Sae was to be complicit in burying the truth.

Riot police buses began to pull up at the perimeter of the site. The blockade, the presence of the police at the site of the building's collapse, invoked a former era. For weeks she had been in a state of shock, suspended from grief. With every body she had seen that was not Jae's, she had felt the timer set back, the ticking quieted and buried underground for a later hour. All of the restraint she had stacked against feeling during these hours and weeks seemed to crack, bursting open. And now she felt a blast move through her, the heat of it transforming the grief to a white rage. A woman offered a clipboard in her direction, and Sae shook her head. No signature, no petition was going to be enough. Nothing short of justice. A volunteer stood by one of the tents wiping at the sweat on his forehead. Sae saw the megaphone in his hand and strode toward him, taking it from him before he could protest. A crowd had gathered around one of the buses, and Sae used the metal bars over the windows to hoist herself onto the roof of the bus. Several protesters looked up at her in surprise. Here, she thought, she would have the crowd's attention. They would be her witnesses. If anything ever happened to her, those in the crowd would know.

"L&S Engineering is not responsible for what happened," Sae began, speaking into the megaphone. "We demand a full investigation of Taehan Group."

• • •

It wasn't until many hours later, when Sae called her mother from the police station to tell her that she was being released without charge, that she was told the news.

Seung-min had gone missing.

Hoon-min's body was rigid in her arms as he sobbed.

"Where is he?" he asked. "Did he go to Appa?"

Sae couldn't hear the police officers' questions over the sound of Hoon-min's crying. She tried to put him down, but he clambered up, scaling her legs, refusing to let go. Carrying him over to the sofa, she sat down with him on her lap. Her mother was pale and her lower lip trembled as she spoke. There was no question of involving the police in this. It was between Kim Yung and herself. And so she needed them to leave, so she could plead for forgiveness. She had imagined that she would be punished; she had flirted with her own death. This was worse.

"Let's go over this again," an officer with pockmarked cheeks said to Sae's mother.

"No, let's not," Sae snapped. They had already been at this for too long. What was Seung-min doing now? Was he with some stranger or alone in a room somewhere? What had he been told about why he was there?

The officers frowned, and one of them scribbled rapidly in his notebook.

"Why are you interrogating her? It's not her fault. You should be out there looking for him," Sae said.

The officers seemed to understand her impatience. "We need

to make sure we haven't missed anything before we begin the search."

"I only wanted to pick up a few things for dinner," her mother said. Her face seemed to spasm from the effort of holding back tears. "I was holding Hoon-min's hand; he never leaves my side. I was mulling over what cut of beef to buy, and when I looked up Seung-min had disappeared."

"He disappeared or he ran off?"

Her mother seemed taken aback by the question.

"Where would he run off to?"

"He's probably lost and unable to find his way home. That's the most likely scenario," the officer said, after a moment of scribbling something on his pad.

"He knows this neighborhood, he knows his way home. He should be back by now," her mother said. "It's not as though someone would take him, would they?"

The police officer tapped the notepad with the tip of his pen impatiently. "Is there anything we should know about?"

Sae shook her head, eager for the police to leave, but her mother shot Sae an inscrutable look.

"He was sad," her mother said. "About the disappearance of his father."

Sae looked at her mother in surprise. Seung-min was unsettled, but had he been distressed? Where had she been all of these weeks? Everywhere but with him. He and Hoon-min were the ones she loved most, and they were the hardest to be alone in a room with. All these weeks she had been in a state of avoidance. She had pushed him into the arms of a grandmother he had never known, abandoning him in a countryside home that was unfamiliar to him.

The officers exchanged looks. "So there's a possibility that his father might have taken—"

"No, he's dead," she said, cutting him off. She wanted them to go. To be able to spring into action, to think less, to not picture Seung-min alone in a room, or Seung-min in the weeks past, distressed and unseen by her. Only motion would allow her distance from these images. "He died at Aspiration Tower."

Hoon-min stiffened on her lap and smacked his head against her chest bone, a low cry building from his throat.

"Seung-min die too?" Hoon-min asked.

"No, no," Sae said, shaking her head, staring up at the sharp light on the ceiling as her eyes began to well up. She needed to move quickly, needed the police officers to leave, she needed to remove the weight of Hoon-min, suddenly unbearable on her thighs.

FORTY-EIGHT DAYS AFTER THE COLLAPSE

All evening, Myong-hee moved from room to room making an inventory of the equipment—television sets, karaoke machines, the heavy marble coffee tables—that might be sold off in the weeks to come. Selling off items individually would mean that she would make less money than if she sold off the whole business with the girls' labor included, but she hoped that the removal of the items would help the next owners to envision a different use for the space. It would also take her more time and require more of her, but she was in no rush; the sale of the items would just about cover the lion's share of her debt, and the money Yung had agreed to pay her would be enough to keep her afloat for decades to come.

Earlier that day, Myong-hee had withdrawn most of her savings to distribute among the girls, hoping that the payment would give them courage to seek a new direction. In the morning she would call a realtor and find a tenant for her apartment. She and Song-mi would find a house—a child would need a garden and space to roam—outside of the city, somewhere in Gyeonggi-do, near the lakes.

The prospect of this new beginning buoyed her. Even the possibility that she might never receive a letter from her daughter felt less punishing. She would devote all of that lost love to

Song-mi's child, giving it the comforts she had been unable to give to her own.

Myong-hee walked into the last room and picked up the mic on the table, feeling the weight of it in her hand. Raising it to her lips, she began to sing. She couldn't remember the last time she had sung only for herself and not for anyone else.

Sae stood in the phone booth. Hoon-min's cries were still echoing in her head as she picked up the receiver.

"It's Sae," she said when Kim Yung answered.

"I was wondering when you'd call," he said dryly.

"If this is about this afternoon . . ." she said, her heart hammering wildly in her chest. "I just need to know that Seung-min is all right. If I could just—"

"I heard about that little stunt of yours. You don't believe anyone will take you seriously? That's not why I had to take the boy."

She pressed her finger against her ear to try to hear him better over the thundering rain.

"I don't understand," she began, squeezing her eyes shut. Whatever she had done she would make amends. "I just need to hear his voice, to know that he's all right."

"You haven't told him about his father. You made it easy for me. He came along without any trouble when I told him we were going to see his dad."

Sae ignored this jab.

"If it isn't about this afternoon then what is it?" she asked.

"You've developed quite the friendship with the madam at Myongwolgwan. She has some tapes that are of interest."

It took a moment to register the impressions of the past few weeks—Myong-hee's permissiveness in allowing her access to the tapes, Song-mi's reference to Myong-hee's conversations with Kim Yung. She was being used in some way she didn't understand.

"There's no way she'll let me—"

"I've always found a mother is most resourceful when it comes to her children," he said, cutting her off.

A bus roared by, and then all she heard was a click before the line went dead.

Myong-hee heard a rap on the rear door of the club and glanced at her watch. It was earlier than Yung had promised—she was not expecting him to arrive with the cash for another two hours. Feeling the wall for the light switch in the darkness, she stiffened at the sight of Sae standing at the entrance, her wet hair clinging to the sides of her face, looking condemned.

In the days since she had seen Sae, Myong-hee found herself turning their last conversation over in her mind. Was it naïvety or bravery that led Sae to believe that Taehan Group could be brought to justice?

"I need the tape," Sae said. The hostility in her voice was sharp and surprising.

"The tape isn't going to bring him back."

"He's dead," Sae said in a flat voice. "I need the tape." Sae pushed past her. Her eyes swept the room as she frantically scanned the surfaces of her office. "Where is it?"

"I can't give it to you."

"He took Seung-min."

Myong-hee saw Sae's eyes fall on the scissors on her desk

and understood the danger, the wildness of Sae's grief. She was a woman now capable of anything. Myong-hee stood rigid, unable to move or speak as Sae pulled out drawer after drawer. When Myong-hee moved toward her, Sae picked up the scissors and pointed them at her, her hand trembling.

"I can take the lies and the years of dishonesty. I don't understand why he had to humiliate me, why he didn't want to tell me the truth. But I won't let them take Seung-min from me. You of all people should understand that."

"Put down the scissors," Myong-hee said calmly, understanding at last. "Yung sent you, didn't he? Don't let him manipulate you into becoming someone you're not. You hurt me and you won't see Seung-min again either."

Sae's eyes widened and she was weeping, her face full of shock and horror. She backed against the wall and the scissors clattered to the ground.

"Then I'll beg you. I am begging you. I need him," she said, on her knees. "They can have Jae, or Geun-ye, or whoever he was in the end. But not Seung-min."

Myong-hee's head snapped up. "What did you say?"

Small nosed and delicate eyed, he had been the smaller one of the twins. The one she had happily handed over, to Secretary Gong. It wasn't until many months later that she read it in the newspaper. They had named him Geun-ye.

He was the one she had sent out with confidence into the world. She had imagined a life filled with tutors, squeaky white trainers at the turn of every season, hand-ground pine nut porridge spooned into the mouth during bouts of mild illness. It was only through Yung's stories that she pieced together a different life. The Chairman's wife's bitter indifference. The Chairman's militaristic austerity. The beatings and harsh punishments. His inhumane demands. Listening to Yung's account of their domestic world had become its own form of torture. She turned away from these stories, searching for hope in her daughter's life.

Geun-ye became the raw wound buried under a mound of salt. She had once believed she could not have offered much better, only a loving touch, an assurance that he belonged somewhere. But when she heard the unlikely story that he had died alone in a car accident, and suspected suicide, it had occurred to her perhaps she had been wrong. Perhaps love and assurance would have helped him to weather the life of poverty he would have faced with her.

Myong-hee stared at Sae in bewilderment, her disbelief that Geun-ye had been alive all this time mingled with the desperate wish for it to be true. Sae was still kneeling before her, her shoulders shuddering. Myong-hee knelt beside her and placed her hand on Sae's face.

Myong-hee had been a fool. Yung had used her. The idea that he would rather take a child and pit another woman against her than pay her a fraction of what she had helped him to earn should have surprised her, but it did not. It was his father's way. She should have known better. The house by the lake, the hours spent in the garden with a toddler, the alleviation from debt, was dissolving from her future. She reached for a hidden compartment in the desk and removed the tape.

"Let's go," she said, grasping Sae by the elbow, helping her onto her feet. "I'll drive you."

Sae looked at her, confused.

"Geun-ye," Myong-hee said, his name catching in her throat. "He was my son."

Myong-hee drove them through the murmuring lights of the leafy residential roads. Yung had inherited the Chairman's old house, and she knew the way by heart, though it had been years since she had been there. Both of them sat encased in silence, Myong-hee unable to look over at Sae but aware of her trembling. For weeks Myong-hee had admired Sae's determination and self-assurance, her smart polish. That Yung was trying to strip her of her spirit by taking the boy enraged her.

They parked in front of a property surrounded by a high gray wall. As a simple iron gate slid open, Myong-hee could see the home in all its monstrosity. A gray and boxy structure, cold and modern, it looked like an expensive prison.

The stone steps led to a modest garden in which nothing seemed to grow—only a few hedges that had been disciplined into stern inorganic shapes. A uniformed woman met them at the door and silently led them to a living room. Two men in suits, presumably security guards, stood in the corners of the room.

The living room had been painted a deep blue, and Myong-hee could smell the underlay of fresh paint expanding in her head, giving her a headache. It was filled with Danish midcentury furniture—a rebellion against the heavy mahogany pieces favored by an older generation, the mix of Western classical pieces with expensive Korean antiques. Yung stood by the window, the top button of his shirt undone, and greeted them like long-lost relatives.

"Well, I wasn't expecting both of you. Nice to see that the ladies are friends now."

Sae let out a little sound, and it was only then that Myong-hee saw the boy in a heap on the edge of the sofa.

Yung stopped Sae from moving toward him.

"You have something for me."

"Why isn't he moving?" she asked.

Yung shrugged. "Kid was making a fuss so I gave him something to shut him up."

Myong-hee's sight grew blurry; Yung's features seemed to melt in her vision. She had been so eager to have access to Geun-ye that she had not seen Yung for who he was. How could Myong-hee have trusted him to be the watchful eye in the Chairman's household? When Yung had worshipped his father as he did? Seung-min was no more human to him than a pawn.

Yung beckoned Myong-hee over.

"Do you have it?" he asked, impatient.

Myong-hee removed the tape from her bag and handed it to him.

"I trust it's the only copy."

"And if it's not?"

He let out a little exasperated breath.

"A person should have a sense of her place in the world. Do you really think you would have come this far without me? I value loyalty, understand?"

"Don't talk to me about loyalty," Myong-hee said.

Yung removed his hand from Sae's shoulder and she lunged for the boy, stroking his face. He was unresponsive, and as she picked him up she struggled under the heavy, sleeping weight of him.

"I hope this will teach you to live quietly. Humbly. Consider this a warning."

It was almost four in the morning by the time Myong-hee returned to her apartment. As she walked through the thin darkness, she saw that Song-mi had fallen asleep on the sofa, the TV remote still in her hand. Myong-hee crossed the room, rolled back the sleeves of her cardigan, and ran the tap. She washed her hands, rinsed her tired eyes, the back of her neck. Stupidly, it was the sight of the creeping mildew in the caulking of the vinyl window frame that brought tears to her eyes. For years she had tried to keep her home meticulously clean, this space she had kept with the hopes that one day she could welcome a guest who was not a guest but family. Tomorrow she would have to vacate the apartment to settle her debts.

She pressed her palms against her face and smoothed the tears across her cheeks, drying her hands on her skirt. She would pack tonight, she would keep moving; there would be plenty of time for rage later. Quietly she gathered a few items—a warm winter coat, the documents she had filled out years ago at the orphanage, several slim gold rings she could sell once she was out of the city. She hesitated at the sight of the business card she had been given by Mr. Byun, who had made her think she could do something about the tapes in the first place, and then tossed it angrily into the trash bin.

She went into the room she had given Song-mi to get the thin envelope of cash she had hidden behind the bookcase. The room was a mess. Several pieces of clothing lay in a pile on a chair—discarded, it seemed, on account of her expanding waist. There was an adolescent touch, too, in the photographs she had taped to her mirror, and the appointment card for her next checkup at the doctor's. Myong-hee placed the envelope of cash on top of the pile of clothes.

Tomorrow they would vacate this apartment and go their separate ways. Myong-hee had nothing to offer Song-mi: no work, no certainty of where she could go; worst of all, she had no hope left to give. What more could she offer her now than a little rest, a few more hours of peaceful, unknowing sleep?

TWENTY-TWO YEARS AFTER THE COLLAPSE

2014

At the end of the courtyard and over the stone wall is a view of the unforgiving sea. At high tide, Ansando appears to be an island, floating independently of the peninsula. It is only as the tides recede that several beaches emerge, uncovering a narrow sandy path leading back to the mainland. Every evening, Sae walks to the top of the hillside along a path of rough fern brush to watch the tide rise, the sea severing its tie to the land. Here she stands overlooking the water, watching nature's act of cleaving, thinking of her mother, of Seung-min and of Jae.

She has lived here for almost two decades, managing a five-room hanok inn where old books collect dust on their unopened wings. She lives in a permanent state of minor emergency. There is much to be fixed; nothing is ever fully repaired. Several roof tiles are missing, the water pressure has slowed to a trickle. Little has been done to update the kitchen—its shelves are cluttered with half-filled condiments, the fridge with ancient pickles and kimchi, fried gochujang. She allows herself only one small stove, using the ancient metal pot to make rice for the lodgers. Her hands are red and raw from cleaning the steel pot, but she does little to simplify her routine, does little to contract time.

• • •

"It's working now," Hoon-min says, wiping his hands on his jeans. He wears his hair long and his horn-rimmed glasses make him look scholarly. Still, she can make out the sweet features that marked his face as a toddler. Unlike Seung-min, who is the spitting image of Jae, Hoon-min is hers—they share the same mushroom nose and round chin. Yet this rare visit from France has presented someone who has matured beyond his years, and she hardly recognizes the long-limbed and lean man before her.

"Come and look," he says.

Sae rubs her hands on her apron and steps into the inn to observe the small box lit up with several flashing lights.

"Here," Hoon-min says, handing her the laptop. "This is how you connect to the Wi-Fi."

He points to an icon at the top right-hand corner of the screen and clicks.

"Why can't I just call you?" Sae says, sitting beside him. "I don't need email. I like hearing your voice."

Hoon-min smiles patiently. "Like I said, this way we'll be able to see each other on video, too. And you can reach me by radio when I am on the boat. You can tune in to the frequency, using this website."

"That would be nice," she admits, stealing a glance at him. It is true that she would like to speak to him as often as she wishes to. Having grown up by the sea, Hoon-min has cultivated a love of marine life, and this love has taken him far away from her. He spends months at a time on a boat on the Atlantic, excavating the ocean floor. He likes to tell her that they know only 20 percent of the ocean, that the rest remains a mystery. She wonders if it is her fault. Whether she is the one who has nurtured this curiosity by holding back so much from him and Seung-min.

"There's also this," he says, leaning over her to type some words in a white box with a blinking cursor. "See here, you can follow news stories in real time."

Sae nods but lowers her eyes, staring at a cracked tile on the floor. She stopped following the news many years ago. Since Seung-min was returned to her, she has learned that she must tread carefully, for many things can tip her back into that darkened place, back to sleeping all day and night, to not eating until she is shaking so badly that she cannot hold a steady spoon to her mouth. As a student, Sae had experienced fear as a physical, animalistic sensation—the quickened beat of her heart, a heightened awareness of her surroundings, a pulsating in her veins—a feeling that receded the moment the immediate danger had been removed. It was only after Seung-min was returned to her that she understood what fear could do to break the spirit. The central instrument of torture was not pain; the central mechanism of interrogations was the dismantling of the spirit. This was how dissidents were disarmed: Fear emptied the body of feeling, until they became mere husks, no longer all there, no longer a threat.

Her world is a narrow one, controlled. She has turned her back to the news, to all of her connections beyond Ansando. There is no need to try to summon her former attachments, no need to *engage*, if she does not know what is happening in the world.

"You could also promote the inn online, get more lodgers," Hoon-min insists, his voice losing conviction as his gaze falls on fragments of roof tile in the otherwise empty courtyard.

"If you think it's best," she says noncommittally. She does not recognize this new digital world, though theoretically she understands its inherent power. In spreading information instantaneously, she thinks that what happened at Gwangju could not possibly happen today. Yet she has also seen the way some of her lodgers talk about their sense of enslavement to their machines and suspects that constant connection may be weaponized in the form of surveillance. Though she longs for more contact with Seung-min, she worries that doing so online will endanger them.

"Let me show you how to make a call," Hoon-min offers.

Clicking a blue icon on the screen, he types in Seung-min's number. Seung-min has not been to visit her for more than three years, first mired by visa troubles, then later claiming he could not get the time off work. It is early in the morning for her, late afternoon for him. They live in opposing rhythms, separated by more than mere latitudes. It is a point of contention that she will not leave Ansando. He resents her rootedness to the place of her dissolution, that she will not leave the island for him. So he does not come to visit, and with every passing year he drifts further away from her.

The computer screen shows that the call is processing. She wishes to see his face, though to see Seung-min is to be flooded with feeling. To look at her son is difficult, like forcing herself to stare into a too-bright light.

"Hoon-min set you up," Seung-min says as soon as he answers. He senses her ambivalence to him, the man he has come to resemble, but she has never told him what it is in him that she cannot embrace. The shadow returns to his face. The withdrawal is subtle, but Sae is aware of it. "I'm in the middle of my workday; I'll call you later."

Before she can say any more, he is gone. He will not return her call. The boys are aware that there is something in their history akin to a buried bomb. They tread lightly in their conversations, like insects on water. But Sae knows that Seung-min has not forgiven her evasions, the way they have made his own memories of his father small.

Hoon-min looks at her, worried. She allows herself to squeeze his shoulder, to reassure him that it is okay. She reluctantly permits herself these maternal gestures. She may have failed them, but she is still their mother.

Shortly after Seung-min was returned to her all those years ago, Sae's mother was killed in a hit-and-run accident. It was late in the afternoon, an hour of light foot traffic. Witnesses reported that a motorcyclist struck her as she was walking home on a wide road. Sae could not let go of the suspicion that it was not an accident but another warning from Yung.

Sae became increasingly skittish, swinging wildly from moments of frantic motion—packing their things, checking for the fifth time that the doors were locked—to catatonic stillness. When Sae had found Seung-min groggy on Yung's sofa, she understood the enormity of her mistake. She had placed her excavation for the truth ahead of his safety. She had not considered the vulnerability of her strong-willed, independent child. She who hardly knew how to keep him safe. It seemed to her that all the truths she held dearly—that she had a husband she was intimate with, that she was a good enough mother, that one should fight to bring the truth to light no matter what the cost—could be turned on their heads. A life of certainty and safety no longer seemed available to her. Better to distance herself, then, from any interest or tendency of her former self.

With dwindling savings and a small payout from her mother's life insurance, they moved to the outskirts of the city. Sae felt they were safer there, but still, they moved every few months, each place more remote than the last, orbiting farther and farther from Seoul, until finally they moved to a village of fewer than a hundred residents. Even then, she could not be sure if this was enough. How was she to know what was best for them? She could no longer trust her judgment.

In the end, her indecision was the decision. The crisis of uncertainty led to paralysis. One afternoon, Sae simply lay down and grew still. At first the boys crawled over her as she lay staring at the ceiling, trying to engage her in play. They tried misbehaving to get her attention. When they could not shake her from her stillness, they became afraid. They tried to revive her by lying beside her, telling her stories as Jae had sometimes done with them. Then finally, they resigned. They had to fend for themselves.

Two years passed. The boys, five and seven, found their way to school and were raised on neighborly pity—donations of food, the stacks of charcoal to heat their floors in the winter, the hand-me-down jackets left on their front doorstep. Despite their mother's silences and refusal to disclose what had happened, they sensed that they were running from some threat. That the world was hostile and dangerous. They were wary of strangers outside of their small community. So when an elegantly dressed older woman with swept-up hair appeared in the courtyard of their house, they were on their guard.

"Is your mother home?" she asked.

The boys exchanged glances. Seung-min shook his head slightly so that Hoon-min understood not to respond.

"I'm a friend of your mother's," she offered.

This confused them. As far as they knew, their mother had no friends. Seung-min kicked the ball to Hoon-min, urging him to continue with their game. Silence, they had learned, was the easiest form of protection. The woman would realize her mistake and move on. Hoon-min kicked the ball back and it rolled into a puddle and splashed her expensive-looking shoes with mud. The boys froze. She seemed not to notice. She was studying their faces with the expectant expression of someone waiting for a loved one to emerge from a crowd. When she caught them staring at her shoes, she stepped forward to kick the ball back to Hoon-min. He hesitated. From the corner of his eye he could see Seung-min shaking his head, but he passed it back to her. She ran to meet the ball, hooting a little as she tried to balance herself on her heels. Seung-min attempted to intercept it, trying to interrupt their play, but she swiftly rolled the ball underfoot and passed to Hoon-min, leaving Seung-min's jaw gaping in surprise.

They played like this for what felt like a long time, until the woman took out a handkerchief to pat at the sweat along her hairline and her upper lip.

Hoon-min approached her with the ball tucked under his arm. "She's inside. My mom. She sleeps all the time."

Seung-min shot him a look but returned his gaze back to her expectantly.

"Well," she said, smoothing her skirt as if undecided about what to do. "Let's not wake her." She looked into the kitchen and then back at them, staring at their hole-ridden T-shirts, their slender calves. "When is the last time you boys ate anything?"

The woman ordered them a feast—deep-fried pork in sweet and sour sauce, dumplings, black bean noodles—that they lapped up like stray dogs. Afterward she hosed them down and scrubbed them mercilessly with a green exfoliating washcloth, rubbing off all that was dead on them.

"You're not here to take us away, are you?" Seung-min asked nervously, as she teased the dirt in his scalp with her long fingernails.

"No," she said, squeezing the water from his hair before drying it with a towel, just like Sae used to.

"Who are you?" Hoon-min asked.

"My name's Myong-hee," she said. "You can call me Emo."

Emo became the one constant of their childhood turned young adulthood. Every week they looked forward to her arrival on Saturday mornings when she would check their homework and prepare banchan and multiple soups—oxtail for their growing bones, miyeok-guk for the iron in their blood, fishbone broth to restore their mother's energy—for them to devour during the week. On Sundays she would take them to the market for new shoes or a haircut. On occasion she took them to gaming arcades in the nearest city and to restaurants. Later, as they grew older, she would give them envelopes of money to spend on after-school classes, encouraging them to work hard, promising to help them if they wished to continue their studies abroad. She let them know they could have any future they chose. They loved her for knowing what they needed before they even ventured to ask, but what the boys loved most was what their emo did for their mother, getting her out of bed, dressing her, in turns cajoling and scolding her into eating, into becoming human again.

Years later, when Sae recovered from her depression, she found that she no longer knew how to talk to the boys. She spoke to them as three- and five-year-olds, when they had already drifted into nine and eleven. They welcomed her back, though the knowledge of her love as an unsteady thing had changed them. They were like survivors of an earthquake, always ready for an emergency, for the earth to come apart beneath their feet, for her to love and retreat.

Even after Sae's recovery, Seung-min felt his mother was an actor who had another life elsewhere, with thoughts and attachments outside of her performance. This other mother was the one he longed for, a part of her that he remembered from childhood, a part that seemed just beyond his reach. She would nurse him if he woke with a fever, would pack his lunches or give him snacks if he was studying late into the night, hug him if he opened his arms to her, but would never look at him.

He became curious about the shape of his face, the thick, wild eyebrows, the eyes which took the shape of cashews when he smiled. It was only when he found a photograph of his parents in between the pages of a book of poetry that it occurred to him that the reason she would not look at him had something to do with his father. In his few scattered memories of him, his father had been warm and loving. Seung-min remembered his mother's laughter, the comfort of her visible happiness. He did not understand what had happened for that love to become a secret thing to be buried quietly and without ceremony.

Whenever Seung-min tried to ask her about the past, Sae would leave the room, grow silent, or take to her bed. To dig for the past was to risk losing her. To seek his father was to abandon his mother.

He consoled himself by drawing, sketching portraits of the photographs he had found of their family. He would leave his sketches for his mother at the kitchen table, but they remained untouched, like a meal for a guest who would never arrive.

As he grew older, practical art beckoned him. If he could not dig, he wished to build. He had hoped that a pragmatic edge to his work would change the way his mother viewed his sketches, but she seemed to like his attraction to architecture even less, until eventually he felt that there was something unlovable in him.

It was Emo who encouraged his work. She seemed to look at him, always, through the lens of second chances. It was Emo who said she would support him if he wanted to pursue a degree in architecture. On the evening he announced that he had been accepted to the architectural school in Berkeley, California, he thought his mother might offer to go with him. But she didn't. Nothing would move her from Ansando.

Hoon-min must return to the sea, to his work. A weeklong visit disappears in a swipe. His presence has revived her senses. The inn seems more porous without him; she feels the wind slicing its way through the gaps in the paper doors. The place is too quiet, more weathered. Sae puts on her glasses and opens the laptop that Hoon-min has given her.

She clicks on various news stories. She learns that chemical weapons have been used in a war in Syria, that terrorists have abducted 200 schoolgirls in Nigeria. In search of lighter news, she clicks on an image of what looks like a whale floating on water. A new window opens and she sees that the whale is in fact a capsized ferry. The news tells the story of the heroic rescue of 350 schoolchildren on board early that morning. She closes her laptop before she finishes reading the article and rises to her feet. She leaves without her coat and begins to walk along the hillside. She surveys the ocean, as if looking for the glide of that ferry in the water, though Jindo-gun is hundreds of miles away.

She closes her eyes and imagines the parents reuniting with their children. Their relief palpable on the docks. She thinks of Seung-min. Her breath quickens as she remembers his delicate bird body pressed against her chest. She steps into the ocean, gasping at the icy grip of the water on her ankles. It helps her to steady her breath, erasing the thunder. The world has evolved, after all; lessons have been drawn from Aspiration Tower. The students have been saved.

Salvation, she thinks, comes for some.

In the office kitchen, Myong-hee places a teaspoon of ginger syrup in the teacup while waiting for the kettle to boil. It is an overcast day that blankets the sun. The traders are attentively looking at their screens; there is a murmur of hushed voices from across the trading floor. She hears the click of the kettle and pours the boiling water; she debates making another cup for Mr. Byun, who is running late. Myong-hee remains in the business of circulating information, making sure Mr. Byun has what he needs to help his clients to make profitable investments. It is a job of her own invention that she crafted when Song-mi refused to leave her.

On the morning that Myong-hee told Song-mi they had to vacate the apartment, Song-mi had blinked at her for a moment as though she was unsure why Myong-hee was telling her this. Then she stretched with one hand, rubbing her stomach with the other.

"When I found out I was pregnant, I went back to the orphanage where I grew up. I was hoping to find the other kids that I had grown up with. Everyone had dispersed, scattered. It wasn't the same. When you asked me to come stay with you, I felt chosen. I finally felt like I had a home. I thought a lot about what home meant. Is it a place? Or is it with people?"

Song-mi smiled at Myong-hee. "You didn't think you were moving without me, did you? Where are we going?"

This "we" changed everything. The first few months were difficult, and if not for Song-mi, Myong-hee thought she might have felt like she had come full circle, back to her days of being a destitute single mother. Scariest of all was the uncertainty of how they were to proceed financially. Myong-hee tried to find employment in offices or shops, but employers seemed to sense something of her history and turned her away. The little money Myong-hee had dwindled to almost nothing when Song-mi gave her Mr. Byun's crumpled business card.

"Where did you find this?" Myong-hee asked her, incredulous.

"I scooped it out before we left," she said. "Thought it might come in handy one day."

The deal Myong-hee had made with Mr. Byun was simple: She would relay relevant corporate information that she heard in the rooms, would inform him of key incipient relationships that would put him ahead of the markets, giving him an edge in his investments. In return he would help her to set up a new club and give her a cut of his investment earnings. Myong-hee was under no illusions that this was a new arrangement; she was forging an old pact with a new devil, but she did what she needed to survive.

Being an experienced manager, Myong-hee found it easy to set up a new room salon, the Mirage, quickly. Clients eagerly flocked to this new establishment when Myongwolgwan was taken over by new management and deteriorated in its services. Myong-hee hired a serious and astute manager to oversee the day-to-day operations so that anyone poking around would not know that she was involved.

Within a year, Myong-hee had found something that resembled stability. Song-mi gave birth to a healthy baby girl, and this new little family gave Myong-hee peace of mind; she was able to imagine, finally, that some stranger had been able to give her daughter the love Myong-hee had for her adopted family.

The new ghost haunting her was Sae. The thought that she had been someone important to Geun-ye, in a life beyond the Chairman's reach, had given her a sense of peace. Myong-hee had hoped to thank her and had gone back to visit the apartment to find it occupied with new tenants. None of the neighbors could tell her where they had gone. They had simply disappeared.

A person lost in the vastness of a foreign country was one thing, but in one's own backyard it was another. With the first paycheck she received from intelligence she passed on to Mr. Byun, she hired a private detective. Within months, she was led to a remote island village.

She finishes the last of the tea and is about to put the cup in the sink when she notices a flurry of activity, with several traders gathering around a single screen. She steps onto the trading floor. There is a news report that switches between footage of the ocean and what looks like a capsized boat. She rises, her heart at her throat, immediately thinking of Hoon-min, who has returned to sea. But as quickly as the fear comes, there is a burst of applause, exclamations of relief at a rescue of sorts. She continues to watch, listening to the harrowing story of the schoolchildren whose ferry capsized while on a school trip. Though the news reports a happy outcome, the story unsettles her. She smooths her dark pants, restless and impatient.

A notification pops up on the phone. It is a text message from Mr. Byun telling her that he will not make it to the office. Myong-hee feels relieved. She cannot shake off this anxiety; she is suddenly in no state to be in a meeting with him. Walking past the traders, who are now settled back at their desks, she finds an empty office and locks the door behind her. She logs on to the website Hoon-min gave her, to find the frequency of his radio aboard the boat. She wishes to hear his voice, if only for a moment, and even if it is to hear Hoon-min in conversation with someone else. She hears angry voices tuning in and out. There is an argument. It takes her several moments to realize that she has tuned in to the radios of Korean fishermen who are on the coast, near the ferry.

"Why are they telling them to stay put if no one is coming?"

"The civilian boats are ready to go, why are we being told to hold off?"

"Big naval effort, my ass. There's nothing out there."

Myong-hee continues to listen, pressing the headphones against her ears, the panic rising inside her like a fever. It is a feeling akin to the one that she had when she went to the orphanage so many years before and could not locate her child among the sea of children's faces. She rises. She must move. It's a lie; the students have not been rescued. Her thoughts swim toward Sae.

As soon as she can, Myong-hee takes a taxi to Seoul station. From Pyeongtaek, an hour away, she boards a train to Mallipo. Three hours later, she arrives to find that she has missed the last ferry to Ansando. She walks along the docks, unsure of what to do. A couple walk leisurely on the beach. Fishermen are reeling in their nets, unhurried. The sea is calm and unworried under the setting sun.

Myong-hee goes to the dock and approaches a fisherman.

"Will you take me to Ansando?" she asks.

He eyes her large ring and expensive-looking coat and shakes his head.

"The ferry leaves in the morning," he says after a while. He picks up the rope and begins wrapping it around his elbow.

Myong-hee hands him an envelope, and he looks at it in disbelief. In half an hour, they are on their way.

When she arrives at the island, she sees Sae walking on the beach with her hands stuffed into a light jacket, a pair of headphones over her head. Myong-hee can tell by Sae's face that the truth about the rescue is now public. She lingers for a moment, listening to the news report from a TV inside a corner store. The ferry has sunk even farther. The captain of the ferry has disappeared. Only 50 of the 476 people have been rescued so far. Children send text messages to their parents, telling them they have been instructed to stay in place on the sinking ferry as the water level slowly rises, that their phone batteries are running low, that they are texting to say *I love you* just in case . . . just in case . . .

Sae spots Myong-hee, running toward her, and the women hold each other, weeping.

TWENTY-FOUR YEARS AFTER THE COLLAPSE

2016

Sae pauses as she slices the zucchini on the cutting board and raises her hand to her head before wiping both hands on her apron. Glancing out of the kitchen window, she sees Myong-hee in the courtyard. There is something heavy in her movements, as if she is weighed down by bad news, but when her eyes meet Sae's her face brightens, her worries folded away. Myong-hee hands her a bag full of groceries and takes over the kitchen. Together they work silently, slicing tofu and onions. Sae dips the floured plaice in the egg batter and drops it onto the pan. Myong-hee cooks mugwort soup, steams fistfuls of spinach down to almost nothing and mixes it with sesame oil and soy sauce. They set up an altar with apples and chestnuts, dried fish and rice cakes. Offer cups of soju for the departed. A feast for the spirits on this anniversary of the Tower's collapse.

They leave the altar, allowing the spirits time to feed. Outside, it has begun sprinkling, a welcome reprieve from the stifling heat.

"Have you been following this news?" Myong-hee says, lighting a cigarette.

"You know I don't," Sae says.

"They're trying to oust President Park Geun-hye," Myong-hee says, studying Sae's face. "No one can say where she was when those kids were in the ferry. All that time when something could have been done."

The wind has picked up in another direction and blows the rain toward them, but Myong-hee makes no effort to step back inside. Sae looks up at the overcast sky. She would prefer to talk about something else.

"Reporters are sniffing around, interrogating the president's closest relationships. You begin to tug on that thread and it leads to predictable places."

Sae realizes that Myong-hee is not just making conversation but is trying to tell her something important. She pictures the boys and imagines where they are; there is a comfort in their distance. They are safer, she thinks, when they are not with her.

"There was a government employee who came into the Mirage. He was talking about the payments that the government has received from all the big conglomerates."

"Some things don't change, I guess."

"Yung's name has come up. This is a minister within the president's party, suggesting that Yung is a financier of sorts for the president, acting as a conduit in extracting bribes from other smaller companies that want a chance to survive in the market," Myong-hee begins, pausing to take a drag of her cigarette.

Sae is uncertain of where Myong-hee is leading her, and places a hand against the doorframe, needing something to lean against.

"If I hand this recording to the authorities—"

"Recording?" Sae asks sharply. She turns away, not wanting to hear any more. "I'm going inside."

"I need you to hear this," Myong-hee says, reaching for her arm. "Sae, we have an opportunity here. To finish what we started."

Sae is confused. "What does that recording have to do with the Tower?" The rain is coming down so hard that she has to raise her voice over the drumming on the plastic awning over their heads.

"People want accountability. We can show them just how deep the rot goes."

"We can't," Sae says, shaking her head continuously. "Yung has that tape. We don't have any evidence. They could use defamation laws against you . . ." Sae trails off, catching the look in Myong-hee's eye. She realizes what Myong-hee wants to do.

Sae's hands are freezing and she wraps her cardigan around herself to try to calm her shaking.

"I can't. You know I can't."

Hours after midnight, after Myong-hee has gone to sleep, Sae sits on the porch watching the trajectory of the storm moving across the water. Her existence is one marked by absences. Absence of love, of people, of guests, of herself, of who she had been. Seung-min and Hoon-min raised themselves out of childhoods taken from them by her grief and fear. She had told herself that she had needed to keep them safe, but they had kept themselves safe without her, or rather, despite her.

On this anniversary evening she allows herself to think of not just Jae but others who lost their lives in the Tower. Ghosts pass through her vision: the mother who left her napping child to run across to the supermarket in the basement, the high school student who had stepped into the atrium to use the phone to tell his mother that he had passed his university entrance exams, the newly engaged couple shopping for wedding gifts. They beckon her, these ghosts, eager to tell their stories.

RELAPSE

1992

It is summer when it happens. On a day ripe and fragrant with promise. The sunshine is like a reassuring hand on the shoulders of those who walk on the streets below. No one expects the worst. Not in the cocooning humidity. Or the stark light of day.

A street vendor closes up his cigarette stall by the subway station. The pressing need to urinate lifts him from his chair and into the searing sun. He crosses the street to use the restrooms in the skyscraper rising high across the street. To look up to try to see its peak is to be filled with vertigo. Aspiration Tower is half a place of commerce, half a monument, a museum of the country's rise to might. Office workers come down from their offices on the upper floors, to shop in beautiful boutique shops during their lunch hour. Wealthy housewives buy expensive premade banchan in the supermarket on the basement floor. Even those who cannot afford the grandly priced luxuries wander in to stand in the warm light of the atrium, to feel a part of this celebration of space. Busloads of excited children arrive on their field trips. They admire the panoramic view of their densely packed city nestled in the crooked arm of majestic mountains. Their teachers will search the horizon, squinting to pinpoint the neighborhoods of their childhoods only to find that they have been ground down. The dust has collected to form the foundations of austere apartment blocks. In their shadow and out of view are the shantytowns with water-stained façades under the low hang of power lines. Seoul is a woman with a past who hides her scars under a garish dress.

The street vendor steps inside and stares at an elaborate window display set up as a savanna scene. Two mannequins—a man and a woman dressed in khaki from head to toe—stand around a stack of progressively smaller suitcases. He is sure he will never go where these people are supposed to be going. It is a practical reality that has not saddened him. Until now. Suddenly he is mesmerized. Longing balloons inside him. For a foreign life beyond his reach. For the first time he feels a sense of loss, homesick in a way he doesn't understand. Staggering backward, he bumps into a young housewife carrying two large bags filled with food for the week.

"Watch where you're going!" she says.

He carries the look of disgust in her eyes as he goes down the escalator to the basement level, to the men's restrooms. He lingers longer than he ordinarily would, examining himself in the mirror, seeing himself through her eyes—his poverty stark in his cheap, worn T-shirt and black plastic sandals. The sight of his reflection fills him with a deep shame.

He does not know that the housewife is annoyed less by his clumsiness than by the waft of cigarette smoke emanating from him, reminding her she has forgotten to buy air freshener to mask the smell of smoke in her apartment before her mother-in-law's visit in the evening. Her time is not her own; it is given to others—to her mother-in-law, her husband, arranging tutorials for her children so that they don't fall behind at school.

Smoking is her most decadent, secret indulgence. Every inhalation is a moment stolen for her alone, reminding her that she still exists. When her mother-in-law caught her smoking she cursed at her as though she had discovered her in the midst of a salacious act. She is already late—her children are waiting to be picked up from school—but she turns and hurries down the escalator to the basement floor, to complete her shopping.

A low groan echoes through the hollow chamber of the building. A small child sits frozen, strapped in his stroller, wide-eyed, feeling afraid—convinced that it is the sound of a monster that his mother assured him does not exist. It's just a cartoon, she had said. Not real. None of the other shoppers seem to share his terror. A few stop and survey the high glass ceilings of the atrium. Most of them are conscious of the noise but give it only a second's thought.

One of them is a recently retired elderly man. It is not the whine of the building that has stopped him but the realization of what he must do to try to save his marriage. Since he has begun spending more time at home, he cannot help but feel that his wife is irritated with him. He wants to buy her a gift. A belated apology for having spent so many hours at the office. Hearing the groan of the building, he looks up but does not expect the worst to happen. In his mind disasters happen to those whose lives are summarized in contracted form in the papers, defined by career title and number of surviving family members. It does not happen to a man like him who has worked for years at a tire manufacturing company and has gone from living in a slum to a house with a corrugated iron roof to a high-rise apartment overlooking the Han River. Like many others, he's come to conflate maturity with affluence, the promise that from now on things can only get better.

So what stops him in his tracks is not the calamitous noise but the sight of a slim gold watch. It is perfect. What could be more symbolic, he thinks, than a watch to say that he wants to make up for lost time.

The walls of the building shudder. A shower of dust falls across the atrium. Shoppers look up. They see there is construction going on across the street and eagerly discard their worries. They mutter to themselves: The management of a landmark building should take care to treat their customers better.

But when the ground beneath their feet begins to vibrate, a common worry begins to coagulate, blame inching away from the building's managers toward a larger, more serious cause. A disaster beyond the building. An invasion. This is, technically, a country still at war. But as the dust spills from the ceiling, it feels more like an earthquake. Necklaces and bottles and diamonds and imported bottles of whiskey begin to quiver and shake on the shelves. The noise the falling dust makes is somewhere between a hiss and a snare drum, and rapidly drowned out by the deafening moan coming from the roof above them.

In the basement, moments before the lights cut out, Jae puts his hand to the wall, feels the vibrations, and immediately understands what is about to happen. They have run out of time. This building is about to collapse under the weight of its own ambition. There are now many things that will never be set right. Things are about to come to an end before he has had a chance to correct his mistakes.

This is not entirely true. He has had many chances. He thinks of Sae, waiting for him to come home. The love he has carried for her like a guilty secret. The giggles of his children, their trust that he will return as he leaves them in the morning. He is about to become a missing name in the index of history, a memory, a speck of light that arrives from a dying star. Frantically, he reaches for the door. It may not be too late. There may be time for one last call. He reaches in the darkness, just as he had reached for her cheek that first night in the library. It was the first time he had felt it, his heart near exploding in his chest. How much he had longed to believe in the kind of love she offered. But nothing in his life has shown him he could trust a redemptive love that sees all and forgives.

As he reaches for the door the first piece of concrete gives way. Above him, in the atrium, the block falls on several young women, office workers. A mushrooming cloud of dust rises in its wake. In confusion people press themselves against the walls before the rush for the exit begins. Heavy air-conditioning units begin to fall from the roof as it caves in. In less than ten seconds all sixty-five floors of the building collapse like a sinkhole. Cement blocks crack teeth and skulls. Rib cages are flattened like cardboard boxes. Femurs shattered. Watch faces broken, the hands of clocks frozen at 5:30 P.M.

In less than a second ambitions contract like an iris against sudden light. He is alone now in the darkness, his arms pinned under the weight of something heavy and damning. Even as other desires shrink back, Jae finds himself doing as he has done every day—bargaining for one more day. To savor the unexpected gift of a life borrowed. Tiny wonders that he never deserved.

All he asks for is one more day:

To feel Sae pressing a cold beer can against his cheek on a too-hot day.

To see the dancing light in her eyes when he enters the room.

To feel the squeeze of Hoon-min's arms around his thigh, Seung-min's slender arms around his waist—"Appa, don't go."

To be the one to tell her, *I'm sorry*.

To have the luxury of knowing that after today there's always tomorrow.

The promise of forgiveness in the days ahead.

ONE WEEK LATER

2016

It has been two days since Myong-hee left, and Sae can't get ahold of her on the phone. Every time she tries the call goes straight to voicemail. The morning after their anniversary rites, Sae had told her that she would not get in the way of what Myong-hee wanted to do, but that she wanted no part of it. She did not have it in her, she said, to restart anything. Myong-hee had nodded sadly but said she understood.

At first Sae thinks that maybe Myong-hee is avoiding her calls, but she knows this would be out of character. When Sae is unable to get in touch with her on the fourth day, she begins to worry. She tries to call Song-mi, without any luck. She moves around the inn, with only one lodger to distract her.

"Well, the economy is going to hell!" her lodger declares over dinner as he pores over his phone. "You know the world's going to hell when they arrest national royalty. The chairman of Taehan Group: He's a national hero. Why the hell would the authorities mess with anything that man has touched?"

"What is that?" Sae takes the phone from his hands. There it is—the news that Kim Yung, president of Taehan Group, has been taken in for questioning amid suspicion of corruption.

She is sure this is Myong-hee's doing. If Yung discovers that they are involved, she does not know what he will do. She thinks of the ghostly visitations, the stories of those buried under the rubble. She thinks of Myong-hee, who has tried, many times, to root her out of this underworld purgatory.

She takes off her apron and throws it on the counter. She wills herself to move, but her feet remain rooted. Her body resists as fiercely as an ox being pulled into a slaughterhouse. All she must do is cross the room, but she cannot do it. Her eyes fall on the cast iron rice pot, which she has scrubbed nightly until her hands were raw. What she had thought to be a stoic practice now looks cowardly. The boys have grown. She is not sure what she is trying to protect. There is no valor in hiding in this isolated existence. Wasn't it worth laying down her life for somebody, to be vulnerable for someone she loved?

She takes a step and then another. Soon she is past the kitchen door. She packs a small bag and leaves the inn, asking a neighbor to look after the guest, who is due to leave later in the afternoon.

She gets on the ferry and finds her way to the train station. In the twenty years since she has been in Seoul, the city has become alien to her. A new bus system has been put in place. Streets have been renamed, districts have been assigned new post codes. It is enough to knock her confidence that she can do this. Once or twice she thinks about getting in a taxi to return to the station.

She finds a bus heading toward Jong-ro, where Song-mi has a shop, and gets on it, only to find herself stuck in traffic. The roads leading to city hall have been closed because of protests. People are milling around at a leisurely pace, some carrying placards with the names of the children they have lost in the *Sewol* ferry sinking. Others demand impeachment of the corrupt president. Sae asks to be let out of the bus and steps into the crowd, feeling the energy of the resistance around her. Myong-hee is right, Sae realizes; there is momentum. If ever there was a moment when they might be able to expose what happened at the Tower, this is it.

Just then she feels a buzzing in her pocket. It is a text message from Myong-hee.

I'm sorry if you've been trying to get in touch, it reads. *Can't talk now. I'll call you later.*

I'm in Seoul, Sae texts back. *I heard the news.*

Before Myong-hee can reply, Sae writes a follow-up text.

I'm here to tell you that I'm in.

Reflexively, Sae calls Tae-kyu, hoping that he might help her to rekindle the old investigation.

Tae-kyu is waiting for her at the coffee shop and rises to greet her as she walks in.

"How long has it been?" he asks, wiping his face. There is an unmistakable tremor in his hand. His face is visibly older; the white roots of his hair belie his head of black hair, and when he speaks she can hear the snapping of his false teeth. "Almost twenty years?"

"You look good," she lies. "I hear you refuse to retire as editor."

Tae-kyu waves this off. "It's not like editing dailies. It's monthly review work, just something to help pass the time."

Sae nods. "It's really something isn't it? All these protests? It's almost like the 1980s again."

"It's a different world now. The *Sewol* ferry sinking has changed everything. You can't hide information like you used to. Not when everyone has the technological means to capture evidence and circulate it. It's not like it was for us. The tide has really turned," Tae-kyu continues. "Some have wanted to get rid of the president from the beginning because she's the dictator's daughter, but I think people just have less tolerance for this kind of entitlement. They're turning against the leaders of conglomerates, too." He tapped the magazine on the table with the back of his hand. "Have you heard about this? Even the chairman of Taehan Group can't seem to hold on to staff these days. His biographer has just quit."

Tae-kyu continues speaking, but she is no longer listening, her gaze pulled to the short article on the table, the photograph of the Chairman in his youth. Her heart is beating furiously, sensing an opportunity, beckoned by a younger, braver self. A small candle between them on the table has dwindled to nothing but a stub, flickering and struggling to stay alight. Every time Sae thinks that the light will go out, it fights, the flame returning.

THREE MONTHS LATER

November 27, 2016

The Chairman stops speaking, his line of vision moving beyond the gray branches of a fig tree outside his window, as if watching a memory crackle and fade on the horizon. The late afternoon light exposes the slack folds of his eyelids, the soft hairs on his chin, the theater of expressions marked by the wrinkles on his forehead. He is older than he appears in the press photographs, more stern and somber. The skin on his hands is liver spotted, translucent with age, and loose over his bulging veins.

The walls of the room are lined with vials of viper's blood, colostrum, ground elephant tusks. The Chairman is a deeply superstitious man. Every hour a nurse comes into the room to give him an injection or bring in a tray with a drink or cup of pills. Even after so many hours with him, Sae cannot separate fact from rumor—can neither confirm nor deny the stories of his famous rages, that he had spat on an employee for spilling a drop of coffee on the edge of a blueprint, that he had had a member of a labor union kidnapped, stripped naked, and set free to walk in the middle of a southern city. Or that he won multiple negotiations by cutting out an opponent's tongue with a steak knife. He is at his most charming and magnanimous in these hours that she spends with him. She suspects, though, a performance in these interviews; there is a rehearsed quality to his monologues. She has had to keep her wits about her. He is a master of diversion, his storytelling like a seductive suitor leading her to places she does not intend to go. He will wax poetically about his loss, his Geun-ye, but he will not speak of Yung.

Becoming the Chairman's biographer was easier than she had anticipated. His former biographer was a university friend of Tae-kyu's and willingly gave them the details she needed to get the job, revealing that an external candidate was preferred because internal publicity teams had so much to contend with following Kim Yung's arrest. She suspects that this biography is a way to avert the public's attention from the ensuing scandal.

The Chairman's admission regarding the false announcement of Geun-ye's death as a car accident is a surprise. It reminds her of something she had once read about propaganda—its effectiveness is in the dilution of lies with a drop of the truth. The moment she has been waiting for has presented itself; it is the opening for which she has been training for months. She shifts a little in her seat and leans forward, gathering her hands on her lap.

"You've expressed your regrets about Geun-ye, sir." She pretends to scan her notepad, knowing that she has his full attention. "But you've said nothing about Yung's arrest."

The Chairman stiffens, his eyes narrowing in the dimming winter light.

"Let's stop here for today," he says, forcing a shaky smile. "I need to rest."

Sae's finger hovers over the record icon, but she does not press it. The phone in her pocket will capture what is to come.

Rising to her feet, she gathers her notebook and pen and the digital recording device. At the door, she stops short of leaving the room and locks the door instead.

"Would it be fair to say, sir, that sometimes we craft a version of our lives that allows us to evade regret, or perhaps shirk our responsibilities?" she says, crossing the room and taking her seat once again.

He looks up sharply, confused that she is still there when he has dismissed her. He grips the sides of his chair as if to stand up, though he cannot do so without assistance.

"I thought I told you that this interview is over," he says in a low voice.

"Would you agree that sometimes we bend the truth to offer the best version of the past to others? A man in your position of authority has the power to write history. But don't you think the public has a right to an account of the past that is free of your distortions?"

"Distortions?" he says. This characterization of his rehearsed speeches seems to upset him.

"You don't comment on what your expectations did to your sons, for example. How Yung went to great lengths to cover for your mistakes, going so far as to implement a dubious plan to fix what you had begun and then going to criminal lengths to cover up what happened."

"Now wait a minute . . ." The Chairman wrestles with the cushion beside him to right himself. He reins in his anger; he seems to decide that it is in his interest to hear what she has to say. "I don't know what you are suggesting."

She takes a deep breath. "Aspiration Tower was never supposed to be a high-rise. The foundations were prepared for a low-rise building when you decided you wanted to erect a commercial building instead of a residential one. It was structurally unsound from the beginning. It was all for show, for the Olympics. The problems were already there. From the beginning, years ago. You and Yung were always aware of the possibility of a collapse. And you did nothing to prevent it."

The last part is hard to say and she stops, swallows hard so she can continue.

"L&S Engineering was hired to fix the structural problems under the guise of building a swimming pool," she continued. "It allowed you to explain the construction in the building without raising fears of safety. And, later, to absolve yourself of responsibility. L&S Engineering—no, Mr. Bae—took the blame."

He paws at the phone beside him and taps at it.

"Tell Mr. Gong to get over here," he says, before slamming the phone down.

Sae continues. "You speak as if the government has coerced you into rushing projects, but it works both ways, doesn't it? Hasn't Taehan Group always been in bed with the government? Is the president of this country the financier of Taehan Group, or is it the other way around?"

"Get out," he barks, shaking the armrests on either side of him, unable to rise from his seat and unwilling to ask her for help.

This is the critical moment. There is, in all likelihood, very little time. In their preparations for this moment, Tae-kyu, Myong-hee, and Sae had discussed that to elicit a confession from him, there must be an element of surprise to disrupt his performance.

"Just one more question, sir," she says. "Was it Yung who told you that Geun-ye died in the factory fire?"

The Chairman stops moving. The shift in the line of questioning has befuddled him, and he grips the armrests tightly, the visible edges of his palms white.

After a moment's silence he seems to resign himself to the fact that he is unable to move and can do nothing but wait for Mr. Gong to arrive.

"Isn't that what I told you already?"

"You don't think Yung could have deceived you?"

He scoffs at this. "You think I'm incapable of knowing when my own son is lying to me? I know my son like I know the back of my own hand. He's a terrible liar."

"Did it ever occur to you that Yung would benefit from Geun-ye's death? You don't think he could have lied to you about the identity of that body?"

Initial disgust at the suggestion is overtaken by a look of growing uncertainty. "What are you saying now, that Geun-ye . . . ? That he—?"

"You said so yourself. The charred corpse seemed smaller than you remembered Geun-ye to be," she says.

"Liar," he roars, erupting at last.

"Yung thought he was doing Geun-ye a favor. Letting him have the life he wanted." She paused. "With me."

Sae removes a photograph from her pocket. It is a photograph of the two of them with their little family on top of Mount Namsan. Aspiration Tower—completed a month after the factory fire—is a visible speck on the horizon. The Chairman stares at her, incredulous. He looks from the photograph back to her. He seems to understand, at last, how they are connected. After a long pause, he swallows hard and asks her: "Do you mean to tell me that Geun-ye is alive?"

It is Sae's turn to pause.

"Yung hired Geun-ye to work in the Tower."

This takes some time to sink in. His bulging eyes dart back and forth in furious calculation.

"Yung isn't capable. He's incompetent. It wasn't even his idea. He was a sniveling mess. Coming to me, talking about how we had to halt operations because of some problem. Do you know how much we would have lost if we had halted our operations in the building? He didn't know how to fix anything! I had to send Mr. Bae with instructions—I told him to beg Yung for a job. Yung wasn't clever enough to come up with a ruse like that himself. He doesn't have the authority, let alone any knowledge of what it means to be in construction. I told you, Yung was never going to be the leader I needed. He wasn't a visionary. There's no way he could pull the wool over my eyes. He isn't capable!"

The Chairman is vibrating with rage; he is a man who cannot stand losing. Her momentary sense of triumph withers into sadness, imagining what it must have been like for Yung and Geun-ye to have grown up boxed in by the Chairman's view of their perceived limitations.

Now she understands that there is another reason why she is here. She wished to see the Chairman as Jae had seen him. To measure the sincerity of his defiance. And she sees him then. A man who will say anything, do anything, to get what he wants. She imagines Jae as a child, in his father's shadow, staring at the height of him against the sun. She had seen only a fragment of the man Jae was, perhaps a man he wanted to be. She understands that Jae's evasions were not those of written history, which narrate a version of the truth to consolidate power. Jae's elusions came from a place of shame.

"The ruse with the pool, then, that was your idea," she repeats. She hopes that Tae-kyu is getting this.

"Isn't that what I've just said? Yung doesn't know how to fix anything. Do you know how much money we would have lost if I hadn't put a plan like that in place?" he says. "You think anyone will concern themselves with what happened all those years ago?"

It is as Tae-kyu and Myong-hee predicted. The Chairman cannot resist an opportunity to marvel at his own genius.

"And what about those lives?" she asks. "The life of your own son?"

"What if Taehan Group went bankrupt?" he says without missing a beat. "It would collapse this country's economy! This is why Taehan Group is untouchable." He smiles, revealing dark stains in the corners of his teeth. "Did you really think your little stunts here were going to be a threat to me? Do you think anyone will take your word over mine?"

"I'm willing to find out," she says, rising at last.

"Or maybe you thought I'd give you money? Did you think that I would give you a cut of the company if you tried to claim some family connection? You wouldn't be the first. You think I got to be where I am by being the kind of fool who gives money to every woman who claims to have a child of mine?"

She reaches the door. The Chairman struggles to stand and falls to the ground with a thud. She hurries past the staff who run to attend to him, hearing him shouting after her as she bursts into the garden.

She slips out of the Chairman's property just as a sedan pulls up to it. She does not turn back until she is on the main road. Protesters are gathered on the car-less road marching toward the Blue House calling for the resignation of the president. She is aware of what they have set in motion: The recorded testimony will launch an investigation, the Chairman will be arrested, the documents that Tae-kyu has been gathering over the past few months will help to build a strong case against Taehan Group. Will it be the end of the Chairman's career or even Taehan Group? She does not know, but there has never been a better moment than this. Even so, it is only as she feels the press of other bodies against her own that she begins to feel her heart slow, safe in the anonymity of the crowd.

There is a touch of festivity in the gathering on the streets; these are not the protests of her youth. Families have brought their children, some young enough to be carried on the shoulders of their parents. Tae-kyu and Myong-hee are waiting for her in the building housing a national newspaper less than a mile away. Sae should feel triumphant; after months of planning and uncertainty, rehearsals and despair, they have succeeded. Despite the odds, they have worked together to get the testimony that will serve as crucial evidence. So she does not understand the feeling that nags at her like an insistent dog, interrupting her steps.

As she turns toward Gwanghwamun, she sees a small boy standing alone on the pavement. Judging by his distraught expression, he has lost his guardian. Her heart lurches. She squeezes between a group of college-aged students to reach him. A protester brushes past her. When she regains sight of the boy, he has been reunited with a woman she can only assume is his mother. He melts into her arms. The sight of them gives Sae a pang of recognition. This is all the comfort Seung-min has wanted from her in searching for her all these years. He has been looking to her for an honest account of their past.

To know something of his father, the hidden pieces of herself. To know the story of their family and, by extension, the story of himself. Her impulse had been to shave off the ugliness of what had happened, the way she sliced away the bruised parts of a fruit to give the boys only the sweetest bits of its flesh. In her tendency toward erasure she sees that she has not been so different from Jae. In realizing she is close to forgiving him, she knows what is unfinished; she is not where she needs to be.

She breaks away from the crowd. On a quieter side street, she pulls out her phone, and dials Seung-min's number.

"Hello?" he says, his voice full of sleep.

"Seung-min . . ." Her voice trails off.

"Is everything all right?" he asks. "Where are you?"

His voice is louder now, tinged with worry at the implied emergency of a call at an ungodly hour.

"There's so much I need to tell you . . ." she begins. It is useless, she thinks, to do this here. There have been many things she has not been able to give him, but there is something he has always wanted that she now has the courage to give. She looks back at the main road, at the families moving together on a sea of candlelight.

"Seung-min," she says. "I'm coming to you."

ACKNOWLEDGMENTS

Two works were essential in informing this work: *The Making of Minjung: Democracy and the Politics of Representation in South Korea* by Namhee Lee and *Writers of the Winter Republic* by Youngju Ryu. I am also indebted to Woojoo Chang, who regaled me with stories of her days as a student protestor.

Thank you to Sharon Bowers, my wonderful agent, for—among other things—telling me that this novel still had a heartbeat when I could not hear it.

Thank you to my warm and supportive editor, Nicole Counts, whose passion and thoughtful advice helped to shape this book into a form that I could not have achieved alone. I am also grateful to everyone at One World for all their efforts in supporting this work.

Thanks also to: Elaine Kim, my literary and academic mentor, who has broadened my horizons while encouraging me to stay on the path towards art; Rachel Richardson and David Roderick and the Left Margin Lit community, who have given me invaluable support and space to work on the long journey to finish this novel; Janet Schneider, Jenny Fosket, Vicky Remler, and Matt Heller, who read parts of this novel more times than seems fair or sane; Grace Zhou and Dilshanie Perera, for the retreats, emotional, and creative support; Kang Young-sook, who coached me through the trials and tribulations of the second novel; Gabriela Blandy, for your reviving energy and creative (re)envisioning; and Rita Amador, for giving me quiet time.

This book could not have been written without the support and encouragement of my family—the holy trinity of Pilwha Chang, Woojoo Chang, and Sangwha Lee.

Last but not least, thank you to my wonderful and patient husband, Chris, for all the hours of support of this very long project. The completion of this novel would not have been possible without you.

ABOUT THE AUTHOR

HANNAH MICHELL grew up in Seoul. She studied anthropology and philosophy at Cambridge University and now lives in California with her husband and children. She teaches in the Asian American and Asian Diaspora Studies Program at the University of California, Berkeley.

Twitter: @HannahMichell
Instagram: @_hannahmichell

ABOUT THE TYPE

This book was set in Jenson, one of the earliest print typefaces. After hearing of the invention of printing in 1458, Charles VII of France sent coin engraver Nicolas Jenson (c. 1420–80) to study this new art. Not long afterward, Jenson started a new career in Venice in letter-founding and printing. In 1471, Jenson was the first to present the form and proportion of this roman font that bears his name.

More than five centuries later, Robert Slimbach, developing fonts for the Adobe Originals program, created Adobe Jenson based on Nicolas Jenson's Venetian Renaissance typeface. It is a dignified font with graceful and balanced strokes.